Praise for Sue Ann Jaffarian's
ODELIA GREY MYSTERY SERIES

"Jaffarian keeps getting better and better at blending humor, suspense, and romance."—*Publishers Weekly*

"Jaffarian plays the formula with finesse, keeping love problems firmly in the background while giving her heroine room to use her ample wit and grit."—*Kirkus Reviews*

"Odelia Grey is the perfect take-no-prisoners heroine for today's woman."—Camryn Manheim, Emmy award-winning actress and author of *Wake Up, I'm Fat!*

"[Odelia] is an intriguing character, a true counter against stereotype, who demonstrates that life can be good, even in a world where thin is always in."—*Booklist*

"Plus-size reading pleasure—try this one on!"
—Lee Child, *New York Times* best-selling author

"Balancing her professional skills as a paralegal with her self-doubt as a sleuth, Odelia is one of the most believable amateur detectives in recent fiction. Strongly recommended."—*Library Journal*

Hide & Snoop

ABOUT THE AUTHOR

Like the character Odelia Grey, Sue Ann Jaffarian is a middle-aged, plus-size paralegal. In addition to the Odelia Grey mystery series, she is the author of the paranormal Ghost of Granny Apples mystery series and the Madison Rose Vampire mystery series. Sue Ann is also nationally sought after as a motivational and humorous speaker. She lives and works in Los Angeles, California.

Other titles in the Odelia Grey series include *Too Big to Miss* (2006), *The Curse of the Holy Pail* (2007), *Thugs and Kisses* (2008), *Booby Trap* (2009), *Corpse on the Cob* (2010), and *Twice As Dead* (2011).

Visit Sue Ann on the Internet at

WWW.SUEANNJAFFARIAN.COM

and

WWW.SUEANNJAFFARIAN.BLOGSPOT.COM

SUE ANN
JAFFARIAN

AN ODELIA GREY MYSTERY ➤

Hide & Snoop

MIDNIGHT INK
WOODBURY, MINNESOTA

FIRST EDITION
First Printing, 2012

Cover design by Ellen Lawson

Midnight Ink, an imprint of Llewellyn Worldwide Ltd.

This is a work of fiction. Names, characters, places, and incidents are either the product of the author's imagination or are used fictitiously, and any resemblance to actual persons living or dead, business establishments, events, or locales is entirely coincidental.

Library of Congress Cataloging-in-Publication Data
Jaffarian, Sue Ann, 1952–
  Hide & snoop / Sue Ann Jaffarian.—1st ed.
     p. cm.—(An Odelia Grey mystery; 7)
  ISBN 978-0-7387-1889-7
1. Grey, Odelia (Fictitious character)—Fiction. 2. Overweight women—
Fiction. 3. Legal assistants—Fiction. I. Title. II. Title: Hide and snoop.
  PS3610.A359H53 2012
  813'.6—dc23

                                                    2012011774

Midnight Ink
Llewellyn Worldwide Ltd.
2143 Wooddale Drive
Woodbury, MN 55125-2989

www.midnightinkbooks.com

Printed in the United States of America

For Diana James.
Thank you for everything.
You are sorely missed.

ACKNOWLEDGMENTS

To the usual suspects: my agent, Whitney Lee; my acquisitions editor at Midnight Ink, Terri Bischoff; and everyone else at Midnight Ink/Llewellyn Worldwide who had a hand in making this book a reality.

And to those people who have become very special to me in the past few years: the members of the Sue Ann Jaffarian Fan Club on Facebook. You folks may not realize it, but your daily support and cheering from the sidelines kept me and this manuscript afloat when I felt I just couldn't write another word. You rock!

A special acknowledgment goes to Cyn Rielley, who started the fan club as a reader and today is a dear friend, and to my niece, Lindsay Jaffarian Holm, who helps Cyn administer the club.

ONE

THE JOINT. THE SLAMMER. The clink. The words trekked through my brain like muddy feet across a clean floor.

The bright light above assaulted my tired, gritty eyes. All I wanted to do was go home and go to bed. I tried to think of synonyms for bed but failed. Instead, my mind kept to its single track like a wheel in a rut.

Hoosegow. Big house. Pokey.

I didn't know how long I'd been in this room. It was small and windowless, containing a sturdy metal table and a few chairs. Was it morning yet? It had to be. Resting my arms on the table, I cradled my head on them, face down, to escape the annoying artificial light.

"Really, Dev, that's all I can tell you." I spoke without lifting my head, the words coming slow, barely above a whisper, as if we were in church instead of jail.

Devin Frye, Newport Beach homicide detective and friend, parked half his butt near me on the edge of the long table. His close presence caused me to lift my head. Dev looked down with a mixture of disbelief and barely reined-in anger. He'd looked that way for hours. "Do you want to call an attorney, Odelia?"

It wasn't the first time he'd asked me that question, but this was the first time I'd seriously considered it as an option. "Do I *need* an attorney?" The question seeped out of me, small and fuzzy, like a gummy bear rolled in cat hair.

I raised my head until I was upright again and looked from Dev to the other detective in the room. She'd been introduced to me as Detective Andrea Fehring.

"I thought I was just pulled in for questioning. I mean, I wasn't Mirandized or anything. That's what they do on TV when they arrest people, isn't it?" Detective Fehring, a trim woman with bobbed black hair and dark eyes, remained silent and studied me like a specimen trapped between two glass slides. Even though there were several other chairs in the room, she stood, leaning against the beige-painted wall.

Dev let out a uneven grumble that started deep in his gut. When he spoke, his usually deep, gravelly voice went up an octave, sounding like a Yahtzee cup shaken with too many dice. "No, Odelia, you're not under arrest. *Yet.*" He emphasized the last word with the sharpness of an awl puncture. "But you were found at the scene of a murder, alone, in the middle of the night, wearing a bloody nightgown."

"I wasn't found at the scene like a lost wallet, Dev." I was dangling over hot water, and I knew it. Mustering what strength I had left, I dropped the whisper, snapping at the detectives like a lobster about to be thrown into a hard boil. "I'm the one who discovered the body and called *you*. Remember? I've only told you that a hundred times."

Dev had been the first and only call I'd made upon finding the body. I'd called him at home. Soon after, Dev arrived in his car, with several police cruisers as backup.

"But why were you there in the first place?" he asked, his face hard and crusty.

A knock sounded on the door. A uniformed officer stepped in and motioned to Dev, who left after giving Fehring a meaningful look.

I was no longer in my nightie. As soon as I'd arrived at the Newport Beach police station, they'd taken it and the hoodie and jeans I'd also been wearing for evidence and gave me an extra-large tee shirt and some sweatpants to wear. Since I'd left the house in my nightgown, I hadn't been wearing a bra, and now I felt naked without one. I crossed my arms in front of my big boobs more out of modesty than defense.

"May I call my husband?" I asked Fehring.

"Detective Frye already did."

"Good." In spite of the word, it didn't feel good. I would have preferred to call Greg myself, after I'd had a chance to rehearse and soften the facts. I'd thought about calling Greg while I waited with the body for Dev but dismissed the idea, hoping I could simply answer a few questions and be on my way. The plan was to tell Greg about my nocturnal activities over a nice breakfast. I would have made him blueberry pancakes with bacon. One of his favorites. Who knows, I might even have woken him up with a booty call before easing into my confession.

Upon receiving Dev's call, I had no doubt Greg sped out of our house in Seal Beach, the tires on his van squealing on the pavement. And I'm sure he was also glued to his cell phone, calling either Seth

Washington or Mike Steele, both attorneys, and begging one of them to meet him at the police station. Greg was going to be madder than hell over this, but at least he'd be on my side. The heated lecture would come once we got home.

Fehring stepped closer to the table, her face deadpan. "So you're the infamous Odelia Grey. I've heard a lot of stories about you."

"You shouldn't believe everything you hear." I squirmed in my chair, which was plastic and not made for someone with a bulky butt.

"Frye has a soft spot for you, but I don't. Remember that." Her dark eyes narrowed into two small ink pools. I noticed for the first time that her dark hair was laced with silver strands, reminding me of a sweater I wear around the holidays.

If she was trying to scare me, it was working. I looked into her face and saw not a hint of warmth, only tired lines and a thin, hard mouth on a face wearing very little makeup. She could have been anywhere between thirty-five and forty-five years of age.

"They call you Corpse Magnet, don't they?" she asked without a smidgen of amusement.

"Who's *they*?" My words had the attitude of a combatant in a playground tussle. My common sense tried to get the upper hand but failed. "It's not like it's on my birth certificate."

Corpse Magnet was an ugly nickname given to me by Seth Washington in a fit of exasperation, and it was only used sparingly by my closest friends whenever I stumbled across a dead body, which was more often than one would think. I didn't know the handle had become public knowledge. Dev must have told her.

"Don't get cute," Fehring warned. "And it's not cute when private citizens get mixed up in serious crimes. You put yourself and others in danger." She pitched forward, slapping both of her hands flat on the table across from me. In my seat I gave a startled little hop and looked down, noticing her square-shaped nails were clean and trim and shined with a coating or two of clear polish. "You can put officers in danger nosing around, and that I take personally."

"Trust me, it's not my idea of a good time. It just seems to happen."

"Are you saying you just *happened* to be standing in someone else's house in the middle of the night when that woman was killed?"

"She was dead when I got there. I told you that."

Fehring stepped back and leaned against the wall again. She stuck her hands in her pants pockets and returned to studying me with laser eyes. "Personally, I think this time you did the killing yourself."

"No!" I cried out in urgency. "I swear I didn't. I—" but my words were cut off by Dev's return. With him was my husband, Greg Stevens, and Seth Washington. Seth isn't only an attorney, he's a close personal friend. His wife, Zenobia, better known as Zee, is my best friend. I was so happy to see them, I nearly cried. But my joy was cut short by the look on Greg's face. If Dev's face looked as hard as day-old bread, Greg's was the truck that ran over the bread. I almost peed in my borrowed sweatpants.

Seth turned to Dev. "I'd like a word with my client."

As soon as Dev and Andrea Fehring filed out, I said to Seth, "I didn't know you were a criminal attorney."

Seth fixed me with his espresso eyes. "I didn't realize you needed a criminal attorney. At least not yet."

Yet. There was that annoying word again. It hung in the air alongside the one Dev had thrown out—a pair of verbal vultures just waiting to pounce and make accusations about my evening.

Greg, in a wheelchair since an accident in his early teens, rolled up to where I was sitting. No hug. No kiss. The pressurized steam coming from his ears could have cleaned a greasy car engine. "What in the hell is going on, Odelia?"

"Calm down, Greg," Seth told him. "We need to get to the bottom of this, and quickly."

Greg looked raggedy, with his light brown hair uncombed and the nighttime stubble sprouting around his usually groomed Vandyke beard. "Seth, was it your wife who sneaked out of the house in the middle of the night to have a slumber party with a dead woman?"

"Of course not," Seth admitted. "Zee has more sense."

I snapped my head around to look at my so-called lawyer. "I beg your pardon? Are you on my side here or not?" When neither Seth nor Greg said anything, I tacked on, "Don't make me call Mike Steele. Please." It was more of a supplication than a threat.

After taking a second or two and several deep breaths, Greg asked, "So who's the stiff this time?"

"Please let me ask the questions, Greg," said Seth, using his lawyer voice. "I think it will go smoother if I handle this."

It was in Greg's nature to take charge, but what Seth said made sense. He was, after all, the only law degree in the room. As soon as Greg nodded his assent, Seth turn to me. "So who's the stiff?"

Greg did a double take but remained silent.

"Her name is Connie Holt," I told the two of them. "She's Lily's mother."

Seth's mouth fell open. So much for his legal composure. "Lily? You mean the sweet little girl sleeping under my roof right now?"

"Yes. Connie is Lily's mother and the sister of my boss, Erica Mayfield. Like I've told the police, I found her—Connie, that is—already dead when I got to Erica's house. I didn't know who she was until the police told me."

Greg groaned. "Please tell me you did not go over to Erica's to beg for your job."

Seth held a hand out towards us, indicating for us to be still. "Back up the bus, folks." He turned to me. "This woman fired you, and you went to her house in the middle of the night?" He took a deep breath. "Why do you do such dumb things, Odelia?"

"I am not dumb." My nose twitched in annoyance while I fought to defend my actions. "I'm impulsive." I turned to my husband for support but could see he was clearly in Seth's camp on this issue. "And I wasn't fired," I insisted. "At least not yet."

"I didn't say you were dumb, Odelia," Seth clarified. "But your actions are often those of an insane person."

Greg was nodding in agreement. I was on my own.

"Maybe I should call Steele," I suggested.

Greg let out a short, dark snort. "If you think he's going to be any easier on you, you've been away from him for far too long."

My hubs was right. If Steele, my former boss, were here instead of Seth, he'd be crucifying me. I just wasn't sure if it would be because of my nocturnal actions or because I didn't invite him along. Steele had grown disturbingly fond of sticking his nose into my amateur murder investigations. Come to think of it, so had Greg, making me believe his anger was more focused on my safety and possible future criminal record than on my actions specifically.

7

"We're wasting time," Seth told us. "According to Dev, they don't believe Odelia is the killer. The woman was shot twice in the chest and may have been dead several hours before Odelia called him."

"I can vouch for her whereabouts," Greg offered. "We went to a dinner party last night given by one of my basketball buddies and his wife. We got home around eleven and went straight to bed. I'd had a few drinks and fell asleep before the Channel Four news ended. Odelia was in bed with me."

Seth knitted his brows as he wrote down the information. "That will help in the event they start looking at her as a suspect."

Suspect? My stomach did a flip. When Detective Fehring suggested earlier that she thought I might be the killer, I thought it might have been more of a scare tactic than something she truly believed, and it had scared the snot out of me. But hearing my lawyer say the word had even more impact. I took a sip of water from the paper cup Dev had brought me earlier. My hands shook, threatening to cave in the thin vessel.

"I think I got to Erica's around one thirty," I added. Seeing no napkin or tissue, I wiped my mouth with the back of my hand.

Remembering how Connie had looked when I stumbled across her, I shuddered. "When I arrived, Connie was staring up at the ceiling, pale and still, the front of her long-sleeved tee shirt drenched in blood. I tried to give her CPR, just in case she wasn't dead. That's how I got so much blood on me." I took another deep breath. "I told the police all this several times."

"I'm positive they're checking your clothing for gunshot residue." Seth stopped writing and looked at me. "Did they test your hands yet?"

"They applied some sort of adhesive strip to them, like they were waxing for hair removal. They also took a swab for DNA. I thought it would help if I were cooperative."

Seth nodded as he made more notes. When he was finished, he put his pen down, folded his hands, and leaned his large body back in his chair. "Okay, Odelia, tell me how you got to Ms. Mayfield's house in the first place."

"I drove."

Greg placed a hand on my arm. It was his first act of affection since entering the room, and it meant the world to me. "He means what caused you to go there."

"Oh."

Of course that's what Seth meant, but the night's events and lack of sleep were taking its toll on my middle-aged brain cells.

I dug through my tired mind for the root of my actions. When had all this craziness started to take shape? What exactly was its genesis? It had started small, of that I was sure. Like a palm-sized snowball, over the past couple of days it had gathered in size with every discussion and situation until it had become a large, heavy orb too big to ignore.

I took a deep breath, ready to start at the beginning.

"It all started with Lily," I told Greg and Seth. This was not something I had told the police, because it really had just come to me.

"The little girl?" Seth asked again with surprise.

TWO

I WAS MESMERIZED BY the snot bubble. It ballooned in and out of one tiny nostril, playing peek-a-boo each time the little girl exhaled.

Normally I don't mind kids, especially since they always belong to someone else and aren't my responsibility. Once, at a summer picnic Greg held for his employees, a woman clutching the hand of a wee tot asked me if I liked kids. I answered, "Absolutely, especially with a little salt and pepper."

With a gaping mouth she had shuttled the child away, lest I slather the tike with barbeque sauce and throw him on the grill, giving new meaning to the phrase *shrimp on the barbie*. Greg, being used to my sense of humor, found it hilarious, but for the rest of the party I noticed people keeping a closer eye on their offspring, especially when I was handing out the ice cream bars and popsicles. I was sorely tempted to climb up on a picnic table with a bullhorn and shout, "It was a joke, people! Get over it!"

The festering petri dish happily coloring on the other side of my desk was named Lily Marie Holt. She was three years old, with an angelic face, fine curly blond hair, upturned nose, blue eyes, and rosy cheeks. The problem was that for the time being she *was* my responsibility.

There's never any salt and pepper handy when you need it.

What had started out this week as simply keeping an eye on Lily one day at the office as a favor to my boss was now turning into full-blown daycare. When I had arrived at the office this morning, Lily was there, as she had been for the past couple of days. But today—in addition to the coloring books, crayons, story books, stuffed toys, blanket, and snacks that usually accompanied her—a car seat, a stroller, and a pink suitcase festooned with various Disney princesses had been added. Either Lily was moving in or preparing for a yard sale.

I was not a happy camper.

As I studied the little bundle of joy with the runny nose, trying to decide what to do about this latest turn of events, I pulled a tissue from the box next to my computer monitor and held it out towards the kid. "Here, Lily."

Instead of taking the tissue, Lily started to drag her left hand across her snot-laden nose while her right hand continued to push the crayon with industry.

"No." The beginning of the short word came out of my mouth sharper than I intended, then spiraled down into a half hush. She looked up from her coloring book, clearly perplexed by my short-lived outburst. I shook the tissue in Lily's direction and was heartened to see her eyes brighten with understanding.

Since law firms don't come equipped with booster seats, I'd pulled a chair up close to my desk. Lily seemed happy to kneel on the seat and color away. If I'd knelt that long, I wouldn't be able to walk for a week. Sometimes she sprawled belly down on the blanket on the floor of my office. She'd proved herself to be a good-natured child, in spite of being cooped up all day in an office. There were a lot of adults in the firm, me included, who could take a few lessons from the kid.

Instead of taking the offered tissue, Lily crawled down off her chair and circled the desk until she stood beside me. Tilting her head back, she presented her wet nose to me as if offering up a precious gift. With a sigh, I held the tissue to her snout. She gave a small toot. I wiped the nostril and the immediate area clean and tossed the tissue into my wastepaper basket. I followed it up with a squirt of waterless cleaner to my hands. As I rubbed my hands together, the scent of the crisp aloe gel wafted through the air.

"Priddy," Lily said, meaning she liked the smell of the antiseptic cleaner. In three days, she was no closer to speaking my language, but I was much closer to understanding toddler gibberish, which appeared to be a combination of babble and real words, or reasonable facsimiles of real words.

I smiled and nodded. It was a ritual—the nose, the wiping, the gel—that Lily and I had shared since she'd been assigned to my care.

My smile faded and my blood pressure started to rise as my eyes once again scanned the pile of Lily's belongings in the corner of my office. Asking me to keep an eye on Lily a day or two was okay, even if it did interfere with my work, but if she were moving in with Greg and me, someone needed to man up and tell me. I'd waited in my office for some explanation, but it had been two hours since my arrival and no one had said a peep about the added baggage.

Getting up from my chair, I held out my hand to Lily. She latched onto it with her own tiny hand as naturally as an infant taking a breast. Together we walked out to the secretarial bay just outside my door.

"Would you watch Lily a moment?" I asked Alyce Allen, who now sat at Jill Bernelli's desk. "The boss and I need to have a 'come to Jesus' meeting, and it may not be something for Lily's delicate ears."

Being a religious woman, Alyce winced at my smart-ass phrase involving her savior, but her disapproval quickly melted into curiosity. She clearly wanted me to expand on my huffiness, but I gave up nothing. Alyce wasn't Jill. I had trusted Jill. The jury was still out on Alyce, though she seemed nice enough.

"Will it take long?" she asked. "I have to get the changes to this agreement done before lunch."

"Depends," I answered truthfully. "What *I* have to say won't take long." I deposited Lily on an empty chair at the desk across from Alyce and started to walk away. A few steps later, I turned back to Alyce. "If I get fired, Lily may end up in your care. Her stuff's in my office."

Alyce looked from me to Lily and back again with the sort of closed-mouth assurance you offer when you tell someone everything's going to be fine even though you know they're probably toast. "I hope it doesn't come to that. The firing, I mean."

Steeling my shoulders for confrontation, I walked the few steps to my supervisor's closed door and knocked. First softly, then again, with more conviction. I never received a call to enter but pretended I did and barged in.

"We need to talk," I announced to the attorney behind the desk. I shut the door behind me.

"I can't right now, Odelia," came the sharp response. "I have something important to do out of the office."

13

The boss in question wasn't Michael Steele, the attorney who'd been a royal pain in my ass for the past several years. Nor was it any of the other attorneys at Wallace, Boer, Brown, and Yates, the law firm where I'd been happily employed for two decades. Woobie, as its employees affectionately referred to the firm, was no more. Shortly after the new year it had entered into a merger with another firm. Woobie was supposedly the surviving entity, but you'd never know it from the way things turned out.

Last June Steele had received an offer from Templin and Tobin to open and manage their new Orange County office, and he'd taken it, leaving at the end of the summer. He'd asked me to go with him. He'd also asked Jill Bernelli, his assistant, to jump the good ship Woobie and sail off to T and T. Jill and I had discussed the offer with our significant others—Greg and her partner, Sally Kipman—and after many separate and joint discussions around our kitchen table and theirs, she decided to go with Steele, and I decided to remain at Woobie. I wasn't sure either of our spouses were happy with our individual decisions. Greg was nudging me to follow Steele, while Sally point-blank told Jill she was nuts to do so without me on board to run interference.

Jill and Steele had departed Woobie nearly seven months ago. A few months later, after the merger was announced, Jolene McHugh, a senior associate, joined them. That move surprised the tar out of me. Jolene never got along with Steele, but she must have sensed the change at Woobie coming like the smell of burning flesh carried on an ill wind. Shortly after the merger took place, Joan Nuñez, another paralegal at Woobie and a good friend, left for a different firm. Sometimes when I walk down the familiar halls and see all the new faces I feel like an alien trying to adjust to a new planet.

We'd merged with a firm that had been downsized over the past few years. With the economy hitting law firms hard, including Woobie, the idea was to join together to form one large, strong unit of legal muscle. The problem was, Woobie joined forces with a firm that had a totally different management and practice style. Along with their client roster, the other firm had brought with them unhappy, caustic employees and foul-mouthed, ill-tempered attorneys. The firm was now called Hamlin, Hawke, Boer, and Yates. I dare you to make a touchy-feely acronym out of that.

Undeterred by the haughty attitude oozing from my new boss, I stood my ground. "I noticed a lot of kid stuff in my office this morning. Is Lily moving in with me or are you using my office for storage?"

Erica Mayfield looked up from the file she was rummaging through and gave me the stink eye. "Michael Steele might have put up with your insubordinate attitude, Odelia, but I will not." She put down the file and latched her eyes onto mine with all the warmth of a hired gun. "In fact, I'm quite tired of your old firm treating you like you're something special. You're not. Get that through your thick skull."

Inside I wobbled for a moment, but outside I held firm. "What's the deal with Lily?" I asked again, trying to infuse my voice with respect, even if it was just for show.

With a deep, exaggerated sigh, Erica stopped what she was doing. "The deal is I need you to take her for a few days."

I stepped closer to her desk, a beautiful and feminine piece that I liked much better than Steele's cold, ultra-modern one. Too bad I didn't like the boss behind it better. "You mean you want me to take her home with me tonight?"

"Yes, and keep her through the weekend. I'll inform you if I need you to care for her any longer than that."

In all my years working as both a legal secretary and a paralegal, I'd been called upon to do a lot of odd and annoying things, especially for Mike Steele, but this took the cake.

Before I could answer, Erica located a piece of paper on her desk and held it out to me. "This is a medical release giving you authority to seek medical care for Lily in the event she requires it."

I took the paper and eyed it. It was signed by a Connie Holt almost a week ago and notarized. "Is this Connie Holt Lily's mother?"

"Yes, that's my sister."

"She doesn't even know me. Why would she turn her kid over to me? Lily's a child, not an unwanted puppy." I shook the paper in my hand at her. "And this was signed a week ago. Clearly this was not a last-minute decision on your part. The least you could have done was given me a heads-up or asked if I could do it. This involves my husband, not just me."

"I had Connie sign two releases, one for me and one for you, just in case I had to leave Lily in your care. I should have given you yours on Monday but forgot. As for advance notice—my bad." Her voice dripped with entitled sarcasm.

Erica stuffed a couple of files into a large designer briefcase and stood. "Now, if you'll excuse me, I have something very important to take care of."

When Erica Mayfield first darkened the doors of our office suite, I had had high hopes of getting along with her. She's in her early forties, smart and organized, with an impressive background. Standing close to five foot ten, with a thick torso and chunky limbs that she dressed to the nines, I thought we might also be able to bond a bit on the big-gal level, as well as over the legal work. But it was not to be. From the moment we met, Erica made it clear I was expendable. She gave all the plum assignments to Mark Baker, the paralegal brought over from her old firm, and went days without acknowledging my presence. It was quite a change from my days with Steele, when he was in my office as much as his own.

I slapped the medical release down on her desk with a heavy hand. "Demanding this of me, especially without warning, is highly unprofessional and inappropriate, Erica, and you know it."

Ignoring me, Erica flipped her dark blond hair over her right shoulder and headed for the door with her purse and briefcase. I followed on her heels, which were expensive and pointy.

"Just a cotton-picking minute," I demanded, but it fell on deaf ears.

She stopped in front of Alyce's desk. "As soon as you have those changes," she said to her secretary in a tone as crisp as a fresh apple, "e-mail them to me."

Alyce nodded. A few feet away, Lily sat frozen in her chair, watching the adults with wide eyes. She made no movement towards her aunt.

"You can't do this," I said to Erica. I wanted to say more, but not in front of Lily. I may not have had children of my own, but I did know they picked things up like sensitive satellite dishes.

Erica didn't seem to care if her niece felt the negative vibes. She turned to face me, standing only a foot way. She was attractive, with large brown eyes, full lips, and a nose just irregular enough to be interesting instead of a negative. "If you value your job here, Odelia, you'll do what I ask. If not, you know where the door is."

The words *I quit* were on my tongue, ready to make the leap into the abyss of unemployment. Instead, I said nothing, knowing I should discuss the matter with Greg first. While his business was doing fine, the economy was not, and a good job wasn't something a person tossed away without serious consideration and a plan.

Erica handed me a smug, confident smile. "I thought not." She turned and marched down the hall towards the front door of the suite, leaving me to steam and boil quietly in front of Alyce and the kid. It took me a few seconds and several deep breaths before I held my hand out to Lily.

"Come on," I told her with a forced smile, "let's leave Alyce to do her work."

Lily and I were barely back in my office when I was called to do snot duty again. I had just wiped Lily's tiny nose when Mark Baker appeared silently at my door.

"Doing Sesame Street duty again, I see." Mark sneered with glee as he watched me with the kid. "Better you than me." The words were pregnant with gloat. Lily moved closer to me.

Like me, Mark is a corporate paralegal. He'd been working with Erica for just over a year before the merger. He's in his mid-thirties, of average height, with a wiry build. He wore his dark hair cropped close to his head, and one brown eye was smaller than the other, like a perpetual half-wink. A small scar ran from the center of his lower lip down across his chin, as if cleaving it in two. It was probably left over from a childhood injury, or maybe from the last paralegal with whom he crossed swords. I could see his smug attitude angering a coworker to the point of wielding a sharp letter opener. Yeah, I could see it easily.

"I have work to do," I told Mark, eyeing my own letter opener with wishful thinking. "Why don't we trade off watching Lily so we can both get some work done?"

Mark laughed. It had a nasty underside to it, like Halloween candy laced with razor blades. "No way." Next to me, Lily buried her head in my soft side.

He looked around my office, his eyes measuring every inch, especially noting my window. Mark had been assigned my old office when Hamlin-Hawke moved in. It was a windowless cell down the hall. He'd made it clear he coveted my larger office with a view. My office was also much closer to Erica's office—Steele's old one. Even Erica had campaigned for a switch between Mark and me, but she had been overruled by management, who cited my seniority with the firm. I have no doubt that if I died today at my desk, Mark would move in before my body was cold and traveling down the elevator on a gurney.

"I hear the firm's thinking of downsizing." Mark tossed the remark out like a live grenade with a pulled pin.

My head snapped up with a quick pop. Lily started to quietly babble something, but I placed a hand gently on her head. Like magic, she stilled. "I haven't heard anything about that," I told Mark as casually as possible.

"Erica told me." He spoke the words with undisguised confidence. "Management's reviewing all duplicate positions. Any unnecessary staff will be laid off."

Duplicate positions—as in two corporate paralegals.

A shudder of fear ran through me. Never, in all my years with the firm, had I feared for my job until this very day. Not even when Steele and I were at each other's throats did I feel this unsettled.

It was becoming clear why Erica was not giving me much work and why she'd saddled me with daycare. It was a setup. With my billable hours slowly sliding into a deep hole, Erica was making it easier for management to decide between their two corporate paralegals. She was stacking the deck in Mark's favor, using the firm's decision to tighten its belt to get rid of me.

Another realization hit me between the eyes. Even the challenge for me to quit a few moments ago might very well have been calculated. Erica knew I would balk at taking care of Lily 24/7 and had laid her trap. Had I quit, I would have walked away with nothing. If they laid me off, I might get a nice severance.

Beneath my desk, my right knee knocked with anxiety. But while it was out of view, I couldn't hide my concern from Mark's eagle eyes. A slow, sardonic smile spread across his face like a smear of dull paint. He raised his mug in my direction in a final salute and left—a competitor assured of a victory.

"Odie," a squeaky voice beside me chimed. I turned to find Lily's nose needing attention again. Not only did I get trapped with a kid, she was a sick kid. Plucking another tissue from the box, I held it to her tiny nostril and was rewarded with a small, wet honk. With Mark gone, Lily returned to her side of the desk, but instead of climbing up on her chair and getting down to the business of coloring, she picked up her latest masterpiece and returned to me, offering it up like a gift.

"For me?" I took it from her.

She put both hands behind her back, screwed up her face in a chubby giggle, and nodded with vigor.

"Thank you, Lily. It's lovely." My eyes fixed on the bulletin board fastened to the wall on the right side of my desk. "Tell you what, how about we pin this up here so I can always see it?" I removed a couple of pushpins from the cork surface, positioned the crayon drawing in a prominent place, and secured it. The child was over-joyed with my art appreciation.

"Don't let it get to you."

I looked up to find my doorway again occupied. This time it was Alyce. She pushed a strand of light brown hair away from her eyes and gave me an encouraging, shy smile. She was petite but sturdy and favored casual business attire with flat shoes.

When I'd showed Alyce the ropes around Woobie—it'll always be Woobie to me, dammit—I'd found her quiet and attentive, and she'd proven herself to be an excellent secretary. She was also sup-posed to provide me with secretarial support, but Mark and Erica made sure I seldom saw the fruits of her labor. I knew little about her beyond the fact that her husband's name was Gary. He was the pastor of a small independent church, and they had two children. Although pleasant enough, she hadn't reached out to make friends with any of the Woobie staff. Alyce was a quiet, private person, which was probably how she survived working with Erica and Mark.

I wiped Lily's nose again as I answered, "It's just a little cold. She doesn't seem to be too bad." I felt her forehead. "No fever."

"I meant Mark." With one finger, Alyce pushed her glasses up the bridge of her nose. They were too large for her face and made her look owlish.

"Oh, that."

I threw the tissue into the trash and squirted some antiseptic gel in my hand. Lily made some indecipherable kiddie sound and held out her hands, making it clear she wanted some. I took her two little paws within my two large ones and rubbed the germ killer on them.

"What do you know about the downsizing, Alyce?"

"About the same as you just learned." Her comment left no doubt she'd heard the entire conversation.

"So it's between Mark and me?"

"I haven't heard that exactly. Is there enough work for the two of you?"

I stroked Lily's head. Her hair needed washing. She started to babble something. She either wanted juice or a jackhammer.

I answered Alyce with blunt honesty. "If you take away my child-care duties, no, there's not. At least not right now. And I'm not too sure I'm doing that good of a job with Lily."

Alyce gave me an almost-warm smile. "You're doing great with her, Odelia. She's in much better hands than if she'd been parked with Mark."

"I'm totally in the weeds here, Alyce. I'm almost never around little kids."

Her nose clean again, Lily leaned up against me. She'd stopped yammering and was rubbing her head, with its fine yellow albeit dirty hair, against my elbow. It felt like one of my cats when they're looking for a scratch behind an ear.

Alyce jerked her chin in Lily's direction. "She really likes you."

"Don't bet on it. More like a case of Stockholm syndrome. That and I'm the keeper of the cookies and juice boxes."

"You're a kick, Odelia." Alyce gave off a small, self-conscious laugh. "It's clear Lily likes and trusts you, that's why she's sticking to you like glue. I haven't even seen her do that with Erica, and she's Lily's aunt."

Lily rubbed against me a couple more times until I was tempted to toss her a kitty treat. Instead, I lifted my arm. Immediately the little girl slid under it and nestled against me like a perfectly joined puzzle piece. It felt kind of nice.

"What's the story, Alyce? Why is Lily with Erica and not her own mother?"

Even though Erica was currently out of the office, Alyce looked up and down the hallway with caution before stepping farther into my office. Maybe she didn't want Mark to hear and tattle to Erica that she'd been talking to me.

"I don't know exactly what's going on, Odelia, but it seems Connie, Lily's mom, brought Lily to Erica and took off. Erica can't reach her anywhere and has no idea when she's coming back."

Under the pretense of fixing her hair, I gently covered Lily's ears with my hands. I didn't know how much she'd understand, but we were talking about her mother deserting her, even if only for a few days. My own mother had done the same to me when I was sixteen, and it had been over thirty years before I found her. You might say I was a bit of an expert on feeling like an abandoned puppy heading for the pound.

"What about her father?"

Alyce shrugged. "That would be Hank Holt. I think they divorced recently, or at least separated. Erica can't reach him either. I'm not even sure she knows how."

After more babble, Lily started dancing around with a pained look. "Priddy," she said to me with urgency. This time I knew she didn't mean the smell of the aloe gel. The kid had to pee. After all, *pretty* and *potty* do sound a lot alike.

Lily was potty trained but didn't have great bladder control. She hadn't yet mastered the art of giving a heads-up with much lead time—something I'd learned the hard way on my first day with her. Without wasting time, I stood up and grabbed her hand. We scooted out the door past Alyce.

"Sorry, Alyce. With Lily, nature doesn't call—it yells ASAP!"

THREE

I F THERE'S ONE THING I'd learned in the past few days, it's that kids need to burn off pent-up energy. You can't stick a kid in an office and expect them to sit still for eight to ten hours. After visiting the ladies' room, I took Lily down the elevator to a tiny area near the parking garage. There were a few small trees and a bit of grass not much larger than an area rug, along with a couple of benches and tables where people could have lunch. To the far side of the area was another bench and an enclosed ash-and-butt-disposal gizmo for the smokers in the building. I'd brought some work-related reading with me so I could get something done while keeping an eye on my charge.

I glanced up at the sky. Thick clouds were approaching like slow-moving cattle herded across a prairie. The weatherman had predicted rain over the next few days. It wasn't supposed to be a big storm, just spring showers. Lily was nattering to herself and hopping on one foot around one of the trees. She was dressed in pint-size jeans and a white turtleneck jersey covered with tiny embroidered ladybugs. Over that was a sweater. I'd left her hooded jacket upstairs. I was contemplating taking her back inside when my cell phone gave off a familiar chime. It was Zee.

"You still doing daycare?" Zee asked after I said hello.

"More than ever." Still keeping an eye on the happy Lily, I gave Zee a rundown of the morning's events.

"Why don't you bring that poor child over here?" Zee offered when I was finished.

"Thanks, but I can't saddle you with a sick kid."

"If she is sick, she should not be at that office. And I've taken care of many runny noses in my day."

Zee and Seth have two children, Hannah and Jacob, both grown now and out of the house. Something told me empty-nester Zee was itching to get her hands on a little one as much as offering to help me out.

"Seriously, Odelia," Zee urged, "bring her over so she can get the rest she needs and you can get some work done."

"Humph," I snorted. "Like I have any work to do."

"Call Mike Steele. He'll give you a job in a heartbeat."

"You sound like Greg. He said the same thing to me last night."

"And we're going to keep saying it until you listen."

Getting up, I went to retrieve Lily to go back upstairs. "But if I wait it out," I said into the phone, "I'll probably walk away with some nice cash when they lay me off."

"I know you, Odelia. Unless that happens soon, and I mean very soon, you'll go insane in the meantime."

"You're assuming I'm not already."

"Well, before you go completely crackers, get that child over here. She doesn't need to witness your descent into madness."

Zee was right. Lily would be better off at her house, although I hated seeing the kid palmed off on yet another stranger. As soon as we returned to my office, it hit me. I couldn't just throw Lily into my car and take off for Zee's. I'd have to get all her stuff downstairs and into the car and set up the car seat somehow. And I'll bet Erica didn't leave instructions. I was developing a headache to go along with Lily's unhappy nose. Instead of dropping her off at Zee's, maybe I should go home sick and call in tomorrow, too.

I was trying to figure out how best to get both Lily and her baggage down to the car in one trip when Stump ambled by with the mail cart. He stopped to drop a few envelopes into my inbox.

"Hey, Stump," I said, eyeing his cart. "Do you have another one of those carts in the copy room? One I can use to get all this stuff down to my car?"

Stump, whose real name is Stanley, eyeballed Lily's stuff, taking quick measurement. "Sure. Give me a minute to finish up my rounds and I'll help."

True to his word, Stump was back at my office in about ten minutes with a two-tier cart. He packed the car seat, stroller, suitcase, and other items onto it like a pro. Stump was tall and angular and pushing thirty. By day he ran our copy room and all aspects of our office services department. By night he wrote screenplays, which he hoped would one day sell and allow him to write full-time.

"Did you hear about Kelsey?" he asked as he made sure the stroller was secure.

My ears perked up. Kelsey Cavendish was the firm's librarian and one of my closest friends. "No, what about her?"

"She was let go."

I froze until Lily said, "Ow." I was holding her hand and had tightened my grip upon hearing Stump's news. I loosened my fingers but never took my eyes from Stump. "Are you sure?"

"Just delivered her mail. She found out, like, two minutes ago."

I started down the hallway to the library, towing Lily behind me, then remembered Stump and the cart. I retraced my steps. "Can you give me a few minutes, Stump? I have to go see Kelsey."

"Tell you what—give me your car keys, and I'll take this stuff down and load it up for you. You still park on the fifth level?"

I nodded and let go of Lily's hand. Going to my desk, I opened my bottom right-hand drawer and retrieved my car keys from my bag. I handed them to Stump.

"Don't worry, Odelia, I'll even install the car seat for you. Got two little kids at home. I'm an old hand at this."

"Thanks, Stump. I really appreciate it." I gently placed a hand on his arm. "How about you? Is your job in jeopardy?"

He gave me a small, sad smile. "I don't think so. The guy from the other firm is only a part-timer. Goes to college the rest of the time." He shrugged. "But you never know."

Stump leaned close. "Watch your back, Odelia," he whispered. "There's a target on it."

Seems everyone had received that memo a day or two before me.

I wanted to run in the direction of the library but couldn't with Lily attached to my hand like a kettle bell. Instead, I walked fast, the tike trotting behind me, her little legs churning up the carpet. If I moved any faster, I'd be dragging her. When we reached the library, Kelsey was just hanging up the phone. She looked like she'd been crying.

"What's up?" I clutched Lily's little hand tighter in my stress but was mindful of not squeezing too tightly.

"I was just about to come over to your office," Kelsey told me. She plastered a smile on her face as her eyes settled on Lily. "I just came from seeing Carl."

She meant Carl Yates, one of the two former Woobie name partners who still remained after the merger. Wendell Wallace had retired years ago, and Katherine Brown had retired this year.

"I heard they let you go," I announced, trying not to cry myself. Hamlin-Hawke had not brought a librarian with them, but Kelsey had told me not too long ago that she feared they might make the librarian a part-time position or outsource it entirely, like a lot of firms were doing.

Kelsey nodded. "Yes, but I was leaving anyway. After this last trip to visit Beau's family in Texas, we decided to move there in a few months."

I dropped Lily's hand and handed her the first magazine I could get my hands on. "Here, Lily," I told the little girl. "Why don't you read yourself a story." She took it happily and plopped down on the carpet.

I plopped my own butt down in a nearby chair. "When's your last day?" I asked Kelsey.

"I have to leave today. Now, in fact. Carl handed me my last check and asked that I be as discreet as possible. He seemed genuinely upset." Kelsey started putting her personal items in a small box while she talked. "That was Beau on the phone. I just told him." She stopped packing and turned to me, this time with a real smile. "We're preggers, Odelia." On that bit of news, her voice tilted up with joy. "I was going to ask you to lunch tomorrow to tell you about that and the move."

Kelsey and her husband, Beau, had been trying for a baby for several years and had nearly given up. She'd had two miscarriages in the past two years, both in the first trimester.

I looked at my friend with concern. "Are you okay? I mean, about the baby?"

She nodded. "I'm about three months along and so far, so good." She patted her stomach. "I should start showing a bump soon. With everything that's going on here, Beau was concerned about my stress level, so he's pleased with this. He was offered a very good job back in Texas when we were there last week and has to start soon. He was going to go ahead of me, but now we'll both move right away. And my severance pay is generous enough that I won't have to look for something else between now and my due date." She took a deep breath. "So although I'm sad and a bit pissed off, it's really a good thing."

I looked down at Lily. As she thumbed through a copy of *California Lawyer*, she jabbered on about kitties and ducks, making up her own legal news as she went along. Soon Kelsey would have one of these.

I got to my feet. As I wrapped my stubby arms around my tall, lanky, and now pregnant friend, my eyes filled with tears of both joy and sadness. I was close to Kelsey. Her moving would be a huge blow, but I knew it would be best for her and Beau.

"Before you leave, Joan and I will have to take you out. Better yet," I told her, "Greg and I will host a party for you and Beau at our house."

"Please don't go to a lot of bother."

"It's no bother. It'll be fun. Jill and Sally will want to come. Carl and his wife. Jolene. Even Steele."

Kelsey smiled and wiped an eye with the back of her hand. "Okay. Thanks."

I didn't want to seem insensitive to Kelsey, but I had to ask. "Do you know if they're laying off anyone else today? I've heard it might be between me and Mark."

Kelsey swallowed hard. "Hope in accounting was told last night, right before she left for the day."

I thought about Hope Spellman, the small birdlike woman who only worked three days a week. She was pushing seventy and had been with Woobie even longer than I had.

"Other than that," Kelsey continued, sniffing back tears, "I haven't heard anything else. It wouldn't surprise me, though. It's the end of a pay period. Today and tomorrow would be the logical days to lower the boom."

I dug into my pocket and checked my smartphone for my firm e-mail account. Nothing. No summons to meet Carl or Tina Swanson, our office manager. No e-mail goodbyes to the firm as a whole from anyone.

"They'd be fools to let you go, Odelia, especially for Mark. He's such an—" she clipped the end of the sentence short when her eyes settled on Lily.

I leaned in close to Kelsey and whispered, "They became fools when they merged with these sharks."

After several more hugs with Kelsey, Lily and I started back to my office to collect my purse and be on our way to Zee's house. We were barely out of the library when Lily emitted a string of high-pitched giggles and shot down the hallway like a runaway pony. I trotted after her, my two-hundred-pound bulk jiggling in every way imaginable, while attorneys and secretaries pointed and laughed. Glad I could provide some entertainment. Maybe the firm will consider keeping me on as court jester when they decide they no longer need my paralegal skills.

We were almost to my office door when my smartphone sounded another familiar ring. I punched the answer button and snapped, "What do you want? I'm busy."

"Uh-huh. That's not what I hear."

"Are you spying on me, Steele?"

"Not at all. I had a beer with Greg a few days ago. He told me you haven't been very busy at the firm."

"I obviously need to talk to my husband about his choice of friends." On Tuesday, Greg came home and said he'd had a beer with a buddy after work. He never said which friend, and I didn't ask. Greg often met friends after work. Usually it was one of his basketball teammates or a client, so I never inquired and he never offered.

It's not like I haven't seen Mike Steele since his departure from Woobie. He's been a guest at our home for a couple of parties and barbeques since then, and he showed up to support Greg during a recent basketball tournament. I just didn't realize he and Greg had remained so friendly on their own. My nose twitched at the thought. I had concerns about my husband and my former boss being close pals. One, it felt like I was outnumbered. Two, Steele has a lot of bad habits I don't want rubbing off on Greg.

"I'm on a special project right now." As I said the words, I watched Lily dance and spin to a tune only she could hear. Either she wasn't sick at all or she was delirious with fever.

"You too busy to have lunch with me today?"

Lunch. Steele had had a beer with Greg and now was asking me to lunch. Greg probably told him how unhappy I was becoming in my job. He was probably going to make me an offer again. This time I'd be sorely tempted to make the jump.

"Did Greg put you up to this?"

"No, he did not." There was a slight pause. "My lunch plans canceled, and I thought why not ask my former paralegal to join me. Is that a crime?"

"Depends on your motive."

Lily was showing signs of winding down. "Look, Steele, I really have to go."

"Have lunch with me today, Grey. You know you want to." I could hear his cheesy grin.

"I already have plans today, Steele. With a very important client, a young up-and-comer."

"Jesus, Grey, I can smell that lie through the phone. You must be slipping."

I sighed as I brushed Lily's fine hair out of her face with my free hand and noted how dirty her face and hands were. Most of the crud she must have picked up playing in the dirt around the tree downstairs, but some of it was just general grime. She didn't smell that fresh either. She'd arrived at my door on Tuesday bright and shiny as a new penny, but as the week wore on she'd become more disheveled in appearance, like she was sliding into neglect feet first. It seemed odd because Erica's grooming was meticulous. Before I could stop her, Lily smacked her mitts down on my thigh, leaving noticeable tiny handprints on my cream-colored skirt. My eyes rolled up into my head like snapped window shades. How did women do this day in and day out? And Lily Holt was well-behaved. What if I'd been put in charge of a miniature Tasmanian devil?

The dirt smudges on my skirt made up my mind for me. After a couple of days watching Lily eat peanut butter and jelly sandwiches and spill milk, I could use a good lunch with some adult talk. My usual lunch companions were thinning out.

"Okay, Steele. You're on, but I have to run by Zee's house first and drop off … um … a package."

"Can't you do that after lunch? I have a meeting in two hours. Meet me in ten minutes at Morton's."

I studied Lily. She was starting to look tired. No doubt she would conk out right after she ate. And I really should give her lunch before depositing her with Zee, not to mention lunch with Steele might be interesting with a tiny third party.

"How about in fifteen minutes?" I said into the phone, my mind made up. I rooted around in my brain for a nearby restaurant with a kiddie menu. "And not Morton's. How about Red Robin?"

"Are you joking?"

"Hey," I protested. "They make great burgers, and they're reasonable. Greg and I eat at Red Robin all the time."

"I rest my case."

"It's that or nothing, Steele."

There was a pause.

"Steele, you still there?"

"I'm thinking."

My office phone rang. The display said it was Carl Yates.

"Take it or leave it, Steele," I said again, this time with urgency.

"Okay, but make it ten minutes."

I looked at Lily's dirty face. "I'll need at least fifteen."

My office phone rang again, and again it was Carl. I ignored it and grabbed my bag and Lily. As we exited the ladies' room with empty bladders and clean faces and hands, I heard my name announced over the PA system, asking me to call Carl's extension. Instead, I punched the down button on the elevator, hoping our receptionist didn't see me making a getaway and try to stop me. There would be enough time after lunch for Carl to kill my legal career. No sense him killing my appetite, too.

FOUR

STEELE WAS WAITING JUST inside the front door of the restaurant, looking handsome and spiffy in his usual combination of designer suit and impeccable grooming. He and Erica shared that trait. I'd seldom seen either with a hair out of place. I had driven the two blocks to the restaurant, ready to take off immediately for Zee's after we ate, and had called her to let her know when to expect us.

When Lily and I came through the front door hand in hand, Steele did a double take on Lily. "I take it that's the reason we're eating here?"

Instead of answering him, I told the waitress seating us we'd need a booster seat.

Once settled, I introduced my former boss to my new boss's niece. "Steele, this is Lily Holt, Erica Mayfield's niece."

"Whoa!" Steele leaned back in his chair, a wide grin plastered on his face. "And you thought I saddled you with wild demands."

"Yeah," I told him. "Who knew I'd wind up with someone who makes you look sane."

The waitress brought over a kiddie place mat and a couple of crayons for Lily. She immediately went to work coloring the cartoon forest creatures on the mat while we looked over the menu. When the waitress returned, Steele and I both ordered salads and iced tea. When it came to Lily, I was stumped.

I looked up at Steele. "What should I order for her?"

Steele held up his hands, palms out, as if the question came with a disease. "Don't look at me."

The waitress came to my rescue. "I have a kid her age. He loves the chicken fingers."

I looked at her with relief. "Then chicken fingers it is."

"Milk to drink and apple slices for dessert?" the waitress suggested.

"Sounds good to me. Thanks."

She returned a minute later with our teas and Lily's milk. Until then Steele had remained silent.

"So," he said after taking his first swig of tea, "seems Hamlin-Hawke is already putting you to work as a sleuth. Has a body turned up yet?"

My attention was on Lily. She was determined to drink her milk while holding crayons in both fists, and I was just as determined not to wear the milk. In the middle of coaxing her to drop the crayons, my head snapped up to stare at Steele. "What in the hell are you talking about?"

"Careful of the profanity, Grey." With his chin, he indicated my charge.

I took a deep breath while I guided the milk to Lily's eager mouth and helped her put down the cup again. I wanted to give Steele my full attention, but it was impossible. As soon as Lily was back to coloring, I tried to focus on his comment. "I repeat, what are you talking about?"

"You don't know?"

"All I know is that Erica Mayfield dumped her niece on me. She didn't say why."

Steele studied me. I knew that look all too well. He had some juicy details about something and was weighing how much to tell me. His eyes settled on Lily briefly before returning to me.

"Mayfield's sister is missing."

That got my attention. "You mean Lily's—" I cut my comment off at the knees before I said the M word in front of the kid. "You mean Connie?" I whispered after making sure Lily was still occupied with her coloring. Even though I'd heard something similar from Alyce, it was the last bit of news I'd expected from Steele.

Steele started to speak, but the waitress arrived with our food. He simply nodded in my direction.

As soon as the waitress left, I asked, "How do you know this?"

"A friend of mine knows Erica quite well. Since she took my old job, my friend finds it amusing to tell me stuff. Seems Connie dropped...," he paused, amending his words for present little ears. "Dropped a valuable package off with Erica and disappeared. Until now, I had no idea you had the package in question."

"I take it this friend of yours is a bed buddy?"

He gave me a sly grin over the rim of his tea glass.

I coaxed Lily into dropping the crayons long enough to start on her chicken fingers. The chunks of deep-fried bird were the perfect size to wrap a small fist around. The eagerness with which Lily tackled them told me it wasn't a new culinary experience for her.

When I spoke, I kept one eye on Lily and one on Steele, both my brain and eyes feeling cross-eyed.

"I thought maybe they had you on the hunt," Steele continued, "considering your colorful past."

Steele took a bite of his grilled chicken salad as he watched me guide Lily through her lunch. "Seems the sis might be into something shady," he said after swallowing.

That got my attention again. "You mean drugs or something like that?"

He shrugged. "Not sure, but I've heard Erica's been worried about her for a long time and doesn't want to involve the police." He speared a piece of chicken with his fork. "That's all I know."

"Well, it's more than I know. I'd heard about Connie missing but not about the other stuff."

"Connie's disappearance isn't the entire reason why I called you, Grey, though it does add a bit of spice to your situation."

I swallowed the bite of salad I'd managed to stuff into my mouth in between babysitting duties. If I had Lily full-time, I'd probably drop a few pounds. "There's more?"

Before I could hear what else Steele had to say, a little hand to my right started pawing at me. I turned to look at Lily, who was holding out a disgusting, half-chewed spear of fried chicken. She'd been tapping me on the arm with it, leaving greasy spots on the sleeve of my blouse. I wanted to scream but held my tongue. I took the gummy crap from her hands and started wiping them with a napkin. With her free hand, Lily pointed to one of the animals she'd been coloring.

"Squirrel," she said, her little digit jabbing at a rodent of some kind. I looked closer. It was indeed a squirrel, or maybe a chipmunk.

"That's right, Lily. Squirrel. What a smart girl."

She pointed her finger at me. "Squirrel."

Steele laughed.

"No, Lily," I told her with a smile. I pointed at myself. "Odelia." Then I pointed at her art project. "That's a squirrel."

She shook her head with determination, setting her blond curls to wiggling. "No," she insisted, pointing at me. "You squirrel. Cheesehead squirrel." She squealed with delight.

Steele laughed again, this time with more gusto. I looked at him, my mind a blank. "How did she come up with that?" He only smirked in response.

I pointed at Steele. "He's a cheesehead squirrel. I'm Odelia."

"Nooooooo," Lily insisted. She jabbed her pudgy finger into one of the grease stains on my sleeve with great accuracy. "You cheese-head squirrel."

"Gotta admit, Grey," Steele said with amusement. "It's better than being called Corpse Magnet."

"Humph, I'm not so sure about that." I reached over and wiped Lily's nose with a napkin.

When I was done, Lily picked up an apple slice and bit into it. She munched with glee, her head bobbing in time to some imagined tune. The child was definitely musical. Between chews, she mumbled a ditty about a cheesehead squirrel.

Steele dissolved into full-blown hysterics. "Oh my God, this is so much better than a stuffy lunch at Morton's."

I tossed him my best scowl. "So glad you're amused. Were you about to tell me something else? You know, like the real reason you asked me to lunch?"

Steele took a drink of tea to compose himself. "Yes, there was something else." He paused. Except for Lily's babble about a squirrel with a cheese problem, the table was quiet.

"There's no easy way to put this, Grey." He paused for effect. "Get ready to be fired."

"You're too late with that, Steele."

He seemed surprised by my lack of surprise. "You mean you've already been fired?"

"No, but the bloodletting has already begun. So far, Hope and Kelsey have been let go. And Erica is making it easy for management to pick me off along with the others."

I fingered Lily's hair while she colored, and pondered the darkness overtaking Woobie. "Did your friend tell you specifically my head was on the chopping block?"

He nodded but said nothing.

"Erica has disliked me from day one," I told him, "and I'm not sure why, except that she brought her own paralegal with her and wants to protect him."

"Makes sense," he said, giving me a small, pained look. "I tried to protect you when I left. I asked you to come along with me."

Anger bubbled up in me like prehistoric tar. "You knew this was going to happen, didn't you, Steele?"

"What?"

"The merger," I accused. "These things don't happen overnight, and you were an equity partner. You knew Woobie was going to merge with Hamlin-Hawke before you left."

"Not exactly. I knew there were negotiations in place. It was one of the reasons I left. I've never liked the people at Hamlin-Hawke, so when the T and T opportunity arose, I saw it as both a viable way out and a good way to expand my career."

"Why didn't you warn me, dammit?" As soon as the swear word was out of my mouth, I regretted it. I looked down at Lily, then sighed with relief. She was totally engrossed in talking to the animals on her place mat. One was a skunk. On the bright side, I could have been dubbed cheesehead skunk instead of cheesehead squirrel.

"I'm sorry, Grey, but I couldn't." Steele looked across the table, and I saw his apology was genuine. Sincere or not, it didn't make me feel better about my situation.

"As a partner, I was bound to very strict confidentiality. When I left, the merger was not definite, just in the negotiation stage, and it was rocky. It came close to not happening at all. If it had been a done deal, I might have tried to warn you somehow."

Giving it some thought, I saw his point. Just because two companies talk merger doesn't mean it will happen. I'd worked on many deals that had gone south at the last minute; so had Steele. Confidentiality or not, it still angered me that he didn't at least drop a few veiled hints. If he had, would I have jumped from Woobie to T and T with Steele or stayed and taken my chances with the new situation? Guess I'll never know, since that ship had sailed. Steele had given me an option, just not a fully informed one.

"So now, based on your bedtime espionage, you're offering me that job again?"

Steele stared at me but made no comment. His jaw was set, his mouth firm, telling me there was no job offer coming. "I hired someone months ago for the spot I offered you. I'm sorry. I held it open as long as I could, hoping you would change your mind."

He'd offered me a combined office manager/paralegal position. I would have been in charge of setting up the new office, including hiring. "And she's stayed all this time?"

His jaw relaxed, and a slow grin emerged. "Amazing, isn't it, but I think Jill has something to do with it."

I fussed over Lily so Steele couldn't see my disappointment in being replaced in his life. In all the years we worked together, I did nothing but bitch and moan about him and his behavior. Now I wanted nothing more than to work with him again. Guess it's true—you don't really know what you have until you've lost it. That doesn't mean he wasn't an arrogant pain in my ass and seriously annoying, but I'd take that over working for Erica Mayfield any day.

Steele took another few bites of his salad before putting his fork down. "You know, Grey, we'll probably have something for you in the fall—a straight paralegal position. The OC office is growing, and we'll be adding a few more attorneys then."

It was currently mid-March. I counted on my mental fingers— April, May, June, July, August, September. Fall was six months away. I did a few more calculations. As a severance, Kelsey said she'd received a week's pay for every year she'd been with the firm. After Hope Spellman, I've been there the longest. A week's pay for each year could hold me over well enough, providing they didn't put a cap on how many weeks an employee could receive.

Or I could just go out and get another job.

My stomach clenched. I put down my fork and rubbed my middle. Whoever had said that change was good was a fool and someone I'd like to slap.

"You okay, Grey?"

"Yeah," I told him, but I really wasn't. I had been at Woobie so long I couldn't imagine changing jobs. Ever since I'd heard about the possible layoffs this morning, I'd considered Steele's new firm my safety net—a place I could go where I already knew folks. Now I'd be starting over from scratch, and being over fifty years old wasn't going to help my employment chances in this dismal economy.

I concentrated on Lily, stroking her hair. Her presence was comforting, like that of my pets. Caressing the top of her little head felt as good as rubbing Wainwright behind his ears. Her soft breathing and babble was as calming as hearing Seamus and Muffin purr. She looked up from her coloring and grinned at me. Food particles were stuck to the milk ring around her mouth, but her nose looked less runny. Taking a clean napkin, I dipped it in my water glass and mopped her face and hands as best I could. I had some disinfectant gel in the car and made a mental note to put it to good use when we left the restaurant.

Lily giggled and jabbed a finger at the place mat she'd scribbled with bright colors and chattered away. She'd named the bird Baby Birdee, the rabbit was Hoppy, and so forth. For each she had a name and a sound or action to go with it. It was a regular Broadway production. She pointed at another creature and giggled again.

"Yes, Lily," I said as I planted a soft, unconscious kiss on the top of her head. "That's me, Cheesehead Squirrel."

FIVE

ZEE'S DARK HAND CUPPED Lily's forehead and cheek. "She has a fever," she announced, "but just a little one. Nothing to be alarmed about, but she should be in bed. She also needs a bath. A warm bath and bed." Zee made the announcement like handing out hardcore medical advice.

I felt like a bad mother, even if it was temporary. "I probably shouldn't have taken her to lunch."

"Nonsense," Zee told me. "The child needed to eat, and it gave me a chance to run to the store and pick up some children's cold medicine, just in case."

Zee picked up a bottle from the counter, shook it, and measured out a spoonful. "Here, Lily, open wide."

Lily hesitated, eyeing the concoction with suspicion. She glanced at me, and I gave her a reassuring nod.

"Go ahead, Lily. It will help you feel better," I said with encouragement. Her little lips pursed in defiance, then like magic she opened her mouth so Zee could dump in the medicine.

Zee held Lily's little face in her palm again and smiled at the girl. "You're such a little cutie. We're going to get along fine, aren't we, Lily?"

Lily grinned up at her new caretaker, probably sensing she'd finally been passed into the care of someone with competence. Lily had taken immediately to Zee. Of course, it helped that cartoons were playing on the TV when we arrived. Zee was armed and ready—cartoons, cold medicine, and kid-type snacks. She'd even dragged out some of her kids' old toys and books. The woman was as ready as a high-end daycare, though I would have expected nothing less. As Zee showed me her arsenal, Lily plopped down to watch cartoons, one of Hannah's old dolls clutched in her arms like a flotation device.

"See," Zee assured me, "Lily will be much better off here than in that office. As soon as you leave, I'll dump her into the tub. After, I'll tuck her in, and we'll read stories together." Zee pointed to the small suitcase. "I trust there are some jammies in there."

"I have no idea what Erica packed. And considering how grubby Lily appears, who knows if what's in there is clean."

"If not, I'm sure I can rustle up something."

I filled Zee in on what was happening at the office and my conversation with Steele.

Zee listened with her usual patience and common sense. "If Woobie lets you go and Steele can guarantee you a job in the fall, it might be good for you to take a few months off in between."

"It is very tempting."

"And who knows, maybe the job with Steele might open up sooner."

I played with the salt and pepper shakers on the kitchen table, occasionally glancing over at Lily, who we could see through the wide door leading to the den.

Zee covered one of my hands with one of hers. We'd known each other over twenty years. She was closer to me than my own family, and there was no one I trusted more besides Greg. "Things always turn out for the best, Odelia. I'll keep you and Lily in my prayers."

I gave her a sad smile and squeezed her hand in return. Zee was the better half of this relationship, just as Greg was the better half of our marriage. While I saw the glass half empty, she saw it over-flowing. I knew things would work out. Maybe not to my personal satisfaction, but in the end the dust would settle, and I'd have a place to go—either with Steele or someplace new. Or maybe a new opportunity would present itself, one I hadn't considered yet. In the meantime, all I saw ahead of me was a road strewn with potholes and land mines.

"I'm not so sure," Zee added, giving my hand a final pat, "that staying at Woobie is best for you, even if they don't fire you. You haven't been happy there since that merger."

"Greg says the same thing."

Zee held up a teapot of Constant Comment tea she'd brewed just before I'd arrived. "Tea?"

I shook my head. "No, thanks. I guzzled a lot of iced tea at the restaurant."

Zee poured herself a cup and set the pot down. "Have you told Greg yet what's going on with Lily and the office?"

"Not yet. I wanted to get Lily settled with you first. I'll call him on my way back to the office." I stared out the window at the back yard. Greg and I had been married there, right next to the swimming pool. We'd met there for the first time, too.

"I really don't want to go back to the office." I groaned—an ailing cow being led to slaughter.

"Then don't," Zee said simply. "Stay here with us today or go out and do something fun to take your mind off everything."

"I have to go back to the office." I continued to look out the window.

"What are they going to do, fire you?"

I turned my head. "Good point."

Zee took a sip of her hot tea. I could see she was giving my situation considerable thought. "Does Carl know you have Lily?"

I raised my head, wondering where she was going with this train of thought. "I don't know. Why?"

"If they lay you off today, what becomes of Lily? They can't expect a fired employee to be saddled with the kid of a partner."

"So I should take Lily back and hand her over to Carl after he fires me?"

We both turned to look at the child in question. Lily was still in front of the TV, sitting cross-legged and half babbling, half singing to the African-American baby doll cradled in her arms.

"You could," Zee said after turning back around to me. "But that's not the best thing for Lily."

I started to get up from the table, groaning as I lifted myself to my feet. "Tell you what, I'll go back and take my medicine, whatever it might be. I'll let Carl know Erica left the kid in my care and ask him what he plans to do about it. Put the problem on him."

"Sounds like a good plan. In the meantime, Lily can stay here and get some rest."

I picked up my purse. "I should have talked to Carl anyway when Erica started leaving Lily with me. It's really inappropriate."

"One thing more, Odelia."

Uh-oh. Zee's voice had changed from supportive to warning.

"You said Lily's mother is missing. Is that true?" she asked.

"That's what I heard."

Zee lifted a hand and pointed an index finger at me. "No matter what happens—no matter what they ask of you—don't you *dare* start nosing around in that business."

I was taken aback by the order. "Why would I?"

"I'm just saying…"

With her words hanging in the air like a bad stench, I left the table. Going into the den, I squatted down by Lily. "I have to go back to the office, Lily, but you're going to stay here with Zee. Okay?"

Lily turned her cornflower blue eyes on me, and for a minute I thought she might start to cry. She clutched the doll tighter.

"I'll be back later to get you. I promise," I added quickly as I stroked her hair. "Be a good girl, and let Zee take care of your cold. Okay?" I offered up another chance for her to agree.

This time Lily surrendered a little nod. Bending down more, I gave the little girl a hug. She wrapped her arms around my neck and clung like a monkey to a vine.

Once I disentangled myself from Lily, I gave her a final pat on the head and started for the back door. I had just given Zee a hug goodbye and a word of thanks when a high-pitched, blood-curdling scream came from the den. Both Zee and I turned to find Lily standing at the doorway, her once-sweet face transformed into a gargoyle. She was screaming at the top of her lungs, rivulets of tears running down her flushed face.

Zee stayed where she was, but I rushed to Lily, holding out my arms. She launched herself into them and latched herself around my neck.

I looked at Zee in total surprise. "What's the matter with her? A moment ago she seemed okay."

"She's three, Odelia. Three-year-olds can be as temperamental as a half-dozen women in menopause."

Great. Lily and I should make a fine pair.

I wrapped my arms around my charge, feeling her warm body melt into mine as her crying subsided. I was lost without a map when it came to kids.

"She's also not feeling well and needs a nap." Zee headed to the kitchen counter with the teapot and her cup. "Not to mention, poor Lily has been handed off quite a bit in the past few days. Maybe one more stranger is her breaking point."

"But she seemed to like you." I put Lily down. She stood straight but clung to my left leg like a plaster cast.

"She does like me." Zee rinsed out her teacup and wiped her hands on a nearby kitchen towel. "And tomorrow she might be just dandy staying here. She'll probably be fine ten to twenty minutes after you leave today. Hard to tell."

I considered my options, then went back to the table to retrieve my phone from my bag. Lily moved with me like a leg iron, not letting go of the choke hold she had above my knee.

I hit the entry for the firm's main line. After two rings it was answered by our receptionist.

"Carl's been looking for you for a couple of hours, Odelia. Where've you been? Isn't your cell phone working?"

I felt a twinge of guilt. I'd left the firm without letting Joyce know, but that had been my plan. "Don't worry, Joyce. I'm calling to tell you I won't be back this afternoon. Lily's not feeling well, so I'm taking her home with me." I paused, then added in a tone of surrender, "Why don't you put me through to Carl."

"Denise Morales is in with Carl now, so you might want to wait a few minutes and call back, or I can put you into his voice mail."

Denise Morales. I wondered how much Joyce knew about the layoffs. One of the positions that wasn't duplicated in the merger was that of receptionist, so I felt confident Joyce still had a job. Denise wasn't so lucky. She worked in our file room, and Hamlin-Hawke had brought over a couple of their own file clerks. In all honesty, they did seem more efficient than Denise. Maybe folks felt the same about Mark and me—that he was the more efficient paralegal when it came down to the work itself.

"Did you know about Hope and Kelsey?" I asked Joyce.

"Yes, very sad." Her voice was low and guarded.

I wondered if Joyce knew my head was on the chopping block, too. Probably she did. Seemed like everyone knew.

"They also let go the Hamlin-Hawke mail guy," Joyce added, "and Susan, the litigation secretary they brought over."

I was sad for those folks, but it was nice to see it wasn't just Woobie employees being tossed out the door.

"Thanks for the info, Joyce. You can put me through to Carl's voice mail now."

I told Carl the same thing I'd told Joyce—Lily was ill, and I was taking her home and putting her to bed. His office was on the other side of the building from mine, so I didn't know if he was aware of

Lily's continuing presence, but I didn't take the time to explain. I could do that if he called back.

My next call was to Alyce Allen. I gave her the same spiel.

"So Lily's with you?" she asked.

"Yes. Erica asked me to take her until Monday."

I looked down just in time to catch Lily wiping her runny nose on my skirt. The skirt was brand new and probably would never be the same. I looked over at Zee, who was watching with amusement, no doubt remembering the clothing she'd sacrificed at the altar of motherhood.

"Alyce, I left my computer on. Would you go in and log it off for me?"

"Sure, Odelia. Glad to do it." She paused long enough to clear her throat. "It's probably best you're not here anyway. A lot of folks are getting the axe this afternoon, both from your old firm and mine."

"That's what I've heard." It was my turn to throat-clear. "Have you heard anything about Mark or me?"

"No, but Mark's been circling our area like a buzzard."

"He's probably waiting for the all-clear signal to claim my office."

"No doubt, but if they have to choose one of you to go, I hope it's him. He's a real pill."

I smiled. While I would have called Mark Baker a bastard or an SOB, Alyce never swore. Calling someone a pill was strong language for her. "Thanks, Alyce. I appreciate that. Any word from Erica?"

"None. I have no idea where she is or when she's returning, and there's nothing on her calendar. Did she say anything to you?"

"I'm lucky she speaks to me at all."

When I ended the call, Zee handed me a small grocery bag she'd been packing during my call to the firm. "What's this?" I asked.

"The children's cold medicine. Give Lily another dose before bed. There's also a plastic baggie of Cheerios in there. Kids love to snack on those. I'm sure you have other kiddie foods in your fridge."

Lily was still clinging to my leg. I patted her head with assurance. "You may be sure," I answered Zee, "but I'm not. We were going to have catfish with wild rice and steamed vegetables for dinner tonight. Think she'll eat that?"

"I doubt it. Little ones can be very fussy eaters. Try mac and cheese, grilled cheese sandwiches, hot dogs, chicken noodle soup, chicken fingers, PB and J, even waffles cut into bite-size pieces. Bananas, apples wedges, and applesauce are also good. I know you have some of those things at home."

Zee was right, most of those items were in my pantry and fridge already, and Greg was the king of grilled cheese. "She had chicken fingers for lunch."

Squatting down, I went face to face with Lily. "Do you want to go to my house, Lily? I have two kitties and a doggie."

The hysteria of a few minutes ago was forgotten as she nodded with enthusiasm. "I go Cheesehead Squirrel's house!"

Zee squinted at us. "Cheesehead what?"

"Nothing," I answered quickly. "Just a character she saw at lunch."

I stood and started rounding up Lily and her stuff for the trip to Seal Beach. The kid did look dog-tired and raggedy. She rubbed her eyes and yawned as I put on her sweater. I'd bet one of Greg's kick-ass grilled cheese sandwiches Lily would sleep most of the way to my house.

We were almost out the door when my cell phone rang. It was Carl Yates. I showed the phone to Zee.

"You have to talk to him sometime, Odelia. Just do it and get it over with."

I took a very deep breath, held it, and blew it out as the ringing continued. Another ring and the call would go to voice mail. At the last moment I caved and punched the answer button. "Yes, Carl?"

"I just got your message." He sounded tired. Carl Yates was a tough lawyer but a very nice man. Throwing people out of work, especially employees he's known for years, had to be killing him. "You're not coming back to work because of a sick kid? Did you and Greg adopt when I wasn't looking?"

"You don't know who Lily Holt is?"

"Enlighten me."

"Lily is Erica Mayfield's three-year-old niece. Erica dumped her on me Tuesday."

I cringed as I said the word *dumped* in front of Lily. I didn't want to give her the feeling she was a nuisance, even though she was. It just wasn't her fault. Zee sensed my concern and picked Lily up and took her into the den. Lily was so tired, she didn't kick up a fuss over the separation.

"I've been taking care of Lily every day since," I explained to Carl. "On the firm's time." I said the last part slowly and with emphasis. "This morning Erica told me I'm to keep Lily over the weekend. She didn't ask me, Carl. She demanded and even threatened my job over it. She unloaded Lily and her things and took off."

Silence as long and lonely as a stretch of desert road came from the other end of the call.

"You gonna fire me today, Carl?" I asked, filling the void with a snotty attitude. Normally I wouldn't dream of speaking to Carl Yates in this manner, but today was special. Today might be my last day at Woobie. Burning bridges had just become my new career path. "Because if you are, be prepared to take Lily home with you for the weekend, runny nose and all."

After more silence and a deep sigh, Carl said, "I need you back here today, Odelia. Can you find someone to take care of Erica's niece for the afternoon?"

When I hesitated, he added, "You're not going to be fired."

"Today or ever?" I asked, demanding clarification.

Another tired sigh. "Just come in, Odelia, and I'll explain everything."

I took a few steps towards the den to take a peek. Zee was seated in an upholstered rocking chair, moving back and forth slowly, softly humming. Lily was bundled in her arms sound asleep, the baby doll clutched in the crook of one arm, the thumb of her other hand stuck in her mouth.

"Carl said he needs me to come back," I whispered.

"Go," Zee told me in a hushed voice. "Lily and I will be fine. I'll tell her you'll be back later."

I mouthed my thanks and stepped back into the kitchen. "Carl, I'll be back in about ten to fifteen minutes."

SIX

"I THOUGHT YOU SAID I wasn't going to be fired."

I was seated in Carl's messy office in front of his equally messy desk. Behind the desk, Carl, a man in his early sixties, sat looking haggard but focused. The sleeves of his dress shirt were rolled up, and his tie was loose. His hair, a thinning mixture of white and yellow like sweet summer corn, was as limp as he looked.

"You're not being fired, Odelia." He ran a hand through his hair. "No one is being fired. People are being laid off, meaning we no longer have jobs for them. It doesn't mean they've done something wrong. Everyone is getting sparkling references, and we're also providing job counseling and nice severances."

"Po-tay-toe, po-tah-toe. It still means folks are unemployed."

"I'm not going to argue semantics with you, Odelia."

Maybe not, but I was ready to argue with him. If I was going down, I was going down hissing and snarling like a cornered bobcat.

"And you're not being laid off or fired—at least not today." Before I could say anything, Carl tacked on, "But don't tempt me."

We took a few minutes to cool down. Carl was the first to break the thick silence. "As I said a minute ago, we haven't made a decision yet about the corporate paralegal position. However, we feel we do need to downsize in that area."

"Why don't you put me and Mark in a cage and let us duke it out to the finish? Last paralegal standing gets to keep their job. He might be younger and stronger, but, trust me, I'd hold my own. It can be the featured entertainment at the next partners' meeting."

Carl stared at me a moment, then broke into chunky laughter. "Something tells me the betting would be heavy in your favor, Odelia. I know I'd take those odds."

I pursed my lips and fixed Carl with narrowed eyes. "Then why aren't you betting on me now? I've been with this firm for decades. Mark hasn't even been with Hamlin-Hawke very long."

Carl leaned forward, not backing down from my challenge. "Who's says I'm not betting on you?" Again silence fell between us. He was the first to blink.

"Odelia, let me be blunt with you. Pretty much everyone was in agreement as to which employees and positions needed to be eliminated except when it came to you and Mark Baker. When it came to you two, it was divided between the firms, with no compromise on either side. On careful evaluation, without regard to alliances, you were the paralegal who fell short. Your billable hours are down, for one thing, and the Hamlin-Hawke folks are digging in their heels about you being a liability to the firm regarding your habit of getting involved in murder cases."

I couldn't believe my ears on the first part. "My billables are down because Erica refuses to give me work. I'm not getting much from other areas of the office either. And for the past several days, she's saddled me with Lily. Do you know how little work I can accomplish with a three-year-old attached to my hip? Try it sometime."

I got to my feet and paced, careful not to step on the files covering the floor. I turned and pointed an index finger at Carl. "Erica Mayfield and Mark Baker are setting me up. As for the liability issue, I wasn't a liability when the firm needed my help a few years back, was I? In fact, I remember not only saving Steele's life, but the reputation of this firm."

My blood pressure was rising to a boil. For the second time today, I was close to telling an attorney to stick this job up their Ivy League ass.

After more silence, Carl asked, "Where's the child now?"

"Zee Washington agreed to watch her today, but my friends should not be used as daycare any more than I should. If Erica's sister has taken off, then Erica needs to step up and take care of her own niece." I stopped my rant long enough to take stock of my words, remembering how scruffy Lily was getting as the days wore on. "Although my guess is Lily is far better off with me or Zee. It's just not right, though."

"I agree."

Carl swiveled around in his chair and looked out the window. I wasn't sure if it was an indication I was dismissed or if he merely needed time to digest the situation. After nearly a minute, I started for the door.

"Odelia." My name came from the chair, but Carl still did not turn around.

I took a careful step back in the direction of Carl's desk as he spun back around to face me.

"I know Erica has been stacking the deck against you. We all know it. She hasn't been very discreet about it. She's even been lobbying the Woobie partners against you on the liability issue and has succeeded in catching the attention of a few. I'm not sure why she's doing that, do you?"

I swung my head back and forth as if on a hinge. "Not a clue."

"Have you tried talking to her about it?"

"Yes, but she shuts me down and won't give me the time of day. I'm practically barred from her office."

I took a seat in the chair across from Carl again, about to unload an unsavory thought. "Carl, do you think Erica's sleeping with Mark Baker? It wouldn't be the first time a boss couldn't keep their hands off the staff."

I knew my remark conjured up thoughts of Steele, who loved getting up close and personal with coworkers, especially secretaries—until we hired him a lesbian assistant. He fell in love with Jill's secretarial abilities and baking skills instead. But as long as I've known him, Steele has never used his influence to help or hinder his lovers.

"I have no idea," Carl answered after giving it consideration. "It could just be a case of her preferring to work with a paralegal she knows. You know, her comfort level." Even though the words came out of his mouth, I could see Carl was thinking there might be more to Erica's motives than mere familiarity.

Crossing my arms, I leveled my eyes at Carl and let loose a barely veiled threat. "If she *is* sleeping with Mark, or has some other personal connection to him, and is going around bad-mouthing me to the partners to get me fired, *she's* the one opening the firm up to liability, not me."

Carl's a smart boy. He knew instantly I meant Erica was exposing the firm to a possible discrimination suit on the issues of sex and gender, with possible age-discrimination allegations thrown in. Not that I'd thought about filing a suit until that very moment, but now that I'd thrown the comment out, it had become part of my arsenal.

Carl's eyes bore into mine to see if I meant business. I didn't crack under the pressure. I had nothing to lose.

"Go back to your desk, Odelia," he finally said. "Do your work in the same efficient manner you always have. It's rather slow right now across the firm as a whole, but I'll rustle up some work to keep you afloat for the time being, and I'll have other attorneys divert billable work to you as much as possible. Don't forget, you have a lot of loyal supporters here."

"What about Lily?"

"I know it's an imposition, but if we can't iron out that problem today, do you think Zee would keep her tomorrow while you're here?"

I thought about Zee cuddling with Lily. Kids were like crack to her. "I believe she would."

Carl reached for his phone. "In the meantime, I'm going to get in touch with Erica."

"Good luck. No one seems to know where she is at the moment or when she's returning. She might even be gone until Monday."

"Hmm." He held up a finger, indicating for me to stay put. After unhanding the phone, he swung around again to gaze out the window to think. Thirty seconds later, he turned back around.

"We've shelved the decision about the paralegals for a few weeks," he told me. "That should buy me time to get to the bottom of this. How about you putting some time into locating Erica? But do it quietly. When you do find her, make sure she gets in touch with me immediately." His eyes were almost glowing. I knew that look. It was how he looked when he had enough evidence to nail an opponent in court.

"More unbillable work, Carl?"

"For now, it might be necessary." Carl picked up a pen and started twirling it between his fingers as he set out his battle plan. "Remember that internal billable code we used when Steele went missing? Use that for your time. If anyone asks, you're on a special assignment for me."

Like with Erica, Carl didn't give me a chance to decline the assignment. "Sure, Carl," I answered as if everything was hunky-dory.

"And while you're at it, find out more about Erica and Mark's relationship. Again, with discretion."

With that order, my task went from locating a boss for a conference call to digging into her personal life like one of those slimy divorce detectives. I had already planned on finding out more about Erica and Mark. After all, if she was slinging mud at me with the partners, I had to be prepared to do battle. From time to time, the firm had called upon me to research the background of questionable corporations and individuals connected to them. It usually involved digging around on the computer through public records and connecting the dots. But this was different. A name partner had given me the green light to burrow into the personal life of another partner. If this went sour, it would taint us both with a stink that would be hard to shake.

Carl put his hand back on the phone, then stopped and looked into my face. "We were all very pleased when you didn't follow Mike

Steele to Templin and Tobin. I think it's time to remind the partners about that."

With one foot out his door, I let loose with my final volley. "Don't you think it's equally important to remind me why I didn't?"

Carl stared at me, grunted something indecipherable, and turned back around to gaze out his window. He was still twirling the pen.

I walked down the hall to the other side of the building, towards my office, thinking how Zee had seen this coming. She'd told me not to get involved, not even if they asked. But what was I to do? I had to find Erica, hand Lily off to her, and hopefully show the powers-that-be that of their two paralegals, I was the keeper.

Truth is, unemployment was beginning to look pretty damn snazzy.

I was barely back in my office when Alyce rushed in. "I got your message that you were coming back."

As soon as I agreed to return to the office, I had called Alyce to keep her in the loop and tell her not to bother with my computer. With Alyce was a tall, thin man I'd never seen before. Due to confidentiality issues, unknown individuals are not allowed to drift through our hallways. My questioning eyes settled on him.

"Oh," jumped in Alyce, noting my attention to the stranger, "this is Gary, my husband. He was in the area and stopped by to say hello and see the office."

I extended my right hand towards Gary Allen. "I'm Odelia Grey. Nice to meet you." He smiled, showing uneven teeth, and took my hand. His shake was firm and dry, his blue eyes serious and intelligent. His face was broad through the forehead and narrow at the jaw, like an inverted pyramid.

"My pleasure, Odelia," Gary Allen said with warmth. "I've heard a lot about you."

Alyce hooked an arm through her husband's. "Gary and I were talking, Odelia. We'd be glad to take Lily back to our house until Monday. Gary works from home mostly, so tomorrow wouldn't be a problem, and we have kids of our own."

Gary patted his wife's arm. "One more child wouldn't make a bit of difference, I can assure you. The Lord provides for all who enter our home."

It was then Alyce noticed I was toddler-free. "Where's Lily?" she asked.

Mark Baker materialized out of nowhere, the three of them crowding my door. Standing slightly behind the Allens, Mark watched in silence like a deadly crocodile waiting in the shallows of a swamp.

"That's very generous of you," I said to Alyce and Gary, "but a friend is watching her."

They seemed genuinely disappointed.

"Carl called me back in for a meeting," I explained, "and I didn't think it wise to have her underfoot."

A hand shot to Alyce's mouth. "You're not ... you know."

"Relax, I still have my job." I took a seat behind my desk and stashed my purse in the bottom drawer. "Carl assigned me a special project he needs done right away." I looked pointedly from Alyce to Mark, letting my gaze linger on the latter. "I'm sure you're *both* relieved to hear I wasn't canned ... yet."

SEVEN

WHEN I PICKED UP Lily after work, she was clearly glad to see me. She was scrubbed clean, top to bottom, including her clothes, and her cold seemed better. She ran to me and threw her arms around my legs, chattering a mile a minute about cookies and trains. Or maybe it was clubs and twine.

"You're a miracle worker, Zee. Lily looks factory new."

Zee was working on supper. "Nothing a nap and a bubble bath couldn't fix. I went through her suitcase to see what was clean and dirty and ended up throwing almost everything in the wash. By the way, there's a baby monitor in there. Make sure you use it tonight."

Lily babbled something and took off like a shot to watch something on TV.

"She was in the middle of *Dora the Explorer*," Zee explained.

"Huh?"

Zee laughed. "You'll learn soon enough."

"I really owe you, Zee." I hesitated. I had two other favors to ask her but didn't want her to think I was taking advantage. One was taking Lily the next day, Friday, so I could go into work. I was sure she wouldn't have an issue with that if she didn't have plans. The other favor was Friday night. Shortly after I left Carl, I had called Greg to update him on everything.

"If I don't locate Erica soon, you and I will be playing Mommy and Daddy over the weekend."

"Sounds like fun, actually," was my darling husband's initial response. "I know Wainwright will love it. But what about Friday night?"

"What's Friday?" I asked, my mind a blank. Before he could say anything, I groaned, remembering we had plans. Isaac and Melina Thornwood had asked us over to dinner on Friday night. Isaac played basketball with Greg. He was also in a wheelchair but was an amputee. Like us, the Thornwoods entertained quite a bit. Usually their dinners were on Saturday night, but this Sunday they were leaving on vacation. Friday night was to be a small birthday bash for Isaac.

"If Zee can't watch Lily, I'll have to stay home with her." I was disappointed but felt very motherly and responsible as I said the words.

"If Zee can't watch her Friday night, maybe my parents could," Greg offered. "You know my mother loves little kids."

That was an understatement. Between Greg, his brother, and his sister, only his sister had produced grandchildren for the Stevens family, and recently she and her brood had moved to Northern California. Renee Stevens was going through grandchildren withdrawal, just as Zee was going through the anticipation of getting her own one day.

I turned my memory away from my earlier phone call with Greg and settled back on the present and Zee.

"I have a really big favor to ask you," I said to my friend as she stirred something in a large pot on the stove. The steam drifted over to my nostrils. It was aromatic, filled with scent of gentle spices and chicken—probably a homemade stew or soup. My mouth watered. Lunch with Steele had seemed like days ago. I hoisted my behind onto a stool in front of the granite kitchen counter.

"You want me to watch Lily tomorrow while you go to work, don't you?" Zee put the wooden spoon down on a spoon rest and wiped her hands on a kitchen towel. She moved from the stove to the counter, standing across from where I sat.

"Could you?"

"Of course," Zee replied in a happy voice. "I figured you might need a sitter for tomorrow."

I fidgeted on the stool, my short legs dangling uncomfortably until I could find the foot rail. "Can you also watch her tomorrow night? Greg and I have dinner plans." Before Zee could answer, I gushed, "If you can't, that's okay—I do have a backup plan, and you're already going above and beyond."

Zee didn't answer the question, instead honing in on the obvious information behind it. "So Lily's staying with you for the entire weekend?"

"If I can't locate Erica tomorrow, she is." I gave her a quick update on my conversation with Carl.

Zee didn't say anything but returned to the stove, where she picked up the wooden spoon and started stirring whatever was in the big pot again. It didn't need it, but Zee needed something to do.

In her head I knew she was stirring the information I'd just given her as vigorously as she was whirling around the contents of the pot.

"So in spite of my warning, you're going to hunt down Erica Mayfield?"

"You forgot, I'm also sneaking around to see if she and Mark are doing the nasty."

Zee didn't say anything. She didn't have to. She fixed me with the two pools of chocolate she called eyes and set her mouth into displeasure.

"I didn't have a choice, Zee," I told her, going on the defense. "Carl gave it to me as an assignment. It could be the difference between keeping my job or not."

"Did you even put up a fight, Odelia? Did you tell him you were out of the attorney-hunting business?" Zee returned to the counter, still clutching the spoon. I worried she might bop me over the head with it. She didn't, but she did shake it at me with determination while her left hand, knotted in a fist, latched onto her bulky left hip. "Well, did you?" Zee's coffee-colored face was stern but not scrunched in anger. I took that as a good sign. Still, I leaned back from the counter.

"No, Zee, I didn't. I'm thinking the sooner I find Erica, the sooner all the crap about Lily and my job will be cleared up. Carl didn't sound the least bit pleased with Erica and her shenanigans."

She put the spoon down on her spotless counter. "Would you really file a discrimination suit against that firm?"

"Honestly? The idea never occurred to me until I found out Erica was trying to influence the Woobie partners against me. If they decide they want Mark over me strictly based on work product, I wouldn't like it, but I could live with it. But Erica is going out of her way to make sure I fail." I paused to think it over. Suing an employer had a lot of risks. "But if I found out Erica had special and personal ties to Mark Baker and that was her motive for sandbagging me, then yes, I'd consider legal action."

Zee issued a deep sigh and looked into my eyes a long time before looking away. From the den came the sound of a children's song and giggles from Lily.

"When you bring Lily over tomorrow morning," Zee said, "why don't you plan on her staying the night. That way you and Greg won't have to worry about how late your dinner runs."

"Thank you, Zee." I breathed a sigh of relief. "We'll pick her up Saturday morning."

She picked up the spoon and shook it at me again. A few drops of broth flew in my direction, landing on the counter with the droplets from earlier. "Just assure me there are no dead bodies involved."

With my right index finger I crossed my heart. "There are no dead bodies, Zee. I just have to locate Erica, so Carl can talk to her as soon as possible, and do some snooping into Mark's connection to her. I'll probably be able to do both tomorrow from the safety of my desk while chowing down on a tuna sandwich."

The spoon pointed at me like a lance. "Just keep it that way, you hear?"

In the beginning, Lily wasn't so sure about wanting to be pals with Wainwright, our big, friendly golden retriever. But he won her over, as he does everyone he meets, and soon she was rolling on the floor in a fit of giggles with Wainwright and Muffin, our young gray cat. Our old man cat, Seamus, wasn't having any of it and had disappeared into our bedroom for a quiet snooze.

Greg was enchanted with Lily and she with him. If Lily were twenty years older, I'd have been a bit worried about her stealing my hubby's heart. Greg loved kids and, like his mother, was grieving over the move of his two nephews.

Kids had been a sticking point when Greg asked me to marry him—not a sticking point to him, but to me. I was in my late forties when we married; Greg was ten years younger. I knew he wanted kids, but for me it wasn't an option. In the end, he assured me it didn't matter, that he wanted me no matter what. For a while we considered adopting, but that never materialized. Now, with me in my fifties and Greg in his forties, children weren't even on our radar, except for the children belonging to friends and family.

When she first met Greg, Lily was fascinated by his wheelchair. She kept wanting him to get up and let her have a turn. Once she understood the chair acted as his legs, she'd asked for a ride. Greg had hoisted her up on his lap and taken her for a spin around our large, wheelchair-friendly house.

Now the two of them were in the kitchen. Greg was whipping up grilled cheese sandwiches with Lily's help and supervision, the planned catfish dinner long forgotten. Lily was kneeling on a chair dragged up close to the counter. Because our counters were built to be accessible to Greg, they were low and perfect for Lily's use, with a little help. They were also perfect for me since I'm on the short side.

Lily was in charge of buttering the bread. Wainwright watched with eager and hungry eyes for any fallout. He'd already snagged a piece of bread that had fallen to the floor—butter-side down, of course. I was at one end of the kitchen table with my laptop. Outside, the threat of rain had finally materialized. It started while driving home from Zee's and had continued, soft and steady, since.

Rain, the warm kitchen, and the happy domestic scene were acting as a balm to the day's events. But watching Greg with Lily brought back the old worry and guilt that I might have robbed my husband of something important. Blinking back the tears threatening my vision, I moved my thoughts back to getting a bead on Erica's whereabouts.

Our firm puts out a personnel directory with everyone's information, such as name, address, telephone number, and emergency contact. I had it on the table beside me. After checking Erica's address, I looked it up on Google Maps. Erica lived on a cul-de-sac in Newport Beach just off Jamboree Road. I knew the area. It was a quiet housing development of nice homes near the Back Bay, not far from Fashion Island Mall. There was both a home phone and a cell phone listed on the sheet. Erica's emergency contact was Connie Holt, Lily's mother. There was no secondary contact. I circled the phone number for Connie, then did a reverse lookup.

A few years ago I had subscribed to an online search engine for finding people. There were some free services out there, but this one had proved to be worth the money and often gave me information most folks thought was unlisted, including things like household income, real estate values, and educational backgrounds. It was paying off right now. Connie's number produced an address in Irvine and her husband's name—Harrison—although I remembered Alyce referring to him as Hank. According to the website, Connie was in her late thirties, Hank in his early forties. The combined household income was just under two hundred thousand a year. It listed one child under five years of age—no name or gender.

"You having any luck?" Greg asked from his spot at the stove.

"A bit. At least I have addresses and telephone numbers, which is a good start." I closed my laptop.

Greg had finished cooking supper and had lifted Lily down to the floor. In her outstretched hands he placed a dinner plate piled with grilled cheese sandwiches. Lily carried the plate with pride and care. When she reached me, I took it from her and placed it on the table.

"Thank you, Lily. What a good helper you are." The child beamed and babbled about how she had cooked the "sand witches."

I settled Lily on top of a couple of cushions placed in a kitchen chair, wrapped a dish towel around her neck for a bib, and pulled her close to the table. Greg rolled over with a large serving bowl of cream of tomato soup.

"How many *sand witches* are you planning on Lily eating?" I asked Greg, casting an eye to the pile on the plate.

"What? There's only five—two each for us and one for Lily." Greg put the soup on the table. "I made three with plain American cheese and two with cheddar and tomatoes."

"And basil?" I asked hopefully.

"Fresh chopped basil, just like you love it."

I got up and went to Greg, giving him a sound kiss on the mouth. He returned the kiss, taking a little longer with his. Next to us, Lily giggled and wiggled. "Me," she insisted. "Kiss Lily, Cheesehead Squirrel."

I leaned over and gave Lily a noisy smackaroo on her forehead. She squealed with delight. Maybe we shouldn't have given up so easily on the adoption thing.

"What did she call you?" Greg asked as he dished soup into two thick mugs.

"Um, Cheesehead Squirrel." I said the name in a quick, low, barely audible voice, hoping he wouldn't notice.

"Don't give her very much," I told him as he spooned soup into a small plastic bowl for Lily. "I don't know if she'll eat it. And let it cool a bit before giving it to her."

Greg put the ladle down. "Cheesehead Squirrel? How did she come up with that?"

"Beats me." I cut one of the American cheese sandwiches into quarters and put two of them on Lily's plate. She grabbed one with the same gusto she'd attacked the chicken fingers with earlier in the day. I was two for two so far on food, thanks to a waitress and Zee.

"Did she say that in front of Steele at lunch today?" my husband asked with a wicked grin.

I sighed. "That's where she came up with it, and totally on her own."

"He must have loved it."

"Yep." I took a bite of my sandwich, letting the flavors of the sharp cheese, cool tomato, and peppery basil melt together in my mouth.

"Cheesehead Squirrel," Greg repeated. "I love it."

"Cheesehead Squirrel. Cheesehead Squirrel. Cheesehead Squirrel," sang Lily, moving her fist with the sandwich like a baton.

I groaned. Greg laughed—far too long, in my opinion.

Wainwright sat at attention next to Lily, his eyes following the arc of the sandwich as it circled through the air. If Lily lost her grip, the sandwich would disappear before it ever hit the floor. I'm sure, if questioned, the dog would have voted for the adoption route, too.

"Wainwright," Greg ordered, pointing away from the table. "Go lay down."

The dog looked from the precarious sandwich to his master with sad, pleading eyes, measuring his training against the hope for buttery bread and cheese.

"Go on, boy," Greg urged. "You know you're not supposed to beg."

Resigned to follow his training, Wainwright left the table and curled up on the floor by the sliding glass doors leading to the patio. He laid his head on his paws but never took his eyes from Lily and the sandwich.

"That's just plain pathetic," I said, trying not to laugh. "You'd think we never feed him."

Lily polished off most of the two quarters of sandwich and managed a few sips of soup before making it perfectly clear she wasn't having a drop more. The patient Wainwright got the other half of her sandwich. He was eyeing the American cheese one I didn't eat with hope, but there was no way Greg was going to let him score that much people food.

"I think it's time for bed, Lily." I held out my hand to her. She'd been playing with Wainwright and Muffin while Greg and I cleaned up the kitchen.

"Nooooo!" She screwed up her face and shook her head back and forth. "No bed." She took off, running into the living room area, coming to a halt in front of the TV. She pointed at it. "Cartoons."

I followed her. "It's too late for cartoons," I told her. "We all have to go to bed. Even Wainwright and the kitties."

Wainwright bumped into her, nudging her with his large head. Lily wrapped her little arms around his neck in a death grip similar to the one she'd given me earlier in the day. "No!" she cried with high-pitched determination. She stomped her little feet on the floor. "No. No. No."

Maybe we'd made the right decision about kids, after all. Wainwright pulled away, obviously rethinking his stand on the issue, too.

I knelt in front of Lily. "Let's get your jammies on, and then I'll read you a story." I felt her forehead. It still seemed a bit warm, so I dug out the medicine from the bag Zee had packed. Lily saw it and set her face in a scowl. I needed to divert her and fast or it might be a struggle getting her to take some.

"Wainwright loves stories. He'll come with us." I reached out a hand to the dog and he came to me. I petted him on top of his head. "How about it, Wainwright, you want a story?" He lashed out his tongue, catching me on the cheek. I was thankful he was playing along.

Lily considered her options. "Doggie read story."

"Doggies can't read, sweetie, but he loves bedtime stories." I stood up and held out my hand. Lily looked from the dog to my hand several times before finally latching on.

"Sweetheart," Greg said from the kitchen area. "Why don't you get Lily ready for bed, and I'll read her the story. That way you can do some more work before we hit the sack."

I looked down at Lily. "You want *Mr.* Cheesehead Squirrel to read you a story?"

She jumped up and down, changing her mood as quickly as I change lunch options.

"Okay, but you'll need to get into your jammies and take your medicine like a good girl."

Bribery worked like magic. In short order, I had Lily in her pj's, her face washed, her teeth brushed, and the medicine down her throat. By the time Greg came in, she was snug in her bed, clutching the baby doll Zee had given her. Muffin was curled next to her, and Wainwright sat next to the bed. Greg brought in the baby monitor and hooked it up while I went in search of something to keep Lily from falling off the queen-sized bed in the middle of the night. When I returned with two body pillows I'd used when I was injured a few years ago, Lily and Greg were discussing which book to read. While I buffered Lily into the bed, they came to an agreement on *The Tale of Peter Rabbit*.

When I kissed Lily goodnight, she wrapped her little arms around my neck and squeezed with delight, then eagerly hunkered down to hear about a bunny who's naughty and disobeys his mother.

EIGHT

With a final look back at the happy scene, I retired to the kitchen and fired up my laptop again. This time I did a map search for Mark Baker's address. According to the address in the firm directory, he lived in Tustin. On the map it looked like Mark lived on top of a very busy intersection in a mostly commercial area. I knew the intersection in question and couldn't remember any apartment buildings nearby. That didn't mean there weren't any, just that if there were, they would be old and small and probably not very nice.

As paralegals at Woobie, Mark and I make decent money. I have no idea what he makes exactly, but we certainly are paid enough to live in better quarters than this intersection suggested. Of course, Mark could be a miser with his money, choosing to live a frugal lifestyle so he could sock it away for the future. Then again, he might also be forced to live economically due to a secret gambling or drug problem. I didn't wish the latter on him or anyone, but if he did have that type of monkey on his back and it came to light, it would make it easier for the partners to choose me over him in the race for continued employment.

I zoomed in, using the satellite feature on Google. Sure enough, the area around Mark's address did indeed look commercial—almost entirely commercial. I enlarged the satellite picture but could not see any sign of residential property. That seemed odd. Switching to another window, I put his address into a reverse lookup program. Up popped a list of names at that address. My eyes widened as I noted not a single individual name, only a couple of business names. It seemed Mr. Baker's neighbors included a massage place, dry cleaner, pizza joint, and mailbox/shipping business. Mark Baker lived at a small strip mall?

I was pondering what this meant when Greg came wheeling out from Lily's room.

"She's asleep," he announced. "It didn't take long. I didn't even get to the end of the book."

Without looking up from the computer screen, I said, "Farmer McGregor gets eaten by zombie bunnies from another planet."

"Uh-huh. That must be the new modern edition. I don't recall that ending from when I was a kid."

"If it doesn't end that way, it should." I kept my eyes on the computer, studying the enlarged satellite photo.

I poked at the screen. "Mark Baker's address is a strip mall. Probably this mailbox place."

Greg scooted up next to me to check out the screen. "A lot of people use mailbox companies as their physical address."

"True, but it makes you wonder where he lives, doesn't it?"

"Not really, but I know it's making *you* wonder about it." Greg winked at me.

"I'm thinking he has something to hide. I'd almost bet on it. He's just too slithery not to."

"I'm bushed." Greg gave my back a gentle, short rub. "I'm heading to bed to watch the news and do a little reading. You coming along soon?"

"Yes, honey. I'm right behind you. It's been a killer of a day, and I have to get up and get Lily ready to go to Zee's in the morning." I dragged my eyes away from the computer to my husband. "By the way, Zee and Seth are going to keep Lily overnight tomorrow so we can go to Isaac's birthday party."

"As soon as this is over, let's take them out for a special brunch or dinner to thank them for all their help."

"Sounds good to me." I blew Greg a kiss. "I'll be in shortly. I promise."

While Greg got ready for bed, I tried to find out as much as I could about Mark Baker. The problem was, the name was too common and I didn't know enough about him to narrow down the possibilities. There were also quite a few on Facebook, but none of the profile photos matched his mug.

After washing my face and brushing my teeth, I crawled into bed beside Greg. He had the bedroom TV turned to the eleven o'clock news, keeping half an ear on it while his eyes were glued to a novel. On the nightstand next to him was the receiver for the baby monitor.

I did a quick count of noses. There were four—two dry and two wet. A wet one was missing. "Where's Muffin?"

Without looking up from his book, Greg answered, "I think she's bunking down with Lily tonight. When I left, the two of them were curled up asleep like long-lost littermates."

"If I wasn't so tired, I'd get up and take a photo of that."

Greg cut his eyes to me and smiled. "I'm sure you'll have plenty of photo ops over the weekend, sweetheart."

I cuddled next to Greg and threw one arm across his solid chest. "Are you sorry we didn't pursue the adoption thing?"

He closed his book and put it on his night stand, then turned to face me, one of his hands stroking my arm. "Sometimes I am," he answered honestly. "I think we would have made great parents." He paused. "But we made the decision not to adopt after long and careful consideration, and I still think it was the right choice." He looked into my eyes. "Don't you?"

I thought about it a moment. "I did until tonight."

"Yeah, tonight was tough. Having someone like Lily around would be great, but it's also a lot of work and sacrifice." He squeezed me tight. "You know, sweetheart, it's not too late. We could probably still adopt."

The snort came out of me unbidden. "They don't just hand out kids to people of my age and with my body-count track record."

"Don't be so hard on yourself, Odelia. We could adopt an older kid. Remember how great you were with Silas and Billy?"

Silas and Billy were young brothers who used to live in the neighborhood with their grandmother. At the time, their mother was in a drug rehabilitation program. The boys often spent time at our house playing with Wainwright. They'd since moved to a new city with their mother, who seemed to have her life back under control. Every now and then Greg received an e-mail from Silas, or the boys would drop by if they were visiting their grandmother. Silas had once stowed away in my car while I was on the trail of a possible murderer.

"Yeah, and I almost got Silas killed."

"It's not like you took him along for a joy ride, sweetheart."

"Still…," I let my voice trail off.

Before I could say more, Greg grabbed the TV remote from the night stand and aimed it at the TV, raising the volume a notch. On screen was a female field reporter wearing a blue rain slicker with a hood. Behind her were the remains of a brush fire.

"I heard about this on the news earlier," Greg said. "Good thing we had this rain today or the fire might have gotten out of control."

"Where is it?"

"Laguna Canyon."

"Isn't it odd to have brush fires this time of year?" I asked as I nestled against my hubby.

"They suspect arson or kids goofing around." The disgust in Greg's voice echoed how he felt about either situation.

Arson was exactly what the perky but wet reporter was telling her audience. With her pretty face furrowed to match the seriousness of the situation, she also informed viewers that the police had just released information that a body had been found near the suspected point of the fire's origin.

Greg and I gave the news our full attention.

When the anchors back in the newsroom asked if there had been any identification of the body, the field reporter said the police did not have an ID yet and that it might be several days due to the condition of the corpse, but that the police believed it to be male. She added that it wasn't clear if the body was the result of homicide or an accident when the fire was set.

I shuddered.

"What do you want to bet," Greg said, giving me a comforting squeeze, "that the fire was set to get rid of the body, or at least to hide its identity?"

"But she just said it could have been an accident. The dead guy could have been the one setting the fire or doing something stupid and it got out of control."

Unconvinced, Greg shook his head. "My gut's telling me it was murder and an attempted coverup."

I raised myself up on one elbow. "Hey, it's supposed to be my gut that talks like that, not yours."

Greg gave me a quick peck on the mouth. His lips tasted of toothpaste. "Guess your gut's rubbing off on mine."

"Could be," I commented, giving it more thought, "but if I was trying to hide a body, I wouldn't light a fire. That only draws attention to the body dump, and it will be discovered right away. Without a fire, the body might not be discovered for a long time, especially if it's buried."

"Good point, sweetheart. But if someone wanted to make sure the identity wasn't clear, burning might be the best way."

I pointed to Greg's cell phone, which was resting on the nightstand next to the baby monitor. "Should we call Dev and give him our theories? I'm sure he'd appreciate them."

Greg let out a bark of laughter. "Yeah, let's do that. You know how much he loves it when we stick our noses where they don't belong. Besides," he added, "Laguna Canyon isn't his territory. Didn't you learn a while back that the county sheriff handles that area?"

"Parts of it," I said, digging through my memory, "and some of it falls under the jurisdiction of the Laguna Beach police."

"Guess Dev will get off easy this time, all the way around. He won't pull this investigation, and he won't have to listen to us play amateur detectives."

I was about to say more when a high-pitched, blood-curdling screech came out of the baby monitor. Wainwright was the first one out the bedroom door. Scrambling to his feet, he took off like a shot towards the origin of the sound. I was second, my feet hitting the floor with such speed and agility, I astounded myself. I ran across the living room and down the hallway of the other half of the house to the guest bedroom.

Lily tossed her head from side to side. Tears ran down her face from eyes squeezed shut. Her little arms thrashed about, beating off an unknown assailant. Muffin was crouched in a corner of the room, watching with wide-eyed feline fear. Wainwright had his two front paws on the bed. He looked to me, waiting for the command to jump on the bed and rescue our charge. I patted his faithful head and gently yanked his collar, signaling for him to get down.

"Mummy!" Lily screamed in her sleep. Wainwright's front paws instantly went back on the bed.

Pushing the dog out of the way, I sat on the bed and scooped the distressed child into my arms. I held her tight. "I'm here, Lily." I knew she wasn't screaming for me, but for the moment I'd have to do.

"Mummy!" This time the cry wasn't as loud, but it was just as urgent. I wondered if Lily had had these nightmares when she slept at Erica's house.

"It's okay, Lily," I told her as I stroked her hair. Around her face it was damp. "It's okay. I'm here."

Lily clung to me, but she still didn't open her eyes. When Greg made it to the guest room, I was gently rocking her and she had quieted down, her breathing returning to the normal pace of sleep.

"What's the matter?" Greg asked, his voice strained with concern.

I shrugged. "I'm not sure if she called for her mother because she was having a nightmare," I whispered, "or if the nightmare is that her mother is not here."

Greg wheeled closer. He had thrown a robe over his boxers. Stretching out a hand, he pushed a lock of damp hair from Lily's forehead. "She's slightly warm. Should we give her some more medicine?"

"I gave her some just a little bit ago." I looked down at the little girl sleeping in my arms, and my heart broke. Where in the hell was her mother? No child should be shunted from one house to another like this. I had the urge to stay home tomorrow and keep Lily close to me. We could bake cookies and play with Muffin. Carl's assignment would just have to wait.

I laid Lily back down and tucked her in. She was snoozing peacefully now, her face smooth and untroubled. It was then I knew I couldn't stay home and play house with this poor abandoned child, as much as I knew both of us would love it. I had to find Erica and, through her, locate Connie Holt. Lily needed her mother, not some chunky squirrel who might not have a job in a few weeks.

NINE

In the morning Lily's cold seemed better, but the weather was not. It was drizzly and cool—unusually cool, even for March. I skipped my morning walk because of it and because I knew getting Lily ready to go to Zee's would take extra time. Just how much extra time made me stagger in disbelief.

By the time I'd showered and dressed myself, then dressed Lily and fed her Cheerios with milk and banana, then re-dressed her because breakfast had hitched a ride on her clothes, and then changed my blouse because somewhere along the line it had been accessorized with milk and a smear of banana, I was already way behind schedule—so much so that Zee had called to see if I was still bringing Lily over.

Greg watched the whole thing with amusement and a closed mouth. Smart man. He'd suggested earlier that it might be prudent to dress Lily *after* she'd eaten, noting that milk on jammies was no big deal. I figured a little milk on her clothes wouldn't kill her any more than milk on pajamas. Like the time issue, I had way under-estimated how much milk could make its way onto her shirt and

84

never considered any would find its way onto my clothing. The happy Wainwright did cleanup detail, competing with Muffin and Seamus for the drips of milk on the floor.

As I handed Zee Lily's stuff, including the baby monitor, I gave her a rundown on Lily's nightmare and the status of her cold. Lily was already in the living room in front of the TV. She'd brought the baby doll back with her. It had been her constant companion since Zee had handed it to her the day before.

"The nightmare doesn't surprise me," Zee said. "Children are creatures of habit, and this little girl's world has been turned upside down."

"She was fine this morning, so I'm not even sure she remembered it. I hope she's okay tonight." I hesitated, not quite convinced I should leave Lily overnight. "Maybe she should stay with us tonight."

"Nonsense," Zee said with assurance. "I can handle a nightmare if it happens. You and Greg have fun tonight. This weekend you can be parents full-time."

I glanced around. Zee seemed to be alone. "Where's Seth? Is he okay with this?"

Zee's face broke into an explosion of white teeth. "He had an early meeting, and *okay* is not the word. As soon as I told him we'd be entertaining a little one tonight, he went into the garage and pulled out Jacob's old wooden train set." She held Lily's jacket. After giving it a slight shake, she draped it over the back of a chair. "Wouldn't surprise me if he came home early today."

Lily only kicked up a little fuss at being left behind at Zee's. Zee quickly defused the situation by telling Lily they were going to make cookies later that day. Hearing that news put a smile on the child's face, and she happily waved goodbye out the window to me as I drove away in the rain. Cookies—that had originally been my plan, now it was Zee's. Driving away from the Washington house, I felt a bit left out, like a kid home sick for the day instead of out playing kickball with her friends.

When I showed up at the office without Lily, Alyce seemed disappointed and made the offer again to take her for the weekend. Mark glanced into my office and appeared disappointed, too, but his letdown seemed more rooted in the fact that I still had a key to the firm's suite.

"Where's the rug rat?" he asked, a mug of coffee in his hand. My office was between his office and the kitchen, which meant he passed by several times during the day. Mark seldom stopped to make small talk, choosing instead to toss sneers through the doorway like flaming bags of dog poop. Two days in a row now, he'd lingered long enough in my doorway to speak. Lucky me.

With a pen clutched in my right hand, I waved him on like a traffic cop. "Move along, Baker, nothing to see here." If my hand had been empty, it might have morphed into a vulgar hand gesture, adding even more work problems to my plate.

He gave me a tight-lipped smile, raised his mug in salute, and moseyed along.

Once settled behind my desk with a mug of coffee of my own, I plotted out my day. In addition to doing more research on the players involved, I wanted to swing by Erica's house and also take a drive out to Irvine to check out the Holt place. With my regular workload almost nonexistent, I didn't think anyone would notice if I took off. I would simply say I was working on something for Carl. I also wanted to tap Alyce for any information that might have popped up since the day before. Maybe she'd heard from Erica.

After topping off my mug in the kitchen, I casually strolled past Alyce's desk. "Have you heard anything from Erica?"

"Not a word," she answered without looking up from her work. Her diligent fingers flew across the keyboard without hesitation. On her typing stand was a document with handwritten corrections and lines and arrows going every which way, like a John Madden football diagram, only more complicated. "She left me a pile of work yesterday and asked that I e-mail it to her when I was done." Alyce took a deep breath, her fingers pausing just long enough to allow time to inhale and exhale before starting up again. "This is the last of it."

"You still don't know where she is?" I took a sip of coffee in an attempt to appear only half interested in the answer. "Maybe she's working at home."

Alyce shook her head and scrunched her nose. Her glasses were slipping down the bridge, but instead of helping the situation, it only made it worse. "Don't think so. Racel, her cleaning lady, called. She's at the house now and also needs to reach her."

I took another sip of coffee, wondering how helpful and forthcoming Erica's cleaning lady might be with information.

"Well, if Erica does call," I said to Alyce as I started for my office, "please let her know that Carl Yates wants to talk to her as soon as possible."

Alyce nodded but kept working.

"Oh, and speaking of Carl," I said, pausing in my tracks, "I'll be out of the office most of today doing research for that project of his."

"Okay," she said, eyes still glued to the document, her fingers scurrying across the keyboard as if trying to catch a train.

TEN

ERICA'S HOME WAS EXACTLY where I expected it to be after checking out the map the night before. From my office, I'd headed down Bristol towards Newport Beach, making a right on Jamboree Road. Then it was a quick right turn onto East Bluff Drive, followed by a left into a housing development of large, well-maintained homes. It was a peaceful, upscale family neighborhood, with manicured lawns and tidy streets and sidewalks.

My destination was located on Ceiba Place, at the end of a very short and quiet cul-de-sac. From the way the house was situated, the back yard probably abutted Jamboree Road and had either sound walls or a bank of tall bushy oleanders to buffer the noise from the wide, busy street on the other side. When driving down Jamboree, you could see such sound-reduction measures coupled with the wall that encircled the entire development.

The stubby street was quiet, with only a few cars in evidence. A new Toyota Sienna was parked in the driveway next to Erica's house, but there was no sign of neighborly life and none on the other side of Erica's either. Could be everyone was at work or the rain was keeping them inside, or both. The home on the right was a two-story, the other a single-story structure like Erica's. The properties were divided from each other by chest-high hedges trimmed to razor sharpness. Erica's house was a cheerful sage-green stucco with white trim and an attached two-car garage. In her driveway was a white Ford Focus—not new, but well maintained. I knew Erica drove a silver Lexus sports coupe. There was no sign of it, unless it was in the closed garage.

I drove my car around the curve of the cul-de-sac and parked just past the house, with the nose of my car pointing towards the opening of the street. Getting out of the car, I smoothed my slacks and adjusted my jacket, thankful it had stopped raining. As I walked up the drive to the front door, my rubber-soled shoes squeaked on the wet concrete.

I had to ring the doorbell twice before anyone answered. On either side of the front door were narrow opaque windows. I tried to see through them but couldn't. I was about to ring a persistent third time when the door was opened by a young, shapely woman in jeans and a long-sleeved, form-fitting tee shirt with the sleeves pushed up almost to the elbows. She appeared to be in her early twenties, and if I had to venture a guess, I'd say she was Filipino.

"May I help you?" she asked, looking me full in the face with sharp almond eyes that dared me to be selling something or campaigning for a political cause. If I had been, I would have lied, because it was easy to see this woman was having none of that. Not today, not ever.

"Um, maybe I have the wrong house," I stammered. "I was looking for the Mayfield residence." When she offered nothing, I prodded, "Does Erica Mayfield live here?"

"Yes, she does. May I ask what is your business?" The question was direct and confident. I wondered if maybe my assumption about Mark and Erica being romantically involved was wrong. Maybe Erica pitched for the other team and this sassy and pretty lass was her main squeeze. She certainly acted like the lady of the house.

Shaking off hesitation, I started on the fabricated reason for my visit. "I'm Odelia Grey. I work at Ms. Mayfield's firm."

"And?"

Apparently my law-firm credentials weren't good enough. "I need to speak to Racel," I added, trying to keep the annoyance out of my voice.

She crossed her arms in front of her in a challenging stance. "I'm Racel."

The young woman standing in front of me did not look or act like any cleaning lady I'd ever met. My housekeeper, Cruz, was a short, squat grandmother in her sixties. Racel looked more like a university coed with a prominent 'tude. I went headlong into the next portion of my story.

"I'm looking after Lily Holt, and she's asking for a doll or something like that. I think Erica forgot to pack it." Lily wasn't asking for anything outside of her mother, but I figured a kid in distress might get my foot in the door a lot easier than simply firing away with questions.

Racel stuck her chin out. "Wouldn't surprise me, the way she handled that kid."

"May I come in and look for it?" I suggested, hoping she wouldn't simply disappear and return with something soft and fuzzy and send me packing. From the tone of her voice, it didn't sound like Racel was any more pleased with the way Lily was treated than I was. If so, she just might spill some information I could use. After a bit of hesitation, Racel opened the door for me to enter.

Erica's home was spacious and beautiful. Once past the foyer, I walked into a humongous open space with French doors lining the far wall. Just beyond the doors, a patio of red brick dominated the small back yard, covering most of the property in place of grass. The patio was partially covered and populated with more furniture than my living room. Flowering plants in pots of various sizes and styles dotted the area. Off to one side was a hot tub, and beyond that the back wall of the property was lined with sentries of tall oleanders acting as a privacy wall and sound barrier. It was the perfect out-door entertainment space.

The wall-to-wall carpet was thick and the color of pale cham-pagne. In one corner of the living room, past the two matching sofas and chairs and assorted polished tables, was a baby grand piano. Another wall was dominated by a large fireplace framed in white wood with a deep mantel. Above the mantel was a Chagall in a gilt frame, and I'd bet my next latté the painting was real. It was a lovely room but very formal and stuffy, like a photo shoot for a glossy design magazine. Every knickknack, painting, and lamp looked appointed and impersonal rather than a cherished memory. There were no personal photos anywhere. I half expected to see red velvet ropes to keep people from using it.

The great room expanded around a wall into a dining area with a large table and six matching chairs covered in cream brocade down to the floor. I started to poke my head out, craning to see the kitchen, which had to be around the next bend, but Racel cleared her throat, bringing me back to the task at hand. I turned to her and gave her a smile I hoped didn't look too cheesy.

"Like I said, I'm Odelia Grey. I'm a paralegal at Erica's firm." I held out my hand to Racel. She took it.

"Racel Barlongo." She softened her look, which enhanced her pretty face and made her look even younger. "How is Lily?"

"She's fine," I told her. "She's with a friend of mine today who is spoiling her rotten with fun and affection. I think they're going to bake cookies this afternoon."

"The kid needs something like that. Erica made her stay in the guest room most of the time, like a prisoner. Occasionally she was allowed in the den." With a sweep of her hand, Racel indicated the immaculate living room. "She was terrified Lily would make a mess in the house." She let out a half snort. "As if Erica would be the one to clean it up."

"How long have you worked for her?"

"About eight months. My aunt used to work for her. When she retired, I took it over." She motioned for me to follow her down a long hallway while she talked. "It's not a bad gig. I'm here almost every day, but my hours fluctuate depending on my school schedule. I go to UC Irvine, biology major. Erica doesn't care as long as the work gets done while she's gone." Once she knew I was Lily's new caretaker, Racel relaxed and became quite chatty. I hoped it would continue.

Racel opened a door off the hallway, exposing a large bedroom. It was nicely decorated but sparse, holding only a queen-sized bed and a dresser. On top of the dresser was a combination flat screen TV and DVD player. "This was where Lily stayed," she told me.

Without asking permission, I started searching for something soft and kid friendly. I needed to at least try to keep up my ruse while I pumped Racel for information.

"Do you know what Lily was so attached to?" I asked while I did my fake search. Lily hadn't seemed to be missing anything important to her, so I doubted Racel would come up with anything.

"I only saw her a few days," Racel said, helping me look for the nonexistent toy. "Long enough to wash her clothes and keep her occupied on top of my other chores. I watched her all last week, but this week I couldn't. I think the only time she was allowed outside to play was when I was here."

I turned to Racel. "That explains her clothes. Lily and her clothes were scrubbed and fresh earlier in the week, then declined after that."

Racel nodded. "Monday was the last day I was here, until today. My mother had surgery and I spent the last few days with her, so I couldn't watch the kid. I'm on break right now, otherwise I wouldn't have been able to stay with Lily last week."

"Makes sense. Erica didn't bring Lily into the office until Tuesday."

I opened the closet and found nothing. The drawers also produced nothing, and I mean nothing. It seemed that Erica had packed all of Lily's things, every last one of them, as if she didn't expect the little girl to return. But then, maybe Lily only arrived at Erica's with the clothes on her back and those in her small suitcase. If her mother only planned on parking her here a few days, that would make sense.

"Did Lily's mother ever call to check on Lily?" I asked.

"Not that I know of."

"And you didn't see Erica's sister drop Lily off?"

Racel narrowed her eyes and studied me like a stain that needed removing. "What's with all the questions?"

I shrugged. "Just curious. I've been watching Lily since Tuesday and haven't heard a peep from or about her mother."

Racel considered my comment. From the way her shoulders relaxed, I could tell she thought my explanation plausible. "Lily was just here one day when I got to work," she explained. "Erica called me the night before and asked if I'd come in early. When I got here she told me I'd be looking after Lily while she was at work. Said she'd pay me for the extra hours." Racel ran her hand across the dresser, checking for dust. There was none. The house was spotless. "I'm always eager to earn extra money when I'm off from school."

Racel got down on her knees, lifted the bed skirt, and looked under the bed. "Hey, this might be what you're looking for." She lowered her body until she was flat on the carpet and reached under the bed, sticking her head under the flounce. When she emerged, she had something small and soft in her hand. It was a stuffed animal of some kind. Once Racel got to her knees, she held it out to me. "I did see Lily hanging on to this."

I took the stuffed animal and studied it. It was a small, light brown bear wearing a ratty pink tutu. It appeared cheap, like a toy from one of those claw vending machines or a prize won at a carnival for breaking a balloon with a dart.

"Thanks," I told Racel as she got to her feet. "I'm sure she'll be happy to see it."

As we started back down the hall, I tried to keep the conversation going. "This is such a large and lovely house. Does Erica live here alone?"

"As far as I know. Sometimes her boyfriend stays over, but not often."

My ears perked up. "Oh, you mean Mark?" I threw the question out as bait, hoping the tone of my voice made it more of a casual comment than an inquiry.

Racel looked surprised at my comment, then cocked her head in thought. "I'm not sure what his name is and I've never met him, but I can always tell when he's been here." She rolled her eyes before adding, "The toilet seat is always left up in the guest bathroom and there's shaving cream and hair in the sink. That's probably why he doesn't use her bath. Erica's a neat freak."

"She's tidy at work, too."

We were closing in on the front door. In a few minutes I'd have to leave, and without many answers. "Do you mind if I use the bathroom before I take off?" I asked, looking for a reason to linger. "I promise I'll put the seat down when I'm done."

At the request, Racel's attitude changed, and she looked about to shove me out the door. A second later she relaxed again and smiled at my little joke. "I'm gonna hold you to that," she said. We headed back down the hallway.

There was nothing of note in the guest bath. I used the facilities, and while water was running in the sink, I quickly opened cupboards and the medicine cabinet to see if there was any trace of a man staying in the house, even on occasion. All I found was extra toilet paper, soap, and a plunger.

I guess in the back of my head I thought I could retrieve hair from a brush or snag a used toothbrush for a DNA test, but the reality is I wouldn't have a clue where to take it for testing without involving Dev. And I'd read that those tests can sometimes take several days to process if they're not for official emergencies. Although

Carl hadn't given me a time limit, I doubted my project deadline was open-ended.

Then I thought about Willie Proctor, my felon-on-the-run pal. If I did grab something for a DNA sample, he'd know what to do with it. Willie was a former financial scam artist who'd fleeced his clients for millions, then took off. He'd built a small empire of legitimate businesses with his ill-gotten gains and ran it from the shadows of the underground. Not too long ago, he'd returned all the money he'd stolen, with interest, but for some investors it had been too late, and they had been ruined. Willie was still on the run. Returning the money didn't make him any less wanted by the police and FBI. Willie came into my life by chance and stuck around, using his considerable talents and connections to bail me out on numerous occasions. Although we didn't like or condone what he'd done, Greg and I found ourselves growing quite fond of him over the years. If he considered you a friend, there was nothing he wouldn't do to help you, showing up at the least-expected times like a superhero with a checkered past.

Clark Littlejohn, my half brother and a former cop, had gone to work for one of Willie's companies in the past year as a security consultant. While Clark assured me what he did for Willie was legal, he didn't go into details. Clark lived in Massachusetts, where he'd grown up, and to be near our elderly mother, who lived in a retirement home in New Hampshire. He divided his time between the East Coast and Phoenix, where Willie's company was located. Of course, there were no tell-tale trails linking Willie directly to Clark's new employer, but it was his company just the same.

I'd bet Clark would know how to get a speedy DNA test done, too. He not only had his own law enforcement connections, he now had Willie's underground contacts at his disposal. It boggled my mind. But a lot of good either Willie or Clark would do me if I didn't have any DNA to give them. But maybe I was getting too fancy; maybe what I needed wasn't DNA but a good old-fashioned fingerprint. I'm sure Clark and Willie could help me with that, too.

There were two deep drawers on the right side of the vanity. I yanked one open, then the other. In the bottom one I found a man's travel toiletry kit and some travel-sized bottles of shower gel and antiperspirant. Bingo! I sent up a silent prayer of thanks that the bag was gaping open. Just inside was a comb. I grabbed it and stuck it in my purse, along with the small tube of Speed Stick, careful to touch only the narrow sides and not the wide side or the top. Then I rinsed my hands, shut off the water, and freshened my lipstick and fluffed my hair, hoping the lipstick and hair repair would explain what took me so long.

When I exited the bathroom, Racel was nowhere in sight, but I could hear her talking to someone. I tuned my ears but only picked up one voice. She must be on the phone. Hopefully that would buy me more time.

With caution, I stepped down the hall, away from the main part of the house. Just past the bedroom used by Lily was another bedroom, but this one had been converted into a home office. The desk was a smaller version of the one Erica had at the office. The room was spotless and tidy. Against the wall were bookcases. Positioned by the large window was a reading chair and lamp. Unlike the living room, there were personal items in this room, including a couple of photos on one of the bookcases. After looking over my shoulder for Racel, I moved closer to examine the photos.

One was Erica's law-school graduation photo. Next to her stood a smiling younger woman who looked like Erica but was slimmer and shorter, and with lighter hair. I wondered if this was Connie Holt. Without picking it up, I studied the photo, trying to burn Connie's face into my memory. I glanced at the other photos. Most were of a younger Erica with friends, maybe taken during college or law school. I saw no other photos of Connie and none of Lily or of Connie with her family. I found this strange. At our house, photos of all our family members were on display, including those of Greg's nephews. There were even photos of my nieces and their families, even though I'd only come to know of their existence in the past few years. Most people liked to keep photos of family nearby. *Most people. Erica Mayfield was not most people,* I reminded myself. Then again, those photos could be on display in a part of the house I hadn't seen yet.

I turned and stepped back into the hallway. Still not seeing Racel, I continued down the hall until I came to the end and the master bedroom. Like the living room, it was straight out of a fancy design magazine and didn't look very used. The furnishings were feminine and expensive—girly-girl all grown up and with a healthy bank account.

My ear caught a sound coming from behind a partially closed door on the opposite wall. It wasn't loud or particularly noticeable, more like a presence than a noise.

I ventured towards it, stepping softly. The sound stopped. I took another step towards the ajar door, thinking it might be the master bath or a closet.

"Odelia."

I jumped at the sound of my own name coming from behind me. With a hand over my chest to steady my racing heartbeat, I turned and faced Racel. She was standing in the hallway, a static duster with a long handle in her hand. I wasn't sure if she was using it as a cleaning device or as a weapon.

"Oh," I said, once I caught my breath. "I thought I heard you in here. I wanted to say goodbye."

She smiled at me, but it seemed forced. "Nope, I was just cleaning up in the den." She looked at my empty hands. "You have the bear, don't you?"

"Yep." I patted the side of my tote bag. "Safe and on its way to Lily." I hoped the fuzziness of the bear didn't disturb any prints that might be on the deodorant container while the items were squished in my bag. The bag was roomy, but still there might be co-mingling. It's not like I carried plastic bags and gloves around like the professional snoops.

Racel escorted me down the long hallway towards the front door. We walked in silence. She seemed to have her mind on something else. It might have been concern about her mother. I had more questions to ask but was worried I'd already used up my allotted time with Racel's patience. But it was Racel who had the next question.

She paused just before we reached the door and gave me a quizzical look. "By the way, where is Lily?"

"As I told you, she's with a friend of mine today."

"I mean," she amended, "if Lily's mother comes back and wants Lily, what should I tell her?"

She had a good point. I dug into an outside pocket of my tote bag and pulled out a business card and a pen. "Here," I said, scribbling my cell phone number on the back of the card. "On the front is my office information. On the back, my cell phone. You can give this to her."

Racel took the card and studied the front and back. She seemed to have something else on her mind. While she tucked the card into a pocket of her jeans, she said, "I've been trying to reach Erica. I've left messages on her cell and with her secretary, but haven't heard back. Could you tell her to call me when you get back to the office?"

Get in line, girlie.

"Sure, except I haven't seen her since yesterday morning."

Racel seemed surprised. "She's not at the office today?"

"Nope. She left the office yesterday and no one has heard from her since." I thought about Mark Baker. Erica might be in touch with him, so I tacked on, "That I know of."

I pointed back towards the master bedroom. "Did she sleep here last night?"

"She makes her own bed unless it's the day to change sheets, so I wouldn't know."

"And she didn't leave you any note or anything saying she'd be gone?"

"Not a word." Racel put the duster down on a table. "I texted her Wednesday that I might be back on Thursday. She sent a text back saying okay. But Thursday my mother wasn't feeling well, so I sent another text early in the morning saying I'd be back on Friday instead. I got a message back from Erica almost immediately saying it was fine and not to worry about Lily, she'd found someone else to watch her."

"That someone was me."

"Seems so. I've heard nothing from her since."

I thought about that. Connie Holt was missing, and now Erica. Although *missing* might not be the best word for the situation. They both probably knew exactly where they were. I began to wonder if Erica was out hunting for her sister.

I asked the same question in a little different way. "And Erica never said she might be out of town for a few days?"

"Nothing at all."

"Why do you need to reach her? Do you need more time off?"

Racel changed into her earlier stern self. "No, but today is pay-day, and Erica didn't leave my money. She's never forgotten that before."

ELEVEN

I<small>T WASN'T OFTEN</small> I went looking for Mark Baker. In fact, today might even be the first time since he came to work at the firm. I walked down the hallway until I came to his office door. It was open, but the lights were off. His office computer wasn't turned on either. Was he late, sick, or taking a vacation day? I was hoping it was door number three, and that maybe we could catch him and Erica off on a romantic jaunt together. Even though Racel didn't seem to recognize his name, it didn't mean Mark wasn't the man Erica was seeing. I was about to head back to my office when I spotted Mark walking towards me from the direction of the kitchen. He was on his personal cell phone and speaking every low. In his other hand, he held a mug of coffee. Slung over his shoulder was the messenger bag he used as a briefcase. He'd apparently just arrived at work. I stood still and waited for him.

As he approached me, he said into the phone, "I gotta go." He ended the call and walked past me into his office. Without a word to me, he turned on the lights and placed the coffee mug on his desk.

"You have a minute?" I asked.

Mark sloughed off the bag and slipped out of his jacket, hanging both the bag and the jacket on a hook behind the door before answering.

"Sure." He sat down and leaned back in his chair, crossing one leg over a knee. A smug grin crossed his face. He probably thought I was here to throw in the towel or to announce my layoff. "What's up?"

He picked up a pen and tapped it on his leg a couple of times before sticking it into his mouth—a nervous habit, to be sure, and similar to Carl's. We all have nervous habits. When rattled, I twist the ends of my hair or knock my knees or devour Thin Mints.

I stepped inside his office but did not take a seat, choosing instead to lean against his doorjamb. I hoped it made me look nonchalant about my visit, even though it was anything but. I took a quick glance around his tiny cell. It had once been my office, and much of the time I'd found its size cozy. It was definitely more private than the one I have now—the one Mark coveted. Maybe if I let Mark have my office, Erica and Mark would back down and I'd be able to save my job. Then again, it might also be that first step down the slippery slope to extinction, like a woolly mammoth slipping into a tar pit. Offering up my office as a peace offering might also be seen as a sign of weakness—a white flag of surrender. And I was not the type to surrender easily. Just ask my husband.

"Have you heard anything from Erica since Thursday?" I asked Mark.

"Maybe," he answered, his face revealing nothing. He'd put the pen down to speak. "Why?"

"Carl Yates is looking for her, and so is her cleaning lady."

A spark shot from his eyes like a tiny ember from struck flint, then just as quickly it disappeared. "How do you know about her cleaning lady? Did you call her house?"

I wasn't about to tell this clown I had been at Erica's home. "No, I didn't call her home," I answered truthfully. "But her cleaning lady has called Alyce looking for her." It was the truth, and I was thankful it could be verified should he decide to check out my story.

He studied me a moment in that unnerving, quiet way he had. I held my ground, refusing to come across like a sick and elderly antelope cut from the herd by a hungry lion.

"I have no idea where Erica is," he finally said. "She only told me she'd be out of the office a few days." He started to say something, then stopped. Putting down the pen, he picked up his coffee mug and took a drink.

"Did you just remember something?" I asked, prodding him to continue. Dollars to donuts, this man was hiding something.

He shrugged as he swallowed his coffee. "I was just wondering about the kid. Is she okay? Is that why you're looking for Erica?"

"Lily's fine. Like I told you and Alyce earlier, she's with a friend of mine." I latched my eyes onto his, staring down the beast. "Carl really does want to speak to Erica, the sooner the better."

I started to leave and had one foot into the hallway when I stopped. My gut told me to keep moving—to go back to my own office and continue with my hunt for Erica and dirt on the two of them. Instead, I turned back to Mark Baker. In anticipation of my departure, he was already sitting up straight and booting up his computer for the day.

I didn't wait to get his attention before plunging ahead. "Why are you and Erica so determined to get rid of me?"

"What?" He looked up, surprised by my confrontation.

I took a step closer to his desk and lowered my voice. "Why are you gunning for me, Mark? And don't say you're not. The whole firm knows it. Erica's been openly campaigning against me with the partners."

He narrowed his eyes in my direction but said nothing.

I narrowed mine right back at him. It was a staring contest of knitted brows and scrunched vision. "When, Mark, when did I ever pee in your Wheaties? When you came here, I was kind and professional and welcomed you."

"It's not personal, Odelia," he finally said, relaxing his face. "I need the job, and I'm willing to fight for it. It's that simple. In this economy, it's survival of the fittest." He eyed me up and down. "Maybe it's time for new blood around here."

It took everything in my power not to pick up his phone and brain him with it, but adding assault to my résumé wasn't going to convince the partners I was the one to keep. I turned and started for the door before I changed my mind about settling this with a brawl.

Just before I stepped out into the hallway, I tossed a warning his way. "Never underestimate a middle-aged woman, Mark. It's the quickest way to be handed your heinie."

Back in my office, there was a voice mail from Carl waiting for me. He was asking if I'd found out anything about Erica yet. I called him back, letting him know no one had seen her since Thursday, and as for Mark, I'd just begun to scratch the surface. Carl told me to dig deeper and faster.

Geez, I'd only been snooping less than twenty-four hours, and part of that time was spent being a mommy. I wasn't a miracle worker.

It was lunchtime, and I was hungry. I also had a stuffed bear in my bag, along with a hairy comb and Speed Stick, that needed attention. There were several secretaries bunched together around small tables enjoying their lunch and gabbing when I entered the firm's kitchen. Another was watching her meal heat in the microwave. They were discussing some of the shows they'd seen on TV the night before. Giving them a quick hello, I opened a drawer and rummaged around for something to protect my heisted booty from Erica's house. The firm supplies paper goods like towels, napkins, and plates, along with plastic cutlery, but they also supply plastic wrap and sometimes baggies for packing up leftovers. Behind the box of plastic wrap, I located the sandwich bags and grabbed a bunch.

Returning to my office, I closed my door and got to work protecting the evidence. No one would think it odd that my door was closed. I often closed it during lunchtime for privacy. Using a tissue, I transferred the comb and the Speed Stick into their own separate baggies and sealed them. Then I put in a call to my big brother on my cell phone.

"Hey, Clark," I said as soon as he answered. "It's Odelia."

"Hi, sis. Nice to hear from you." From the upswing in his voice, I knew he meant it.

"How's Mom?" I called my mother every week. They were trying calls. She'd never been warm and fuzzy, and old age had made her even more cantankerous. "When I called her last Saturday, she said she was ready to die. Said something about if she was still alive come winter, she was stepping in front of a snow plow."

"Humph," my brother snorted. "She's fine. So fine she's planning a bus trip to Branson, Missouri, with a bunch of other geezers. That old bird will outlive both of us."

"I sincerely hope not," I said, then quickly added, "not that I want her dead, but considering the age difference, it would be nice for us to go after her, don't ya think?"

"Affirmative."

I paused before jumping into the reason for my call. Taking a deep breath, I forged ahead. "I was wondering if you could give me some help, Clark."

"Oh, Christ," Clark groaned. "What are you up to your neck in now?"

"It's for work," I added quickly. I gave my big bro a rundown of what was happening at the office and how I'd been given the task of saving my own job.

"So what can I do to help?" The groaning was gone, replaced by sincere concern.

"I need to find out if the other paralegal has been spending time at Erica's. I...," I hesitated, searching for the right word. "I *appropriated* some personal items from her guest bath that I think might belong to him."

"You mean you *stole* them, don't you, sis?"

"Po-tay-toe. Po-tah-toe."

Clark chuckled, the snarky phrase going over better with him than it did with Carl Yates. "Uh-huh. Continue."

"I have hair on a comb and possibly fingerprints on the deodorant. Can you ID those for me?"

"Tests like that don't grow on trees, Odelia."

"But I've seen ads online for quick DNA testing."

"True, and those can run you anywhere from a few hundred to a couple of thousand, and the results can take time. Plus you would need a sample from the suspect and a good sample to match it against," Clark clarified. "Does the hair in the comb contain follicles?"

"Beats me." Through the baggie, I checked out the comb. For the first time, I noticed the few short hairs caught in the comb were fair. Mark's hair was dark.

Crap. That meant someone else was a possibility.

"Without the follicles, that hair will probably not help. The best DNA samples come from a swab of the mouth. Is that other paralegal going to let you swab his mouth?"

The sarcasm in Clark's question made me wiggle my nose with annoyance. "Then how about the fingerprints?" Even though the hair wasn't a match, I wasn't ready to give up on nailing Mark.

"We might be able to lift a set off, but I'm not sure how clear it would be. This stuff isn't as easy-peasy as they make it look on TV, you know."

"Between your law background and Willie's connections, I thought this might be fairly simple." My shoulders were starting to droop with disappointment.

"Willie has a lot of information at his disposal, but I'm not sure access to a national fingerprint bank is one of them. But with him, you never know." He paused. I hoped it was to come up with a solution and not the beginning of a goodbye.

"Tell you what, sis. Can you get that guy's fingerprints? Then we can try to match them against the ones you might have stolen. That would be easier than trying to find a way to match them against unknowns."

I wrinkled my nose at his second suggestion that I was a thief but sat up straight, ready to grab at the assistance Clark was offering. "I can certainly try." As I said the words, I wondered how in the hell I was going to accomplish my mission. I'd already made one uncharacteristic visit to Mark's office, and I'd left with flair. At least I thought I'd left with flair. Going back so soon would ruin the effect.

"As soon as you get the prints," Clark continued, "overnight them to me at my Phoenix office. I'm actually at the airport on my way there now. And send it for Saturday delivery. Someone will be there to receive it."

"How long will you be in Phoenix?"

"Not sure, but at least a few days. Maybe I can pop over to see you and Greg when I'm done."

"We'd like that, Clark," I said with encouragement. "Please try to make it."

TWELVE

For the most part, during lunchtime our office empties out. Secretaries and other staff members congregate in the kitchen or go out to eat. Attorneys do the same or, like me, eat in their office with the door closed. Sometimes folks work through lunch when there is a court filing or rush projects. But today was Friday, and we'd just been paid. A lot of folks went out for lunch together on Fridays.

Almost everyone was gone from their posts as I made my way down the hallway. I hoped Mark would be, too. He'd come in late, so he might be working through his lunch hour. It was a chance I'd have to take. Before leaving my office, I grabbed a yellow legal pad and a pen just to look like I was on official business in case anyone saw me. I also had an expandable file tucked under the yellow pad. If I did find anything worth pinching, I could open the file and slip it in.

When I reached Mark's office, I glanced around. Every nearby secretarial bay in the area was empty. The attorney office on his left was empty, the one on the right had its door closed. Mark's office was vacant.

Before stepping inside, I took a quick glance around to pick my target before I plunged inside. If Mark came back unexpectedly, I sure didn't want him to find me inside his office rummaging around. I would identify an item from the doorway, then make a quick snatch. I believe in jewelry holdups they call this smash and grab, but I didn't have any intention of smashing anything, not that I didn't feel like it at the moment. This was simply a grab job, and I didn't plan on taking anything of value.

Mark's coffee mug was on his desk, just to the right of his phone. It was one of the generic ones the firm supplied, not a personal one like mine. I had two mugs I kept on my desk and rotated. One was a double-size mug from one of our attorney services. The other, which I used less often, was a gift from Steele. On its white porcelain side, emblazoned in red block letters, were the words PARALE- GAL DIVA. I was glad Mark didn't have a personal mug. If one of the firm's went missing, I doubt he'd kick up a fuss. He'd probably just think he'd put it in the kitchen and forgot.

With one last glance both ways down the hallway, I ducked into Mark's office and carefully grabbed the mug by its handle, using a tissue to keep my own prints off of it. It still had some coffee in it, and I nearly splashed it on his desk but managed to corral the coffee into behaving. I opened the file and stuck it inside, careful not to tip it. Then I tucked the file under my arm to hold it steady during my getaway. At the last minute, I spied his chewed pen and snagged that, too.

Back in my office, I emptied the coffee dregs into my own mug and dropped Mark's mug into one of the extra baggies. The pen went into another. The whole operation from start to finish took just over four minutes, and I was a wreck.

After scooting into the mail room to find a suitable box, I packed and taped the whole shebang and shipped it via Federal Express to Clark in care of Willie's company in Phoenix. Clark hadn't given me much hope of a speedy or accurate match, but at least it was something.

I spent the next thirty minutes munching on a sandwich and soup I'd grabbed from the café on the first floor of our office building. While I waited for my food, I noticed Mark Baker seated at one of the tables against the wall. He was alone, reading the newspaper while he ate. It looked like he was almost done. I breathed a sigh of relief that I'd taken care of collecting evidence when I did.

After lunch, I called Zee to check on Lily. Zee said she was fine, though still a little stuffy, and was taking a nap to be rested up for cookie baking that afternoon. I thanked Zee for the hundredth time for looking after Lily.

"Clark may be coming to town next week," I said into the phone. "If you and Seth are free, maybe Greg and I could take you all out to dinner."

"It would be lovely to see Clark again," Zee answered with enthusiasm. She and Seth liked Clark as much as Greg and I did. "Have you found out anything yet on Erica?"

"Not much, except that no one has seen her since Thursday. I swung by her house but didn't learn much."

"Maybe," Zee suggested, "Mark isn't her boyfriend, and she went away with whomever she is really seeing?"

"Could be. I threw out Mark's name to Racel, Erica's cleaning lady, and she gave no sign of recognition at all. And I mean none, as not even recognizing the name as being one of Erica's coworkers at the firm."

I hesitated about telling Zee about the mug and other stuff I'd sent off to Clark. Zee, while being closer to me than my own skin, could be a real stickler for law and order. She wouldn't be happy knowing I'd lifted a few items from Erica's house. When I'd done similar stuff before, she'd scolded me. Thinking back on a few of my investigations, I guess I did have a history of sticky fingers.

"Too bad you couldn't pick up anything at Erica's to test for prints," Zee said.

Huh?

I shook my head to clear my brain and my hearing.

"Are you suggesting, Mrs. Washington, pillar of church and community, that I should have stolen something?"

"Well, it's not like you've never done it before, Odelia."

I cleared my throat.

"You did, didn't you?" my friend accused. "You took something from Erica's house."

"Just some men's antiperspirant and a comb," I admitted, leaving out the mug and pen from Mark's office. "Clark's going to see if he can get some prints and whatever off of it."

"Good thinking."

"Geez, Zee. One day you're crabbing at me for … um … collecting evidence, and the next you're giving me a gold star for the same thing. Make up your mind, will ya?"

"I'm not judging you, Odelia. I just know you. And I doubt you're going to go to hell for deodorant and a few hairs on a comb." I detected a smile in her voice during the last sentence. I'm not very religious and neither is Greg. If there is a God and a hereafter, I'm banking on getting in on a glowing reference from Zee.

After my chat with Zee, I called Greg and caught him up on the latest, including my plan to visit the Holt home.

"Good thinking, sweetheart, asking Clark about prints and all." There was a long silence before my husband added, "But I'm not sure I want you going out to the Holt house by yourself."

"I'll be fine, Greg," I assured him. "I'm just going to take a run out there and see if anyone's home. Who knows, maybe Connie Holt dropped Lily off with Erica because she needed some 'me' time. Just being around Lily for a few days has been exhausting, so I can imagine how bedraggled a full-time mom would feel."

"Why don't you call the number you found on the firm's emergency list?"

"I did and there was no answer, just voice mail. If I was supposed to be out of town but was staying home, I'd wouldn't answer my phone either." A thought nipped my brain. "You know, Greg, if I left my young daughter somewhere, I wouldn't be totally out of touch. I'd want to be reachable in case of some type of emergency. Wouldn't you?"

"Absolutely."

"I'm going to call again. The first time I just hung up. This time I'll leave a message and my phone number and tell her it's about Lily. I'll bet that will get a call back quick enough."

"Just make sure," Greg cautioned, "you don't make it sound like Lily's in some sort of serious condition, like an accident or something. You don't want the woman to panic needlessly."

"Good point, honey. I want Lily's mom to call, not have a heart attack." I paused. "And you know, maybe Zee's right. Maybe Erica went off for the weekend with some secret boyfriend who is not Mark Baker. It could have been planned before Lily arrived, and she wasn't about to change her plans for her niece."

"It still wasn't right for Erica to drop the kid in our laps, even if it has been fun, but it does make sense. Erica does sound like the type of person who only thinks of herself."

Before telling my husband I loved him and giving him a quick phone smooch, I rattled off the Holt address just in case. Greg then extracted a promise from me to call him right after my trip to Irvine.

I again called the number listed as Erica's emergency contact and once more got voice mail. It was a basic message letting me know I'd reached the cell phone for "Connie" and instructing me to leave a message. I quickly came up with something that was urgent but not life threatening.

"Hi," I said after the beep. "This is Odelia Grey, a paralegal working with your sister. I'm taking care of Lily and was wondering about any allergies she might have. She has a little cold, and I didn't want to give her anything without checking with you first." I left my cell phone number and the firm's.

After leaving a note on Alyce's desk saying I had to leave the office and didn't know when I'd be back, I took off for Irvine.

It took me about forty minutes to get to the Holt home from my office, with a quick pit stop along the way. They lived on a street called Mallard in an upscale residential section reminiscent of the neighborhood where Erica lived. When I'd Googled the address and did a closeup on the street, it looked like a collection of large houses crammed on too-small lots. I wasn't wrong. The homes were very large, with very little space between them.

I parked a few doors down from the Holt residence and made my way to the front door. If I found Connie at home, my plan was to grill her on her sister's whereabouts. Or maybe I'd run into another chatty cleaning lady.

The Holt home was a split-level the color of light brown suede, with river rock accents on the small porch and around the support pillars by the front door, which was painted a dark chocolate brown. The front door, window casings, and garage were painted white. The garage faced the street at the end of a stubby driveway, along with the front door and one downstairs window. Upstairs, three windows faced the street. The roof was tile. In front of the house was a postage stamp–sized patch of grass. It appeared well tended, as did the young shrubs and trees around the house.

Overhead, dark clouds scooted by on an important errand. The rain had stopped, taking a short breather, but the weather report said it would last most of the day and could be quite heavy in the afternoon.

Thanks to TV, the rest of the nation seems to think those of us who live in Southern California all wear sunglasses and spend our days lounging on pool chaises next to movie stars. Or that we all surf. Or that we endure drive-by shootings from warring gangs and drug lords on a daily basis. Today was a dreary, rainy Friday, like any you'd find in most suburbs across the nation during March.

I made my way down the sidewalk to the Holt house. An SUV drove by and turned into a driveway a few houses down. Its back doors cracked open and two children spilled out like stuffing from a sofa. They took off for the front door while engaged in high-pitched chatter. A woman got out of the driver's side and scurried after them, pausing only long enough to aim her key fob at the vehicle until she heard the beep of the set alarm. Another car drove down the street and turned left at the intersection. A US Postal truck was parked farther up the street. I scanned the neighborhood until I located its driver—a man bundled against the dampness, with a large bag over his shoulder, going from house to house with the mail, moving away from me. Otherwise the street seemed quiet.

I approached the Holt house casually, as if I did it every day, just in case the street had a neighborhood watch or nosy occupants. When I reached the door, I rang the doorbell and waited. Nothing. I rang it again and waited. Again, nothing. Something was sticking out of the mail slot in the center of the front door. After a quick glance up the street in the direction of the postman, I tugged on the protruding piece of mail.

It was actually two pieces of mail stuck together. One was a power bill, the other a postcard from a local boutique. I shoved the power bill back through the slot and studied the advertisement. It came from a women's clothing store that, according to the copy, specialized in "artisan clothing and vintage wear." The store was called Golden Quail. Below the printed text, someone had hand-written: *Connie, we miss you! Stop by for lunch. A & J*. The ink on the words "miss you" was partially smudged. I stuck the postcard in my tote bag.

The downstairs window that faced the street was off the small porch. For that, I was grateful. It enabled me to peek inside without crawling over shrubs and attracting undue attention. Horizontal mini blinds covered it but were half open. Cupping my hand around my eyes and the glass, I peeked in. Dim light streamed into the house from the other side of the house, possibly from patio doors, which made it possible for me to get a good, albeit squinty, look.

On the other side of the window appeared to be a small breakfast nook. Beyond it, a good-sized kitchen led into a larger dining area with large windows. There appeared to be no sign of life inside. Something was off, though I wasn't sure what it was.

I leaned back from the window to readjust my eyes, then put them back to work, trying to focus on details in the room beyond. On my second pass, I thought I could make out open drawers and stuff on the floor, like it had been ransacked or maybe someone had been looking for something in a hurry.

I left the window and did another quick surveillance of the immediate neighborhood. If the weather had not been so gloomy, I'm sure the streets and front yards would have had more action. I checked my watch. I had no idea when school got out but was sure it wouldn't be long before kids started returning back to their individual motherships. The earlier SUV was just the beginning. Whatever I needed to do, I had to do it now, before curious eyes noticed me.

Leaving the porch, I walked past the garage and checked the space between the Holt house and the neighbors. It wasn't very wide, but it was large enough to have a fence dividing the properties and gates leading to each separate back yard. The neighbor's garage mirrored the Holt's, so there were no windows to worry about on this side. The Holt door was a metal gate that allowed a partial view of the back yard through its vertical bars. The neighbor's was a solid piece of wood. Both were high enough to discourage anyone from climbing.

"Here, boy," I called in a loud whisper through the gate. I hadn't heard any dogs but wanted to be careful. The last thing I wanted was to come face to face with a watchdog. I clucked a canine come-hither through the bars a few more times, but nothing raised a territorial ruckus. Neither did any animal noises come from the neighbor's back yard.

Getting into the Holt back yard was going to prove difficult. Even if I placed a foot on the lower part of the gate frame, it wouldn't be high enough to hoist my butt over the top. Not to mention the vertical bars were topped with ornamental fleur-de-lis spikes that were pretty to look at, but also pretty deadly should some non-agile intruder become impaled upon them. Since nimble hoisting and jumping isn't one of my strong suits, I decided picking the lock might be the better choice. Not that I was any great shakes at picking locks either, but at least it wouldn't leave me stuck like a marshmallow on a pointy stick.

Before I went any further, I reached into my tote bag to retrieve the purchase I'd made on the way here. It was a pair of thin rubber gloves that I picked up at a drug store. I'd only wanted one pair, but they came in boxes of either forty or ten. I'd gotten the idea for the gloves on my way to Irvine, although the seed had been planted about the time I was trying to put Mark's mug and the other items into baggies without slathering my own prints all over them. I'd bought the ten-pack, opening the package as soon as I was back in my car. Taking out one pair, I stashed them in my bag. I stowed the remaining gloves in the glove compartment.

If I was going to illegally snoop around someone's property, I really should wear gloves so I wouldn't leave behind bushels of my own prints. But as I stood outside the Holt back gate, it occurred to me that I was really standing on the precipice of premeditated actions. Buying and using the gloves had put me in a different class of snoop, and I wasn't sure I was comfortable with the upgrade. I was also pretty sure Greg wouldn't be, even if he did enjoy playing Ned Nickerson to my Nancy Drew.

Pushing criminal intent to the back of my brain, I slipped on the gloves, glad I'd opted for the large size. With a furtive glance back over my shoulder, I made ready to examine the lock on the gate.

I'd once picked a lock using the underwire from a bra, but that had been indoors, and my life and Steele's had been in danger. Today I would have to make do with whatever I found in my tote bag—a large purse Greg often referred to as my magic bag of tricks.

Placing a hand on the gate, I gave it a gentle jiggle to see how sturdy the latch was and discovered magic was already at work. One slight wiggle and the latch slipped out of its catch easy as pie, making me wonder if it had been locked tight in the first place. Whoever entered or left last through the gate might not have pulled it tight enough to engage the lock. Our back gate had a similar problem. We had to pull it tight and test it before leaving to make sure it was closed tight. If not, the lock was useless. With continued caution, I pushed the Holt gate open wider and stepped into the back yard.

The back yard was small, with young trees and several trimmed bushes. In the middle of the space was a colorful playset with swings, a slide, and stuff to climb on. Off to one side was a small, sturdy playhouse. On the covered patio a toddler's bike, along with other toys, took refuge from the rain. Lily was certainly not deprived when it came to outdoor playthings. I was almost tempted to scoop up the little bike and take it home with me for her.

Crossing behind the garage, I tiptoed onto the patio and made my way to a small door with a window and took a peek. It looked to be a laundry room. There was another small door just past the washer/dryer set that I was sure led to the garage. The washer and dryer looked like the latest models. I knew because Greg and I had been shopping for a new set for ourselves recently. If my eyes weren't deceiving me, the set on the other side of this door was the Mercedes of washers. The unit in question did everything but fold and mend your clothes, and I'm pretty sure it had a feature to take the place of ironing. I had coveted it like Wainwright covets Snausages, but Greg's level head took one look at the price tag and went into convulsions. In the end, we bought a very nice set on sale that came with a lot of great features we didn't have on our old washer. With one last wistful sigh, I turned my eyes away from the king and queen of laundry and scanned the small room. It looked messy, like the kitchen. I tried the door handle, but the door was locked. I was about to move to the sliding doors when a scratching sound to my right made me jump.

Snapping around, I flattened myself against the door and fumbled around in my tote bag until I located a small inside pocket. Yanking out a small pepper spray canister, I held it at the ready in my right hand. I'd never used the spray before. Clark had given both Greg and me a couple of discreet canisters for Christmas, saying he'd feel better if we had it on hand. Clark had even instructed us on how best to use it, but he hadn't instructed me on how to find it quickly in my purse while under pressure. If I'd come face to face with a killer just now, I'd have been toast before I'd even had a chance to touch the spray.

Fortunately, I saw no one. I heard the sound again and held my breath. Slowly turning my head, I saw the origin of the noise. A long, untrimmed branch of a rose bush was moving against the screen of a window on the far end of the patio. The cool wind that had accompanied the rain had picked up and was pushing the thorny, thin branch back and forth against the screen like cheese against a grater.

After taking a few deep breaths, I scooted several steps to my right, closer to the rose bush, and stopped in front of the sliding patio doors. These ran most of the width of the living room and were partially open. Not just ajar, but open enough for a person to slip through. The lock not grabbing on the gate was one thing, but I doubted Connie Holt had gone off and left the slider open on such a cold, rainy day.

Grasping my pepper spray, I ducked inside.

THIRTEEN

THE LIVING ROOM WAS long rather than deep and ran across most of the back of the house. Off to the right was the dining area, and through an arch I spotted a fragment of the kitchen I'd seen earlier through the front window. As soon as my eyes adjusted to the soft, dull light allowed by the cloudy day, I saw that the living room and dining room were in the same shape as the kitchen. The rooms had been ransacked. Cushions were off the sectional sofa and chairs, drawers and doors on cabinets and the breakfront in the dining area were open, and the contents pulled out and scattered. Paintings and photos were pulled off the walls. Someone was looking for something important—at least important to them—and I don't think it was Connie or Hank Holt.

I stopped moving and listened for the sound of anyone else in the house. I heard nothing. Armed with my spray, I made my way through the house in a slow, shuffling two-step—step, step, listen; step, step, listen. Along the way, my focus was derailed as one theory after another entered my brain.

Was Connie in trouble? Had she parked Lily with Erica to keep her safe and out of the way? Were the Holts in the middle of a marital battle that had turned violent? Did Erica know what was going on and take off to help her little sis, or was Erica taking a long weekend to play footsie with some unknown lover?

A hallway led to the laundry room I'd spied earlier, a guest bath, and a den. All had been pillaged. I opened a door in the laundry room and, as I had suspected, it led to the garage. There was no car, but even here, things had been overturned. Next to the door was a keypad for an alarm system. An alarm—I hadn't thought of that. A lot of folks had them. Greg and I didn't have one, but I had one on the condo I owned before marrying Greg. Either Connie hadn't set the alarm in her haste to leave or the people who had trashed the place had managed to disarm it. A set alarm would have notified the alarm company when that back door had been opened by an intruder, let alone was allowed to hang open.

Even under the chaos, I could see that the Holt home was nicely furnished, yet not in an untouchable way like Erica's house. This had been a comfortable, user-friendly family home. There was a fireplace in the living room, along with a sectional sofa with matching coffee and end tables. Twin lamps, now on their sides on the carpet with their shades caved, had once graced each end table. In the den, an old black leather recliner was aimed at a very large flat-screen TV, along with a comfy-looking overstuffed sofa now missing its cushions. The seat of the lounger was well worn with a concave indentation on the seat, which I was pretty sure would fit Hank Holt's butt like the glass slipper fit Cinderella. On the floor by the recliner were several issues of *Sports Illustrated* and the remote to the TV. No doubt this had been command central for the man of house. A few toys had also been scattered on the floor of the den.

In spite of the wreckage, it looked as if Hank Holt was still in residence, or maybe they hadn't been separated that long. Maybe Connie had left the chair, remote, and magazines as a shrine to her skedaddled hubs in the hope that he would return. If she didn't want him back, I would think that eyesore of a chair might have ended up in the garage or by the curb even before Hank had pulled out of the driveway. Or maybe the man-cave setup was Connie's favorite place to hang out and not Hank's.

With caution, I made my way back to the living room. The length of the room was cut midway by the entryway leading to the front door. I stepped into the foyer. To my right was a doorway to the breakfast area of the kitchen; to my left, a staircase led to the second level. Against the wall shared with the kitchen was a small table on which sat a large, pretty bowl. It was probably where they dropped their mail and keys when they returned home. Greg and I had a drop-off place like that, but it was a wicker basket on the kitchen counter. The bowl and table looked untouched, probably because it didn't have any drawers to search.

On the floor in front of the door, just under the mail slot, various envelopes, ads, and magazines had dropped onto a small area rug positioned in front of the door. As I stared down at them, my gut told me something was off. Directly below the slot in the door was the bill I'd dropped through minutes before. The other mail was off to the side, scattered, some on the rug, some not. I put my back to the door in front of the slot and looked down at the bill I'd stuffed through, then at the other mail. There was no way that bunch of mail landed in that position on its own. Someone had to have picked it up, sifted through it, and dropped it piece by piece as they went. If Connie had picked it up, she would have put it on the table or in the kitchen. It also told me that whoever ransacked the house had been there in the last twenty-four hours.

I picked up a few of the envelopes, glad I had gloves on my hands. Several were from local businesses like the cable company. I checked the postmarks. It generally took one to two days for local mail to be delivered. Some of these postmarks were from several days ago; one envelope from a local medical group was dated a week ago. It was a good bet Connie had not been home since she'd dropped off Lily. Given the state of the house, I was leaning towards the theory she was running from trouble. But was Hank the source of the trouble, or was it something else—or someone else?

Placing the mail back on the floor, I stared up the staircase and listened for any sign of life. Nothing. I put a foot on the first step and stopped, worried that if I went upstairs and someone came in, I'd be trapped. At least downstairs there were several doorways. Not that I could escape easily, but at least there were options. Upstairs there would be none, except for squeezing out of a second-story window.

With the pepper spray in my right hand, I took the steps one at a time, ready to spray and bolt at the first sign of life.

There were three bedrooms and two baths upstairs. All the rooms had been ransacked. One of the smaller bedrooms was obviously Lily's. It was decorated to look like a cheerful garden, complete with a wallpaper border of a white picket fence and fluffy lady bug and frog pillows. Her bedspread was a blanket of flowers. Again, I was tempted to take something familiar for her to use while in exile at my house. I eyed the clothing spilling out of her little green dresser and the closet and quickly picked out a several pairs of clean panties, two knit shirts, and two pairs of long pants. From the look of things, Lily might not be returning home anytime soon and would need more clothes.

After tightly rolling the clothes and stuffing them into my bag alongside the bear with the tutu, I stepped carefully around the debris on the floor and made my way to the master bedroom. The sacking had been worse here. I peeked into the walk-in closet and snapped on the light. Hanging and thrown on the floor were both men's and women's clothing. I stopped short when I spotted the wall safe. Built into the wall of the closet, it would have been hidden by hanging clothes had the clothes not been tossed to the floor. It was smallish, and the door was hanging open. It was also empty. The question was, had it been emptied by Connie before she left or emptied after by whoever had vandalized the house?

Tiptoeing into the master bath, I did a quick check of the medicine cabinet. A man's razor occupied the lowest shelf, along with a can of shave gel. It still wasn't hard evidence of Hank's presence. He could have a travel kit with duplicate items. Greg always kept one packed for when he traveled so he wouldn't forget anything.

Since I didn't have a clue what anyone was looking for, I couldn't look for it myself. And the empty safe indicated that whatever they were looking for might have been found. It was time to get out of the place before someone returned and I had some explaining to do or, worse, a neighbor called the cops to report a break-in.

I didn't have any convictions about breaking *out* of the house, so it took me a lot less time to get down the stairs, out the patio door, and through the back gate than it had taken me coming into the place. Before stripping off my rubber gloves, I closed the back patio door and made sure the gate was locked tight. The place had been tossed, not necessarily robbed, and I wasn't going to make it easy on any burglars that might be interested in an unoccupied house.

Back in the car, I stashed the pepper spray into a slim outside pocket of my tote bag for ease of finding if the need arose again. Who knows, maybe that's what that seemingly useless space was for—to hold pens and pepper spray. Stripping off the used gloves, I threw them onto the floor of the back seat. I had a decision to make. My original plan was to head to the mailbox place I suspected was Mark's address. Pulling Lily's clothing and the bear out of my tote bag, I tossed them on the passenger's seat, then went back in for the postcard from the Golden Quail. I wondered if maybe a visit to the store might be a better use of my time. It was closer and might yield more about Connie, who was moving to the top of my curiosity list. Carl had told me to find Erica and look into her relationship with Mark. Yes, doing that might save my job, but something told me the more important question here was what had happened to Lily's parents. It also might lead me to the elusive Erica.

I checked my watch. I had to make sure I got home in time to dress for Isaac's party tonight. I had promised Greg I wouldn't get so caught up in snooping that I'd forget about time.

The Golden Quail was a charming shop in an upscale single-story mall that housed, among other things, a wine and cheese shop, an antique store, an art gallery, and a few chain restaurants, both pricey and mid-level. It was not the sort of shopping center that catered to the hot-dog-on-a-stick crowd.

"May we help you?" asked a woman with a pink streak in her long, dark hair. She was dressed in a lovely black dress that looked right out of an Audrey Hepburn movie. It suited her slim figure, although I doubted many women from that era put Day-Glo streaks in their hair.

"Yes," I told her, casting my eyes around the store. "A friend recommended your store to me. I understand you carry vintage clothing." I eyed the tailored dress she was wearing. "That's a lovely dress, by the way."

"Thank you," she said, beaming. "It's a favorite of mine."

"You must be one of the owners," I commented, making the assumption that an hourly clerk wouldn't be wearing prize stock.

"Yes. I'm Amanda Quinn." She held out a manicured hand.

Ah, there was the A in the A & J on the postcard.

I took her offered hand and shook it, giving her a smile. "And I'm Odelia."

"I own the store with my sister, Jennifer," she explained.

And there was the J.

"What exactly does *artisan clothing* mean?" I asked, moving the conversation along. "Is it safe to assume handmade articles?"

"That's exactly what it means." Amanda moved over to a display of beautiful sweaters. "We carry a nice selection of hand-knitted, one-of-a-kind sweaters and scarves, as well as hand-stitched articles."

I caressed a gorgeous plum-colored sweater with an interesting pattern. It felt like a cloud under my hand. "Do you carry plus sizes?"

"If you see something you like," a voice said from behind me, "we can ask the artist to make it in your size."

I turned towards the back of the store to see a woman bringing in an armload of sweaters. She put the sweaters down on the counter and stepped forward.

"This is my sister," Amanda told me. "Jennifer Quinn." The two women stood next to each other like bookends. They were in their mid-thirties and identical twins, except that Jennifer did not have a color streak in her hair.

Jennifer extended her hand, and we shook. The Quinns gave off the vibe that they knew their customers well and provided excellent personal service, something that was sadly lacking in most retail stores.

"I handle the artisan side," Jennifer explained. "Amanda is more into the vintage." And indeed, Jennifer was wearing a spectacular cream sweater. Seeing me eye her top with a hunger usually reserved for cheesecake, she indicated the pile she'd just left on the counter. "We just received several new items from our designer in Portland. Please feel free to look them over. There's a smashing teal short-sleeve sweater that would go great with your hair and eyes. It's a small, but we could have one made to fit you. It wouldn't be identical, of course, considering each item is handmade, but close."

Jennifer walked back to the small pile and plucked out a sweater. Waving me over to a three-way mirror, she held it up to me and invited me to take a look. She was right, the sweater was perfect with my coloring and as light and soft as a marshmallow. I could feel my credit card itching to come out and play, until I found the tag and checked the price.

Yikes!

Before I succumbed to a buying coma, I lowered the sweater and forced my focus back on the missing Connie Holt. "It is indeed lovely, but I came in to ask you about someone."

The Quinn sisters looked at me with interest, but Jennifer made no move to take the sweater from me. She knew the longer I held the silky item in my hand, the more tempted I'd be to order one of my own. And I made no move to hand it back.

"I learned about this store from Connie Holt," I told them.

"Oh, Connie!" Amanda brightened. "How is she?"

"We haven't seen her in ages," Jennifer added, "have we, sis?"

Amanda gave it some thought as she straightened a rack of pristine dresses that was already perfect to my eye. "No, it's been at least a month or so. She's always been a regular. How is she?"

"That's just it," I said, still holding on to the teal sweater. "I can't seem to reach her or Hank."

"That's odd." Amanda tilted her head. "Maybe they took Lily and went on a little vacation."

I was about to let them know I had Lily but caught my tongue at the last minute. If I had their daughter, then I should know where the Holts were, and I felt the sharp Quinn sisters would catch that little misstep. I didn't feel a full-blown explanation was in order. "I'm sure you're right," I said instead, infusing my voice with a casualness I didn't feel.

Jennifer smiled. "That Lily is a cutie. It was such a blessing that Hank and Connie were able to adopt her."

My ears pricked. Still holding the sweater, I turned away from the mirror. "I didn't know Lily was adopted." I handed the sweater back to Jennifer with some reluctance. "I haven't known Connie very long, but she's never mentioned it."

"Lily was adopted maybe a year ago, I think." Jennifer turned to Amanda for confirmation. "Is that right?"

Amanda nodded. "About that, maybe a little longer. She and Hank had been wanting a child for so long. They are both over the moon about that little girl."

I moved over to a display of silver jewelry, all of which looked like handcrafted original pieces. Jennifer stepped over to the counter and set the sweater down. "Those are done by a designer in Santa Fe. Exquisite, aren't they?"

131

"Yes," I admitted. "May I see those earrings?" I pointed to a pair in the upper left-hand corner of the display. Jennifer reached for the wrong pair. "No, those, to the left," I directed. "To your right." Her fingers finally touched the correct pair. "Yes, those."

As soon as I had the earrings in my hand, Jennifer moved a mirror over so I could take a look. After pushing my hair behind one ear, I held one of the earrings up to it to see how it looked. Amanda moved over to the counter to watch. The silver was swirled in an interesting pattern, almost as if it had been melted, then captured mid-drip. At the end was a nice-sized teardrop of a blue-green stone.

"The stone is kyanite," Amanda informed me.

The earrings were beautiful and would go with several of my outfits. I turned the card over to check the price. It was reasonable. I didn't want to pump the Quinns for information, then leave without buying something. It didn't seem right. At least that's my excuse, and I'm sticking to it.

Another customer entered the shop, and Amanda went off in her little black dress to help her. From the way she greeted her, the customer must have been a regular.

Jennifer tapped the sweater on the counter. "Those earrings would go great with this sweater."

I looked up from my reflection in the mirror. "Oh, you're good."

Jennifer smiled, knowing I meant it as a compliment.

I put down the earrings and pushed the pair towards her. "I'll definitely take these." I eyed the sweater but didn't touch it. "How long would it take if I special ordered my size?" She knew I meant the tempting knit.

"A few weeks, depending on how many orders she has ahead of you."

I considered the time frame involved and used it to apply the brakes to my shopping impulse. This was Southern California. It might be wet and dreary today, but in a few weeks we may be in the grip of a heat wave. Hell, in a few days it could be in the upper seventies. It was hard to tell. If I'd discovered the sweater in November, I would have been more tempted. If they had it in the store in my size, no doubt I would have grabbed it today.

"I think I'll hold off on it and just take the earrings."

While Jennifer rang up my purchase, I asked, "Have you met Erica Mayfield, Connie's sister?"

Jennifer's omnipresent smile melted. Just as quickly, she plastered it back on, but this time the smile was forced. "Yes, she's been in the store a few times with Connie."

When the other customer left the store, Amanda joined us. "Cora stopped by," she told her sister, "to see if we had any new arrivals. I told her by the end of next week we'll have several new pieces from that estate sale." She turned to me. "We just purchased a bunch of new inventory from this old estate—fun stuff, strictly old Hollywood glamour—but it takes time to mend, clean, and prepare the items for the store."

As she spoke to her sister, Jennifer pushed my credit card slip across the counter for my signature. "Odelia here just asked if we've met Erica Mayfield."

"Humph," was all Amanda said.

Seems Erica was just as good at making friends outside the office as she was at work. I decided to push and see what happened, even if I did have to lie my ass off. "Connie once told me she and Erica didn't see eye to eye on much."

"That's an understatement." Jennifer placed my earrings in a small cream-colored bag and handed them to me along with my receipt.

Amanda nodded, her streak of pink rippling in a sea of dark brown. "Erica's always been hard on Connie, but I think the real falling out started when Connie and Hank adopted Lily." She looked to her sister for confirmation.

Jennifer agreed. "She wasn't happy at all with the adoption. Frankly, I think she's jealous of Connie and Hank's happiness, and always has been, even before Lily."

"Remember," chimed in Amanda. "That friend of Connie's threw her a baby shower, and Erica refused to come."

I thought about how Erica treated Lily like a nasty boil that needed lancing. Did she not like the idea of adoption or children in general? And I could see Erica being jealous of her younger sister's marriage. Erica struck me as the green-eyed type—like the Wicked Witch of the West being jealous of Glinda. Yet, when Connie needed her to, Erica took Lily into her home.

Or rather, into my home.

Before leaving the parking lot at the Golden Quail, I called Zee to check on Lily. She was doing fine and didn't seem to miss me at all. I was relieved and sad at the same time.

"I just found out Lily's adopted," I told Zee. "She's been with the Holts for about a year or so."

"Poor baby."

"Yeah, given up for adoption, only to land in this mess. I went by the Holt home and it looks like no one's been around for days." Zee can be a worrywart, so I left out the part about the ransacking by parties unknown and me breaking in while wearing gloves.

"Are you talking while driving, Odelia?"

See what I mean? Imagine what she'd say if she knew the truth about the Holt house.

"No, I am not talking while driving," I insisted. "I'm in the parking lot of a shopping center, about to head home. I wanted to make sure it's still okay to leave Lily with you tonight."

"Sure, no problem. We're having a great time. Pick her up tomorrow anytime you like."

I patted the side of my tote bag. Just before leaving the Golden Quail, I had spotted a pair of sweet silver earrings set with peridot, Zee's favorite stone. I had Jennifer ring them up as a thank-you gift to Zee for babysitting Lily—and me.

FOURTEEN

I DECIDED TO WEAR my new earrings to Isaac's birthday party. Greg liked them and considered it a small price to pay for the information I'd gleaned from the Quinns. While we got ready for the party, I brought him up to speed.

"I'm not happy about you going into that house alone," Greg said as he slipped into his shirt and started buttoning it. "Not happy at all."

"You know you would have done the same, if you could have."

Greg stared at me, then shifted his eyes away. He seldom let being in a wheelchair limit him from doing anything, but there were some things he couldn't do. Sneaking into a house was one of them.

"Yes, I would have, but I still don't like you being there alone," he argued. "You should have waited so we could do it together. I could have provided watch and backup."

"You knew I was going over there, Greg." I slipped on a light gray sweater with a bold argyle print on the front and looked in the mirror. It was nice, but the sweater from the Golden Quail would have been nicer. I sighed, not sure if I was mourning the fact that I didn't wear a size small or that it would take weeks to get the right size.

"Going over there, yes," he continued, unwilling to let it rest. "But I didn't think you'd break into the house. What if the people who trashed the place had still been there?"

After slipping into some shoes, I went to Greg and placed my hands gently on his shoulders. "But they weren't, honey. And I didn't just bust in there. I made sure no one was around. And I had my pepper spray."

He seemed somewhat mollified, or maybe he was saving his strength. Greg was more of a "win the war, not the battle" type, while I had trouble understanding that big-picture concept. Not that I hadn't seen my hubs rise to the occasion on a few battles. Underneath his good looks, intelligence, and decency beat the heart of a born warrior—a general able to lead troops into battle. People see the wheelchair and immediately think *disabled*. Trust me, there is nothing disabled about Greg Stevens. His legs just don't work.

Greg looked deep into my eyes, then picked up my hand and kissed the palm, letting his warm mouth linger against my skin. I wondered if we might be late to the party or skip it altogether.

"I'd be lost without you, Odelia. You know that."

"We'd be lost without each other, Greg. But I'll promise to be careful if you will." I leaned down and kissed his mouth.

By the time we got out the door, we were running very late.

"So, what do you think?" Greg asked as we drove to the Thornwood party.

I shrugged. "Tell them I was held up at work." I was driving my car for two reasons: it was easier to park in a crowded neighborhood than Greg's van, and Greg would probably be kicking back several beers tonight with his basketball buds.

Greg laughed as he reached over to pat my thigh. "I'm not talking about being late," he clarified. "I'm talking about the mess with Erica and her sister. Do you think Erica knows the trouble Connie and her husband are in and is trying to help, or do you think she took off so she wouldn't have to take care of Lily?"

"Hard to say. I just don't understand why Erica would be so hard-nosed about Lily's adoption. It's not like it affects her."

"You never know, sweetheart. Maybe the family has a lot of money and Erica didn't want to share the wealth with a non-blood relative." He glanced over at me. "Do you know anything about their family?"

"All I know is that they don't have any other brothers and sisters and that their parents are retired and live somewhere in the Caribbean. Alyce once let that slip."

"There could be some money involved, then. Maybe Connie took off to see her parents. If she's in trouble, she might have gone to them to get help."

"But if she was going to do that, why didn't she take Lily?"

"Maybe her parents aren't that thrilled with the adoption either."

We drove in silence before Greg added, "Considering what happened at the house, maybe Connie left Lily behind so she could move faster and with less notice."

I nodded, understanding that idea made a lot of sense. In just a few days, I'd learned you can't move quickly with a kid in tow.

"Do you know what Hank Holt does for a living?"

"No, but they had a nice house in a very good neighborhood."

Greg stared out the windshield, his eyes narrowed in thought. I could see him processing everything, looking for common threads. "Maybe Hank's in trouble—drugs or something—and that's why he left the house."

"Meaning the people he screwed over came looking for him, so Connie took off?" I suggested, adding my two cents' worth.

"Something like that. And maybe Erica's trying to help them out of the jam."

That idea sounded plausible. Whether Erica liked Lily or the idea of Lily or not, Connie was her sister, and she might be inclined to help.

"Could be," Greg added, "Erica followed her sister to wherever the parents live to give Connie some support."

"More likely, Erica followed her sister there to argue against any support from Mom and Dad."

He squeezed out a small chuckle. "You really don't like Erica, do you? Even Steele at the height of his most obnoxious behavior didn't command this much disgust."

"Greg, do I have to remind you that this is the woman who is going to great pains to get me fired?" I shot a scowl his way. "Really, do I?" I took a deep breath. "Steele would never have done that, no matter how much he huffed and puffed about it."

We lucked out and found a parking spot just a house away from Isaac and Melina's place. Before we got out, I dug out my cell phone and started texting, my index finger jabbing the screen of my phone at high speed.

"What are you doing?" Greg asked.

"Texting Clark. I'm giving him Erica's name, along with Connie's and Hank's, and asking if he or Willie are able to check if any of them left the country or took flights anywhere."

"It's a tall order, but if anyone can do that off the grid, it would be Willie."

Finished with the message to Clark, I started to open the car door. Greg stopped me by putting a strong hand on my arm. "Sweetheart, we're about to go to a party with our friends. Let's put this aside for the rest of the night and just enjoy ourselves."

I started to argue but stopped. Greg was right. Lily was in good care, and there was nothing I could do tonight about Erica and her sister or about my job.

"Deal," I said, giving him a kiss. "And if Clark answers tonight, I'll just wait until morning to respond."

"That's my girl." Greg winked at me, a gesture that always turns my innards soft and gooey.

FIFTEEN

THE DOG LOOKED AT me with great expectations. He was standing by the back door where we kept his leash, wagging his tail and giving me a big dose of saucer eyes.

"Go back to bed, Wainwright," I whispered to the eager animal. "It's not time for a walk." On the mornings I walked for exercise, I took Wainwright with me. He loved it and so did Greg, because it gave Wainwright more exercise. Greg stayed behind in bed with the two snoozing cats but was usually up by the time I returned.

That's where Greg was now—in bed, with both cats curled up somewhere in the folds of blankets. Thanks to all the booze he'd had at the party, he had fallen asleep almost as soon as his head hit the pillow. I, on the other hand, sober and with a head filled with ideas and concerns, couldn't fall asleep to save my life. After the news ended, I watched Jay Leno for a while but was too antsy to pay attention or to drift off. Getting out of bed, I took my mental pacing into the living room, where my feet could join in on the fun.

I felt guilty when I looked at Wainwright. He'd followed me out to the living room and then to the kitchen while I made some tea. He stayed hot on my trail just in case I decided to take that walk. Had it been morning, I might have done it to burn off some of my anxiety.

I tiptoed back into the bedroom to grab my cell phone from the charger on the nightstand, but it wasn't there. I swore to myself. I had forgotten to plug it in after we got home from the party. Going back into the kitchen, I grabbed my purse from the kitchen counter where I'd dropped it. The phone was in its little pocket. I yanked it out and checked to see if Clark had texted me back. He had. The phone also alerted me that I had very little power left. Crap!

I opened Clark's text message. He said he didn't know if they had those resources, but he'd check and let me know. Again, he said it might take a day or so to find out. I was sending him a reply when my phone shut itself off for lack of power.

Dead phone in hand, I turned off the lights and headed back to bed. A disappointed Wainwright trailed after me. After putting the phone on the charger, I scooted back under the covers, but sleep still eluded me. I had ants in my pants and way too many ideas in my head about what was going on.

I tossed and turned, finally deciding to go into the living room again before I woke Greg. The ever-hopeful Wainwright followed me. Plopping down on the sofa, I pulled an afghan over me and opened a book. I read a few pages but couldn't concentrate. My skin was crawling. Termites of doubt and anxiety chewed away at me, relentless in their damage to my nerves.

I kept going over everything I'd done, heard, and learned today. It had been a busy day, with lots of new faces and information, feeling more like five days squeezed into the past eighteen hours. There was something I'd missed—something I needed to revisit, like a movie that is so complicated you need to see it a few times before finally comprehending the plot. I kept telling myself to sleep—that it would come to me in the morning when my brain was rested and not so crowded. But, like most of my body parts, it wouldn't listen. Instead, it nagged at me, flaunting that ghostlike piece of half-remembered information like a hooker strolling in front of a prison yard.

Casting off the afghan, I stood and started touching my toes. Up. Down. Up. Down. From his position on the floor, Wainwright stared at me like I'd lost my mind. Then I started in on lunges and arm twirls. I needed to wear myself out and clear my mind. If they weren't so noisy, I'd be doing jumping jacks. Since I don't exercise much outside of walking, I figured I'd be pooped in no time.

No such luck.

Huffing and puffing, I threw myself back down on the sofa. We'd have Lily tomorrow and she'd wear me out, but I needed that relief now. I considered hitting the liquor cabinet or, at the very least, taking a shot or two of NyQuil. Instead, I closed my eyes and took several slow, deep breaths, concentrating on fluffy clouds and soft kittens and raindrops on roses and all the other junk Julie Andrews sings about.

It worked, at least sort of. I felt my body relax and my head loll against one of the sofa pillows. *Finally.* Sleep couldn't be too far behind. I smiled to myself as my mind organized my thoughts and put them all way, each in their own little cubby, until later.

All but one.

It stood there inside my head like the last kid picked for kickball. Looking for attention, it waved at me. *Yoo-hoo, remember me?*

I bolted straight up, my eyes wide, my brain on turbo, but instead of many ideas buzzing around inside my head, there was only one: Erica might still be in the area. She didn't say she was leaving town, and no one said she'd told them she was leaving. We all assumed it when we couldn't reach her.

My brain rewound until it came back to my visit to Erica's house and my encounter with Racel Barlongo. I'd heard a noise in Erica's closet when I was snooping, I was sure of it. And Racel had taken a long time to come to the door. She could have been helping Erica hide. The call to Alyce looking for Erica could have been a ruse, along with telling me Erica hadn't paid her. I wished that I'd been able to look in the garage to see if Erica's car was there.

I let out another deep sigh. Finally I had cracked what had been bothering me. Maybe now I could get some sleep and head back over to Erica's in the morning to investigate. Greg and I could go there before we picked up Lily.

I was halfway to the bedroom when another thought hit like a slap. By morning Erica could be gone off somewhere or in hiding again. What I needed was the element of surprise. I had to catch her off guard when no one else was there to give her time to hide. I had to go there now.

Slipping back into the bedroom, I grabbed the jeans I'd worn to the party off the chair where I'd tossed them. Greg moaned and changed positions. I froze. He'd have a shit fit if he knew what I was up to, but I didn't want to wake him and ask him to come along. He needed to sleep off his buzz. With no traffic, I could get down to Newport Beach, check it out, and be back in no time. If Erica wasn't there, it would be a quick in-and-out. If she was … well, I'd cross that bridge when I got there.

Back in the living room, I pulled on my jeans, then snarled quietly when I realized I needed to go back into the bedroom for a bra and top. That would mean possibly waking Greg. I thought about checking the dirty laundry, but it was in our bathroom, just off the bedroom. Not to mention every time I went into the bedroom Wainwright followed me, his dog tags jingling in the silence and his toenails tapping on our hardwood floors like Gregory Hines doing a dance routine.

Giving up on the idea of dressing properly, I tucked my nightgown into my jeans. It gave me a bulky, diapered look around my butt, but this was not the time to be fussy. I stuck my feet into the old sneakers I kept by the back door and grabbed my jacket off the hook above it. As I slipped into it, I realized it wasn't going to work. The jacket was bulky and sometimes made noise when I moved. I sloughed it off and grabbed the gray fleece hoodie on the peg next to it. It had stopped raining earlier, and I was mostly going to be in the car. The hoodie would have to do. I thought about snagging my cell phone, but that was a lost cause. It was in the bedroom, and it was dead.

Wainwright stood at attention, waiting for the signal we were heading out for our morning walk. It didn't matter to him that it was still pitch-black outside. When I didn't grab his leash, he let out a low whine.

"Shh," I whispered to the animal. Tiptoeing to a low cabinet, I opened it and pulled a few Snausages from a box. Wainwright's tail wagged with enthusiasm.

"Here, boy," I whispered, holding out my hand. The happy dog gobbled them up. Then I pointed to his thick, pillowy bed set where the living and dining room areas met. "Go to your bed," I commanded in a hushed voice. The animal looked at me with great disappointment. "Go on," I urged. The obedient, loyal dog, his big yellow head lowered, made his way to the bed and lay down with a heaviness that just about broke my heart.

I MADE IT FROM Seal Beach to Newport Beach in record time, thanks to the lateness of the evening. As I expected, the streets in Erica's neighborhood were dead. Except for security lighting, most of the houses were dark, but every now and then I'd catch a glimpse of a light in one of them—maybe someone with insomnia like me. I made my way to Ceiba Place but didn't turn onto the cul-de-sac. Instead, I turned around and parked on the street that intersected it, heading back out of the development. If Erica was home, I didn't want to alert her to my presence by driving up to her house.

The damp chill of the night penetrated the hoodie and my nightgown as I walked the short block to Erica's house. I stuck my hands into the pockets of the sweatshirt and shivered as I scurried along soundlessly on my sneakers, keeping as much as possible to the shadows.

There was definitely a light on inside Erica's house, and it was too bright to be a night light. It shone through the closed blinds of two large corner windows as a testament to my theory that Erica hadn't gone anywhere. One window faced the street; the other, the neighbor to the left. I tried to remember the layout of the house to get an idea of which room this light might be in. My recollection was that the living room was in the back, same as at Connie's house, so that it looked out onto the patio. The kitchen was in that direction also and off to the right. That should make these windows part of the master bedroom.

Light also shone through the frosty narrow windows that framed the front door. I halted to study the bright glow, then looked back at the location of the bedroom windows. Lights had to also be on in the living room or the foyer for it to be this bright by the door. I could also hear music through the door. Someone had to be home and definitely was not in bed.

Should I knock softly or ring the bell? If I did, Erica might shut off all the lights and pretend she wasn't home. She might also call the police. The element of surprise might be best, providing she didn't keep a gun in the house. Then the surprise would be on me. It also crossed my mind that I should have brought along my pepper spray. When I was here this morning, I hadn't noticed an alarm system, but I hadn't been looking for it. And the keypad could have been by the back door that led to the garage. That's where I'd seen it at the Holts'. In the end, I decided to ring the doorbell. It might ruin the element of surprise, but at least I wouldn't be in danger of getting my ass shot off.

I was having a bad case of déjà vu. No one answered the bell, just like this morning. I rang it again. Nothing. I pressed my determined finger against the glowing plastic button next to the door and leaned in, letting it ring for a full ten seconds. I could even hear it on my side of the door. Still, nothing. Either Erica was ignoring it or wasn't home at all. Maybe Racel was in residence, using her boss's home as a private getaway, and didn't want to get caught. I glanced at the driveway. This morning a Ford Focus had been parked there while Racel was here. Now the drive was empty. I rang the bell again, followed by a soft knock.

"Erica," I hissed in a low tone. "It's me, Odelia. Please open up. It's important." I waited. Nothing. I repeated my actions, but again there was no response.

I went to bedroom window. It was no help. The blinds were shut tight. I returned to the front door. I'd already broken into one house today; why not go two for two?

I reached down to put my hand on the doorknob to the front door, then stopped. I'd forgotten to bring my gloves. I'd stashed the package in the glove compartment of my car. Looking back down the street, I weighed whether or not I should go back and get them, then decided against it. I was cold, and it was late. Sticking my hand into the pocket of the hoodie, I used the fleece to keep my prints off the doorknob. Much to my surprise, it turned.

I should have realized something was wrong right then and there, especially considering what I'd found at the Holts', but instead I forged ahead.

Gently pushing the door open, I called out, but not too loudly, "Erica, it's Odelia." I took a step inside. "I tried the bell, then saw the door open." Okay, it was a partial fib. Getting no response, I stepped fully into the foyer. "Erica?"

I glanced down the hallway that led to the bedrooms, then back in the direction of the living room. The place seemed empty and as neat as when I'd seen it this morning. I stopped and listened. Stepping slowly into the living room, I followed the sound of music, which seemed to be coming from the kitchen.

"Oh!" My voice stuck in my throat as I almost stepped into something on the carpet. It looked like blood. Lots of it. It was smeared and going in the direction I was heading. I followed the trail with my eyes as it led into the adjoining dining area and ended where a woman was lying in a pool of blood.

I dashed to her side. It wasn't Erica and it wasn't Racel, but whoever it was, she'd been shot in the chest more than once. Digging through my pockets, I swore as I remembered my cell phone was at home, recharging. I darted into the kitchen, looking for a land line and hoping Erica had one. A lot of folks were dispensing with home phones and only using cell phones. I spotted a cordless phone nestled in its cradle on the kitchen counter and grabbed it. With shaking fingers, I punched in 911.

SIXTEEN

"So that's the whole story?" asked Seth. "And by 'whole,' I mean everything?" He glared at me, eye to eye, to make his point about full disclosure, breaking the steely stare only when necessary to adjust his large frame in the small plastic chair. It wasn't made for his size any more than it was made for mine, though Seth was definitely not stout, just tall and broad. He was folded into the chair, not seated. I guess most criminals are tiny. Either that or discomfort was part of the interrogation process. No wonder Dev, a man the size of Paul Bunyan's blue ox, had opted to sit on the edge of the table.

"Yes, Seth," I answered, tilting my chin up in defiance. "That's everything. And it's exactly what I told the police." I paused. Both men, knowing me well, gave me looks that let me know they didn't believe me. "Well," I admitted, "I told *you* everything. I didn't tell Dev, or anyone else, about searching the Holt house." I paused. Again, they waited for the next confession. "And I didn't tell them about taking stuff from Erica's and the office and sending it to Clark for prints."

"Thank God for that." Greg dragged a hand through his thick hair. "No sense adding 'breaking and entering' and 'theft' to your rap sheet." His sarcasm was as jarring as an off-tune piano. "And no sense getting Clark involved."

I slapped the table with the palm of one hand. "I don't have a rap sheet, Greg! The police are just questioning me."

"Still," my husband persisted, "I wished you'd called me or Seth immediately, Odelia, before you started spilling your guts to the police."

I turned to my husband, my mouth open like a frog waiting for a fly. "I have nothing to hide, Greg. I didn't kill that woman. And—"

"I know, sweetheart," Greg said, cutting me off. "But cops have a way of twisting information until it sounds like a confession. Dev may be our friend, but he's still a cop and has a job to do."

Seth held out his hands as if breaking up a street fight. "All right, you two, simmer down."

He turned his attention to me specifically. "Greg's right, Odelia. You should have called as soon as they brought you in. With that said, let's move on. What else didn't you tell the police?"

My brain was dangerously close to shutting down from exhaustion, but I cajoled it into staying open a bit longer while I sifted through my memory of the last few hours. What had I said to the police? When they first brought me in, I'd been careful, but as time went by and their constant questioning wore me down, had I let slip something that might incriminate me? Hard to say. Detective Fehring had circled my every word like a vulture, just waiting for me to drop my guard so she could feast.

"I'm pretty sure I told them nothing about my snooping at Erica's or at Connie's. I told them I went to Erica's to find a toy for Lily and to see if Erica was really at home, but I'm sure I didn't say anything about going to Irvine at all."

Seth shifted in his seat while he thought it through. "But you did tell Dev and the other detective that Carl Yates wanted you to check out Erica's whereabouts and her relationship with this Mark guy?"

"Yes." I looked from Seth to Greg and back to Seth. "Shouldn't I have told them that?"

Seth shrugged. "It's something they would have learned from talking to Carl anyway. So at least they know you weren't lying about your motive for being at her house."

My heart stopped, then restarted just as fast. Of course they would talk to Carl. Why was I so surprised? I was found in the house of one of Woobie's partners, standing over a dead body, and I'd said another partner had given me the green light to snoop.

"Looks like Mark Baker and Erica can stop their campaign to get rid of me." I said the words out loud and in a soft voice, almost to myself. "There's no way the firm would keep me now."

"You don't know that," Seth assured me.

"But why couldn't you have waited until morning, Odelia?" The question came from an exasperated Greg. "We could have gone together. Maybe someone else would have found the body before then."

"You mean, someone other than me, right?"

Greg's face was flushed, and his voice climbed. "It would have been a nice change of pace."

I was about to say something rude to my darling husband when there was a knock at the door. Before we could say anything, the door opened, and Detective Fehring waltzed in with Dev behind her. Dev glanced at each of us, but his face remained a blank. Fehring dropped something on the table. I groaned inwardly, pleased I'd hadn't been verbal in my dismay. On the table was a plastic evidence bag. Inside were the gloves I'd purchased and stashed in my glove compartment.

"You recognize these?" Fehring asked.

I nodded, then looked at the two detectives with indignation. "You searched my car?"

My lawyer piped up. "You get a warrant for that?"

Dev pulled a piece of paper out of his jacket pocket and waved it at half-mast. He was doing his job and at the moment not liking it one bit.

"How did you even know where the car was?" I asked.

Dev answered, his face still a blank wall. "You said yourself that you drove to the Mayfield house, and I know what you drive."

"Lots of people drive the same make and model," I protested, in spite of Seth poking me under the table.

For the first time all night, a teeny-weeny smile threatened to crack Dev's tight mouth. "And how many of those folks have a license-plate frame that says *I brake for Thin Mints*?"

Seth leaned in and whispered, "Let me do the talking before you fry. Please."

On my other side, Greg reached a hand under the table and squeezed my knee. From the pressure, I knew it wasn't a gesture of affection but a request to keep my mouth shut.

Seth answered for me. "A lot of people buy rubber gloves, Detectives."

"According to the receipt found in the bag," Fehring announced with smug satisfaction, "these were bought yesterday afternoon at a Rite Aid in Irvine."

"And?" prodded Seth.

"And," answered Dev, "Connie Holt lived in Irvine."

Detective Fehring dropped another evidence bag on the table. It contained a single pair of crumpled rubber gloves. "And these appear to be used. We found them discarded on the floor of the back seat of your vehicle, Ms. Grey. Could you tell us what you used them for?"

Dev rephrased the question. "What were you doing in Irvine, Odelia, during a workday?"

"Don't answer that, Odelia," Seth told me. He looked at the two determined detectives. "Are you charging Odelia with anything?"

"Depends," Andrea Fehring said with a slight snarl, "if we find gun powder residue on the used gloves, or anything else incriminating."

"You won't," I shot back at her, "and I think you know that."

Seth started to say something, but I held up my hand, stopping him in his tracks. Under the table, my husband squeezed my knee so hard, I'm sure he was leaving a bruise. But I didn't care. I'd had enough. Let them put me in a cell and throw away the key. At least I'd be able to get some sleep. This was Newport Beach, not South Central. How hardened could the female criminals be in here?

I fixed my eyes on Detective Fehring, willing them to look hard and determined instead of bloodshot and drooping. I didn't want to look at Dev. Cop or not, he was too close of a friend for me to feel antagonistic towards, even under these circumstances. Fehring and I had no such bond, and I doubted we ever would.

"I went to Irvine to see if the Holts were home. I told you Connie dumped poor Lily on her aunt, Erica Mayfield, who, in turn, stashed the kid with me. Last night—" I paused to realign my dates.

"Actually, the night before, when Lily stayed at our house, she had a nightmare and was calling for her mother. With Erica nowhere to be found, I got to wondering if maybe Connie was around—you know, maybe taking a little break from being a mom—so I drove over there."

"And the gloves?" Fehring asked.

I hesitated, knowing I was about to admit to breaking into someone's home. My brain did some painful calculations, trying to figure out a cagey way around the truth, but it was no use. I was beyond exhaustion, and my brain was mush. I stole a glance at Dev Frye. He was watching me, weighing my facial expressions and eye movements like the pro he was, and I knew he'd detect any lies before they passed my lips.

Next to me, Seth was quiet, almost holding his breath. On the other side, Greg had a death grip on my knee. Had he been able to move his legs, I'm sure they would have been jiggling from nerves, as mine were.

After a big sigh of surrender, I plunged forward. "I bought the gloves because I needed them at home."

My brain had decided on a compromise—half lie, half truth. I might be ready to admit I was inside the Holt house, but there was no way I was going to admit to it being a premeditated break-in.

I pointed at the bag with the unused gloves. "If you check the receipt, you'll see I also bought ibuprofen. I had a headache and decided to take something before I got to the Holt house. While at Rite Aid, I spotted the gloves and picked them up at the same time."

"So where's the bottle of ibuprofen?" asked Dev.

"In my tote bag. At home."

"And what about these gloves?" Fehring jabbed a finger at the evidence bag containing the used gloves.

"When I got to the Holt house, no one was home, but through the front window it looked like someone had trashed the place. I was going to try all the doors, then remembered the gloves and went back to my car to get a pair."

"So you wanted to help, but didn't want to leave prints?" Fehring pulled out a plastic chair across the table from me and sat down. Her trim ass fit it perfectly, giving me another reason to dislike her. "This is fascinating," she said with a sneer. "Please continue."

"No need to get snotty," I snapped, rallying my own snarky attitude. "I'm trying to help here."

"If you were trying to help, Odelia, why didn't you call the police when you noticed the Holt house had been broken into?" The question came from Dev, and it was a damn good one.

Quiet filled the room. The cops were waiting for my answer. My husband and lawyer were dreading it.

"Because I wanted to search the place first," I finally admitted. "To see if I could find out where Connie was. I knew once the police came in, I'd never be able to check anything out, but I also didn't want to leave prints that might confuse the police when they did investigate." My explanation sounded plausible to me, even if it was on the fly. "I didn't know for sure the house had been broken into until I got inside."

I held up my right hand and index finger to emphasize my next point. "*And*, I want you to know I didn't break into that house. The back gate was unlatched and the back sliding door was open when I got there. Once inside, I saw that the whole house had been ransacked. When I left, I locked up."

Dev slowly shook his head with disbelief and displeasure. "Did you take anything, Odelia?"

"Yes," I confessed. "I took some clean clothes for Lily, but that was it. From the look of the place, I figured she might be with us longer than expected."

"And you didn't think to call the police even after you were inside?" This question came from Detective Fehring. She and Dev were playing Ping-Pong, with my brain as the ball.

"Whoever trashed that house meant business," I said, looking straight at her again. "I got in, took the clothes, and got out. Connie and her husband are up to their necks in something nasty, and I didn't want to get involved any more than necessary."

Fehring laughed. She actually leaned back in her chair and laughed. It was low and laced with amusement, like a hungry snake inviting a field mouse to tea. "And how's that working out for you?"

The thought of reaching across the table and slapping Fehring crossed my mind. Then I remembered she carried a gun.

Before I could do or say anything monumentally stupid, the door opened and someone motioned to Dev and Fehring. They both left.

Once the door was closed, I looked to my left, then my right, and said, "That went well."

"In what universe, Odelia?" Greg took his hand off my knee. I'm sure if he'd been able, he would have been up and pacing the room. "You're in jail, being questioned about a murder, and you've just confessed to breaking and entering."

"The door was open, Greg," I corrected. "I broke into nothing. Both houses had their doors unlocked."

"It's still trespassing, Odelia," Seth chimed in.

Before the three of us could muster enough energy to get into a verbal brawl, the door opened again, and Fehring and Dev walked back in. There was nothing bland about Dev's face this time, and even Fehring's usual smirk was wiped clean.

"How well did you know Harrison Holt?" Dev asked without preamble.

"Who?" I responded.

"Hank Holt," added Fehring. "Connie's husband."

"I don't know him at all. In fact, I'd never even set eyes on Connie until I found her dead." My eyes widened with horrible possibility. "Why? Do you think he killed his wife?"

"No," answered Dev. "Holt did not murder his wife. He was found dead a few days ago up in Laguna Canyon."

Greg and I gasped at the same time, but he found his voice first. "You mean that guy burned in the fire?" Before they could answer, he added, "We saw it on TV the other night. I thought they didn't know who that was."

"They identified his body late yesterday," Dev told us. "The sheriff just notified us when they got the report about Connie Holt this morning."

I slumped in my chair, all thoughts of saving my own skin gone. "Poor Lily."

SEVENTEEN

As SOON AS WE got home, I crawled into bed. I didn't even bother to change out of the clothes the police had given me. All I wanted was to sleep for a few weeks and wake up to find this was nothing but a bad dream. But sleep eluded me once more.

Not too long after, I heard Greg wheel in, undress, and lift himself onto our bed. He positioned himself and rolled towards me. I was on my side, my back to him.

"You're not going into the shop today?" I didn't turn to face him. As a rule, Greg worked every other Saturday, trading weekends with his manager.

"I called Chris. He said he could cover today."

Chris Fowler was the manager of Greg's California shop, Ocean Breeze Graphics. Greg and his partner, Boomer, owned several graphic design and print shops—one in Colorado, one in Phoenix, and the original shop here in Huntington Beach. Boomer lived in Denver and ran that one. The location in Phoenix was operated by Boomer's brother.

"I just fed the animals," Greg added. "So they should leave us alone while we grab some more sleep." He snuggled close and put an arm around me.

"You're not mad at me?" I asked, still not turning to face him.

"I'm pissed as hell." The words were harsh, but his voice was low and soft. "But I'm also exhausted and thankful you're safe." He gave me a gentle squeeze. "But let's get some sleep and talk about it more later."

"But what about Lily? She can't go into foster care." I started to cry. "She just can't!" This time I did turn around. "We can take her. She can live with us until this is all sorted out."

"It's not that simple, sweetheart." Greg wiped the tears off my cheeks with his fingers. "Her parents are dead, and you were found with the body of her mother. I don't think the county is going to just hand her over to us, considering the circumstances."

"But we can try."

Greg studied me a full minute before turning away. Grabbing his cell phone from his nightstand, he punched one of his speed dials. "Seth," he said when the other party answered, "I'm sorry to disturb you, especially after what you just did for us, but I have a question. Is there any way we can get temporary custody of Lily? We don't want her going into foster care if it can be helped."

Greg listened for what seemed an eternity but was really only a few seconds. "What's he saying?" I hissed with impatience. "Put him on speaker."

"Seth, I have you on speaker," Greg told him after punching the phone's feature. "Odelia's here."

"Like I was telling Greg," Seth said, his voice coming through the speaker low and tired. "Zee and I feel the same way about the girl.

Zee's done a lot of volunteer work and fundraising for the Orange-wood Children and Family Center over the years, and she put in a call to the head honcho. She called him at his home as soon as I got back. Got him out of bed and everything."

"And?" I pushed with impatience.

"Nothing's final yet, but he's going to pull some strings and see if Lily can stay with us for the time being."

"She can stay here," I suggested.

"I'm sorry, Odelia, but they won't go for that. Not with you being so involved. They're stretching it for us as it is."

Greg gave me an I-told-you-so look that made me want to pinch him, but joy at Lily not going under the care of the county overrode my annoyance.

"What does 'time being' mean?" I asked, wanting clarification.

"It means," Seth explained, "until they can find members of her family who can take her. She has at least an aunt that we know of."

"And," Greg added, "Odelia said the girl's maternal grandparents are alive and living somewhere out of the country."

"In the Caribbean," I called out in the direction of the phone.

"It won't take long for the authorities to hunt them down to tell them about Connie and her husband. And I'm sure the county would rather keep Lily in a stable home than put her in Orange-wood, where they are already filled to capacity."

"I want to come over and see Lily later today," I told both men.

There was a long pause, both on the phone and in the bed next to me.

"Sweetheart," began Greg, "as much as I know you want to see Lily, and so do I, I think we should lay low today."

Seth was of the same mind. "Greg's right, Odelia. Let everything settle down and get some rest. You've had quite a shock and no sleep. Lily will be fine with us."

"How about tomorrow?" I pushed.

"Odelia, it's me." Coming from the phone now was Zee's voice. She sounded concerned and dead serious. "Odelia, the child has been through a lot, and the worst of it is just beginning, with both her parents now gone. Let her have today without confusion and being torn in several directions. If you come here, she'll want to go home with you, and we can't allow that. It will be difficult for both of you."

It made sense, but I still didn't like it. After a long silence, I squeaked out, "I understand. We have to do what's best for Lily." And I meant it.

"Tell you what," said Zee, softening her voice. "Let's see what happens today. If everything calms down and the county doesn't object, you and Greg can come over tomorrow for Sunday dinner. You can have a nice long visit with Lily, and I know she'll be happy to see you."

She was throwing me a bone, and I snatched at it like Wainwright. "Okay. Let's see what happens." I followed that with something else on my mind. "Did Lily have a nightmare last night? Did she call out for her mother?"

"No," answered Zee. "At least not that we noticed. She slept like a log."

Maybe it was only our house or my mothering that brought out Lily's night terrors.

I looked at Greg and saw he was reading my thoughts. Sometimes I love that he knows me so well. Other times, like now, it felt like an annoying invasion of privacy.

"Don't you dare blame yourself for that," my husband whispered, his breath warm against my ear.

When Greg and I woke up, it was just after noon. We dawdled around the house with no real purpose, neither productive or relaxing, until Greg suggested we go out for lunch, then a movie. I knew he was trying to keep my mind occupied, and I loved him for it. While we showered and dressed, I asked Greg if he thought the police would question Carl Yates today or wait until Monday when the office opened. The idea of going into the office in two days made my stomach churn.

Greg carefully shaved around his beard. He stopped long enough to give the question a few seconds' thought before airing his opinion. "I'm betting they try to contact him today or tomorrow. Seems they'd start asking questions sooner than later, and the police are going to do their damndest to find Erica. You can bet on that. I'll bet one of their first stops was to that housekeeper of hers."

I ran a brush through my hair while standing at the sink next to him. "Do you think Erica killed her own sister?"

"Hard to say."

He rinsed the remaining scraps of lather from his face before burying it in a clean towel. I love watching Greg shave. It's like comfort food for the eyes.

He pulled the towel down, revealing his tidied face and beard. "You've said yourself she's a cold piece of work."

I nodded. "That she is, but I'm not sure she's a cold killer."

"If Connie came to the house looking for Lily, they might have gotten into a fight." While he spoke, Greg wheeled into the bedroom to get dressed.

I followed and sat on the edge of the bed to pull on my socks. "True. If I had a sister and she'd pawned my kid off on strangers, I'd be mad as hell." I stood up and reached for my jeans. From the bed, the two cats watched with bored expressions. Wainwright was in the back yard. "But would I be mad enough to kill? It's not like Lily was sold into slavery."

Greg shimmied into his own jeans. "Who else could have had access to Erica's house? For starters, there's the housekeeper, Racel."

"Connie might have had a key. At least you would think so, given they have no other family and lived in the same area."

Greg agreed. "Makes sense for emergencies. Mom and Dad have our key, as do Seth and Zee. And we have both of theirs."

"Racel mentioned Erica having a boyfriend. He might have a key, depending on how close they were." I slipped a gray nubby sweater over my head. "I hope Clark can determine if it's Mark or not."

Greg popped his head through the neck of his sweatshirt. "Maybe the killer was waiting to kill Erica and not Connie. If so, do you think they'd really need a key to get in?"

Stopping short while fastening my watch around my wrist, I turned and looked at Greg, my eyes wide. "That means it could have been anyone. And the killer could have been after them both."

Greg ran a hand through his hair, pushing it back from his face. Beyond washing and drying, that was his idea of combing. "My money's on the thugs who trashed Connie's house and torched her husband."

"Ya know," I said, sidling up to Greg. I put a hand on his shoulder. He put a hand on my ass, his earlier anger with me apparently gone. "Could be, whoever killed Connie was actually there to kill Erica."

"Could be," my hubs added, giving my butt a gentle squeeze, "both sisters were in hot water and on someone's serious shit list."

EIGHTEEN

We went to one of our favorite cafés near the beach. In spite of the cool, overcast day, we sat on the patio so we could keep Wainwright with us. Greg wolfed down a bacon cheeseburger with sweet potato fries while I picked at a spinach omelet and a bagel. Both of us drank extra coffee. After receiving tidbits from our plates, the dog happily napped out of the way under the table. Not once during the meal did either of us mention Connie Holt, Erica Mayfield, Lily, my job, or the police. The conversation was carefully kept to the mundane items of our life, like who was going to take Wainwright to the vet for his annual checkup next week and should we ask our gardener to plant new shrubs in the front of the house. We didn't agree ahead of time to keep the conversation away from murder, but we both seemed to be craving the normality of our usually simple life. We munched our food in peace until Greg broke the unspoken topic taboo.

"I have something I need to say to you," he said after the waitress took away our plates and refilled our coffee mugs.

I braced myself to be lectured on my behavior last night.

Greg reached over and covered my hand with his. "I want you to leave Woobie."

A coarse laugh of relief escaped my lips. "I think after last night, I'll probably get the heave-ho anyway." I set my free hand over the top of his, making a hand sandwich. "My head was already on the chopping block, honey; this will just make the decision final."

"But you didn't kill Erica's sister."

"No, I didn't, but law firms are very conservative, as a rule, and skittish about such things. Trust me, as soon as the police contact Carl and the questions begin, there will be a pow-wow about this, and I'll be determined an unsavory employee. That's why I asked you earlier if you thought the police would wait until Monday."

Something wasn't resting well with Greg. I could tell by the way he turned his head and looked off to the side, as if he'd find the answer to his troubles sitting on the sidewalk like an abandoned kitty.

"What is it, honey?"

Without turning to face me, Greg said, "Carl Yates is bothering me, that's what." He turned back and looked at me. His eyes were two dark clouds in a stormy face. "You were investigating Erica because Carl asked you to do it. The bad judgment of going over to her house in the middle of the night rests totally on you, but he asked you to find the evidence to save your job."

"Yes, that's about right."

"So," Greg stabbed the table with the index finger of his right hand. "So, why would you lose your job over this? You were just following up on something Carl assigned to you."

Color me confused. "But I thought you didn't want me to stay at Woobie."

"I don't, but it frosts my ass that you might get canned for following the orders of a partner."

I tilted my head back and let out a short, sharp bark of laughter. "Welcome to the world of working for lawyers."

Greg was not amused. "First you're on the chopping block because of the backstabbing by one partner, then another gives you orders that might seal the deal."

"But if I had proved that Mark and Erica were involved romantically, Carl probably could have turned the layoff decision in my favor."

"It's a game, Odelia." Greg shook his head slowly. "They're the kings and queens, and you and Mark are the expendable pawns. Trouble is, you're not playing a game. This is your livelihood. Do you think I would ever treat my employees like that?"

I didn't have to think long to answer that question. "No. Never."

"Damn right, I wouldn't." Again, Greg punched the table with his finger. I half expected it to leave dents in the plastic top. "Carl should have done his own dirty work. Makes you wonder what he said to the police and his partners, doesn't it?"

When I looked puzzled, Greg explained. "You told the police that Carl wanted you to look into Erica's relationship with Mark Baker, correct?"

"Yes, of course. I told them the truth."

"And I'm sure the cops asked or will ask Carl about that when they question him. Even if he tells Dev and Fehring the truth, will he honestly tell his co-owners what he had you doing? Or will he throw you under the bus so he doesn't lose leverage with the other partners?"

I took a big swig of my coffee and gave Greg's words a quick turn through my gray matter. "Outside of the fact that I have no reason to mistrust Carl, you have a point. In all the years I've worked at Woobie, he's always had my back and the backs of most of his employees. But it's true, the other partners will not like the fact Carl was behind my snooping, especially without their knowledge, and especially not the partners from Hamlin-Hawke. The Woobie partners sanctioned it when Steele went missing a few years back, but that was to save the firm's reputation."

"I'm just saying, sweetheart, leaving Woobie or not, I don't like the way Carl might have left you hanging in the wind. It would be his word against yours, and I honestly don't think the other partners will care much about what you have to say."

I wrapped my hands around my coffee mug. Greg had given me a lot to consider. "Here's how I see this playing out, Greg, based on my experience with the firm and what you've just said. If the police don't question the other attorneys, they might not find out about me being at Erica's house or about my arrangement with Carl unless Carl tells them. But if they do find out about it, the e-mails and calls between the partners will start flying, especially from those attorneys not supporting me in the layoff issue. The partners will then set a meeting to hash it out or have a conference call. The question isn't whether they will act but if they will do anything over the weekend or wait until Monday." I drained the coffee in my mug. "Everything hinges on what they find out and when."

Greg picked up his own mug and tilted his head back, draining it. When he was done, he fixed me with a look of determination. "Even if they don't fire you, I still want you to leave that job and as soon as possible. And this isn't something new on my wish list."

I weighed his request, not sure if it was a suggestion or a demand. Greg knew how I dug my heels in on demands, no matter how much love and concern was behind them. It was the surest way to get me to not do something, even if doing it was in my best interest. I was just wired that way. But this was different. He'd already laid out a compelling argument. If Carl no longer had my back, it was time to leave because my trust would be shattered.

"Look, Odelia," Greg continued, dialing his passion down a notch, "this mess with Erica aside, until recently, both of us loved our jobs and the people we work with. I think it's one of the things that added to our happiness as a couple. But ever since this merger at the law firm, you've been unhappy. All that stress hasn't been healthy for you, and I'm concerned." Greg paused, looking into his mug as if more coffee would magically appear. "These past few weeks, I was actually hoping they would lay you off. I wanted you to lose that job." When I looked at him with surprise, he added, "Come on, sweetheart, you know yourself you wouldn't have been that disappointed."

"But we need me to work."

"Not really. As I've told you before, we'll be fine. Thanks to the trust from my grandfather, I paid cash for our house when I bought it. My business will support our other needs. We might not be able to save as much and might have to cut back on a few things, but we'll be fine. Besides, Steele said he'd probably have something for you later in the year, right? But even then, if you don't want to go back to work, then don't. Or maybe you'd rather work just part-time. It will be your choice. And whatever you decide I'll be cool with, as long as it's not at Woobie."

My head nodded on its own, but my brain thought it premature. "After finding this latest body, I doubt T and T will let Steele hire me, even part-time."

Greg smiled. "Aren't you underestimating Steele's persuasion abilities?"

Greg was right. Even without the drama of Connie's murder, it was time to leave Woobie, or what was left of it, but it had been such a major part of my life that it felt as if I were thinking about a divorce. "Tell you what," I told Greg. "If they don't fire me by the end of Monday, I'll give my two-week notice first thing Tuesday morning."

"Why not give them the notice first thing Monday?"

"Because I'm betting they fire me or lay me off on Monday, and if they do, I'll probably get some sort of severance package. Better to leave with something than nothing."

"And what if they fire you with nothing?"

I took a deep breath, knowing my decision was not an easy one. "Then I will kick up a fuss and sing like a bird about Carl's involvement. Trust me, I will not go quietly if I'm betrayed."

My husband raised his empty mug in my direction. "To you, sweetheart."

The rest of the day went by without incident, though every time my phone rang I jumped, thinking Carl and the firm were pulling the trigger faster than anticipated. I really didn't want to take Carl on and hoped it wouldn't come to that, but Greg was right, Carl shouldn't have asked me to snoop into an attorney's private life, especially not to save my own job. Not that I wouldn't have done that on my own, but having an attorney send me off to do something that could ultimately get me fired gave it an icky pallor. Of course, Carl had no way of knowing that Erica's family members were involved in something sinister and would end up murdered. You just can't make contingencies for things like that like you can for earthquakes and other natural disasters.

The murder made the TV news. A perky reporter wearing a jacket against the cool air was positioned in front of Erica's house. Greg and I watched from our living room sofa, where we'd each been reading while half listening. Both of us dropped our books and tuned in to hear what the reporter had to say. Ironically, it was the same reporter who'd reported on the death of Connie's husband. They didn't say anything I didn't already know and even left out some large chunks of information, such as the name of the victim. Nothing was said about Erica Mayfield except that the police were searching for the owner of the house for questioning.

My phone rang near the end of the newscast. I picked it up off the end table. It was Steele. I showed it to Greg and made a face. "I'll bet he just saw the news."

"You know if you don't answer that, he'll call the house phone, my phone, and probably even Seth and Zee until he finds someone."

I punched the decline button on my phone and placed it back on the table. Sure enough, a few seconds later Greg's phone rang. He pulled it out of his pocket. It was Steele.

"Don't answer it," I hissed. "Let him call all over the world. I don't care."

Greg smiled and answered the call, putting it on speaker. "Hey, Steele. How's everything?"

"Where's Grey?"

"She's right here, pretending she's not." Greg winked at me. I stuck out my tongue.

"Grey," Steele's voice came from the phone. "Did you have anything to do with that body found at Mayfield's place?"

I sneered at the phone. "There was a body found at Erica's?" I forced surprise into my voice.

"From your tone, I know you're dodging the question," my former boss said with a slight laugh.

"How do you know that was Erica's house on the news? They didn't say anything about who owned it."

"I've been to that house with my friend."

Greg, clearly amused by the conversation, continued to hold the phone while Steele and I bantered.

"Does your friend have any idea where Erica might be?"

"Not a clue."

I twisted a chunk of hair in one hand. "Hang on, Steele, there's another call coming in." I motioned for Greg to hit the mute button.

"What's up?" he asked after he cut Steele off from hearing us.

"It just occurred to me that Steele might be Erica's elusive boyfriend, not Mark Baker." I continued to torture my hair. "What do you think?"

"Do you really think he'd sleep with Erica, knowing she has it in for you?"

"Oh, please—Steele would sleep with a yak if it turned him on. I don't think any loyalty to me would stand in the way of his need for sexual conquest." I stopped twirling my hair. "And he did know about Erica's attempt to get rid of me." I motioned for him to turn the sound back on.

"Steele, I want you to answer me something truthfully."

"I'd never lie to you, Grey. I might not say what you want to hear, but I'd never lie."

"Are you sleeping with Erica?"

"Absolutely not! I told you I know a friend of hers."

"People sometimes use *friend* as a smoke screen."

"Well, not in this case, Grey. I'm telling you the truth. I'm dating someone she knows well, someone from law school, and that's the honest-to-God, cross-my-heart truth. Erica's not my type."

"Why? Because she's fat?"

Steele grunted. "No, not because she's fat, but because she's a Class A bitch on wheels and not a nice person. I do have some standards, you know."

It was nice to know that even the yak would have to have something going for it besides good looks.

There was silence on both ends before Steele asked, "So, did you find the body? And if so, do you need a lawyer?"

Greg fielded the second question. "Seth Washington got Odelia through the questioning."

"Aha!" came through the phone loud and clear. "So you did find the body. Who was it?"

"You mean your *friend* didn't tell you?" My sarcasm lit up the phone line.

"I just saw it on the news, Grey. I haven't talked to my friend about it yet. You were the first call I made."

"The stiff was Connie Holt, Erica's sister and Lily's mother," Greg told him.

"Oh, no—you don't mean the sweet little girl that was with Grey at lunch?"

"Yes," I confirmed. "The same."

Greg chimed in. "To make matters worse, it was Lily's dad who was found dead in Laguna Canyon recently."

"Jesus," Steele said, his voice low and sad. "How do you break something like that to a kid?"

"I have no idea." My throat tightened as I wondered if Lily had been told yet, and who did the telling. And if she had been told, did she comprehend what it meant? "She's with Seth and Zee right now. The county had issues with her staying with me since I'm involved."

"That's a good place for her," Steele decided. "Zee knows how to handle kids."

"Oh, and I don't?" I was sorry we were talking on the phone so I couldn't snarl in person.

"Come on, Cheesehead Squirrel, you were over your head even in happy times. Admit it."

"He's got you there, sweetheart."

I aimed my snarl at my husband.

"Okay, Grey, it's my turn to ask you a question and get an honest answer." Steele's voice had turned serious on a dime. Both Greg and I noticed and stared at the phone, waiting.

"What in the hell were you doing at Erica's house in the first place? Did you get it into your thick head to confront her about your job?"

"Yes and no," I answered. "I couldn't sleep and had the bright idea she might be home and just pretending she was somewhere else. When I got there, I found Connie's body."

"Hold the phone," Steele snapped. "You couldn't sleep? What in the hell time did you go over there? On the news it looked like the body was found this morning."

"It was this morning," added Greg. "About two this morning."

Steele groaned. "Dammit, Grey, what possesses you to do these things?"

"Like I said, I got the idea into my head that Erica might just be pretending to be gone to avoid taking care of Lily, so I went over there to find out. What better time than in the middle of the night to catch someone in a lie? And I wanted to find out—" I chopped the sentence off before ending it.

"Find out what?" Steele prodded.

"Go ahead," Greg urged, "tell him why you were really skulking about in the middle of the night. I'd like Steele's opinion on this."

"We've already discussed this, Greg. Steele doesn't need to be involved."

Greg ignored me. "Steele, would you ever, and I mean *ever*, ask Odelia to spy on one of your law partners while she was in your employ?"

There was silence on Steele's end of the phone for a full minute. Greg checked to make sure the call was still connected.

"Who sent you over there, Odelia?" Steele demanded. His earlier amusement had taken a hike.

"No one sent me there, Steele. I went under my own steam."

Greg didn't like my answer. "Carl Yates has Odelia trying to find out why Erica has it in for her, specifically whether or not she's sleeping with Mark Baker."

Again, a long silence.

"If Carl wants to know that," answered Steele, "he should ask Erica himself, not send you to do his dirty work."

"Bingo!" Greg jerked his chin at me in an annoying way. "That's exactly what I said."

"Let me get this straight," Steele said, lining up his mental ducks. "You went to Erica's to catch her with Mark Baker, and Carl Yates sent you? That's rich!"

"No," I insisted. "Carl didn't know I was there or that I was going to go there. He and I talked about why Erica was campaigning so hard with the partners to get rid of me and save Mark's job. We both wondered if it might have something to do with a personal relationship, so he asked me to do some quiet checking."

"Freaking unbelievable!" After a slight pause, Steele added, "I hope you don't have plans on retiring from that firm, Odelia, because it's not going to happen. Even if Carl was behind it, once this gets out, the other partners will never trust you again, especially the partners from Hamlin-Hawke."

"I'm thinking they'll either fire me or play the layoff card this week."

"If they're smart, they will lay you off. Less controversy than a firing, especially since they've been laying off people already and it's common knowledge your position was targeted. If you kick up a fuss, they'll be able to prove it was already in the works before this happened."

Greg nudged me with his elbow.

"And even if they don't," I continued, rubbing my side where Greg had gently assaulted me, "I'm going to give my notice this week. It's time for me to leave Woobie."

"Now that's the smart-thinking Grey I know." We could almost hear Steele smiling through the phone. "As I told you at lunch, we'll probably be able to take you on in late summer or early fall. Can you hang tight until then?"

"She'll be hanging tight," Greg answered for me. I didn't mind it when Greg and I finished each other's sentences. A lot of close couples did that. But this acting as my mouthpiece was really irritating and made me feel like a slow kid that needed looking after or I'd get on the wrong bus.

"In fact, don't go in on Monday." Steele spoke in rushed words, his habit when his mind was spinning so fast that his mouth had trouble keeping up. "Call in sick or take some vacation days. Tell them your great-aunt Suzie died. Something. Anything."

"I don't have a great-aunt Suzie," I pointed out.

Greg jumped onto Steele's bandwagon in a flash. "Great idea, Steele." Greg turned to me. "You're not busy, so why not take some time off, sweetheart?"

It did sound nice. I wouldn't have to face Carl or Mark or the stares of my coworkers in the event they knew what had happened. And I could go to Zee's and spend more time with Lily.

"And while you're home, Grey," Steele said, "do you think you could stay out of trouble? Maybe you could grout your bathroom tile or something like that."

NINETEEN

SUNDAY TURNED OUT A lot like Saturday. Time dragged. Greg was going to stay home from his twice-a-month basketball game, but I urged him to go. He even asked me to go with him, but I declined, saying I could use the time to catch up on laundry and other stuff. Of course, since I was going to be unemployed soon, I'd have plenty of time to do the wash and clean the house. I could even do it anytime during the next few days.

Clean the house—now there was an unwelcome thought. When Greg and I married, Cruz Valenz, the housekeeper I'd had for years, started working her magic at Greg's house. He'd been using a service with spotty results and was thrilled with Cruz. Her husband, Arturo, who had been taking care of the few plants and shrubs I had on my patio, migrated to Greg's with Cruz. Arturo was happy to see we had a real lawn, both in the front and back, and lots of greenery. Now that I'd be off work, I might have to go back to cleaning my own house. Cruz had spoiled me. The idea of taking care of this house, which was much larger than my condo, was not appealing. It's not that I don't know how to clean, it just wasn't my strong suit.

Greg kissed me goodbye and underlined Steele's admonishment to keep out of trouble. As soon as he got home and showered, we'd be off to see Lily. I couldn't wait to see her, even if it was under tragic circumstances.

Before I did anything, I placed a call to Tina Swanson, the office manager at Woobie, and left a voice mail to let her know I would need to take a couple of unplanned vacation days. Tina's position seemed safe since Hamlin-Hawke had not brought any management positions over with them, but she definitely seemed the worse for wear since the merger. I'd heard a rumor she was shopping around her résumé, and I wasn't surprised.

I didn't give Tina an exact day I'd be back but simply said an emergency had come up and I would be in touch. I also told her in the voice mail that there wasn't anything on my desk that couldn't wait until my return. That was a laugh. There wasn't anything on my desk at all to speak of, and what was there was routine. Erica and Mark had seen to that. Normally I would never do such a thing as take unscheduled time off like this except for a very serious reason. But I wasn't busy, and I did have quite a few vacation days accrued and didn't want to face the office. Last night Greg and I did the math. I had enough vacation days that even if I gave Woobie a two-week notice, I'd never have to go back to work before officially leaving the firm. Steele had encouraged me not to pull the trigger so fast on quitting, but to wait it out for a few days to see if they'd make me an offer to leave with cash, so we shelved the plan for me to give notice on Tuesday.

I had just thrown a load of towels into the washer when the front doorbell rang. Usually Wainwright would echo the chimes with barking, but he was with Greg. The cats were both useless when it

180

came to announcing people at the door. I glanced at the clock on the microwave. It was just after eleven. Greg would be home shortly after one. Sunday dinner with the Washingtons was at two thirty.

"Hi, Odelia," said a familiar voice when I opened the door. Standing on the other side of the locked screen door was Alyce Allen and her husband, Gary, both dressed in their Sunday best. "I hope you don't mind the intrusion," Alyce said, "but when we heard what happened to Lily's mother, I wanted to see for myself that you were okay."

"You know what happened?" I remained dumbstruck, not moving to invite them in.

Alyce nodded. "The police came by our house yesterday." She glanced at Gary as if awaiting permission to say more. He gave her a small smile of encouragement. "They asked a lot of questions about Erica and"—she paused—"and about you."

I shook off the surprise of their visit and unlocked the screen door. "Please come in."

The Allens came into my home and awkwardly looked around. I invited them to sit down. They sat side by side on the sofa like a mismatched set of salt and pepper shakers but didn't take off their coats. "Can I get you anything to drink?" I offered.

"No," Gary answered for the two of them. "We're fine."

"I'm surprised to see you," I said to Gary. "Especially since you're a pastor. Shouldn't you be behind a pulpit about now?"

He gave me a slow, calm smile, the same type he gave his wife. I'll bet the man had great bedside manner when it came to comforting the sick and grieving. "Our worship service is at nine in the morning. It's a small congregation of early birds."

"Usually we go out for brunch after," Alyce chimed in, "but today we left our kids with friends and came to see you. I hope that's okay."

"I appreciate your thoughtfulness, Alyce. Have you heard from Erica at all?"

"Not a peep," she answered. "And I don't think the police have found her yet either. Under the circumstances, I'm getting pretty worried about her." Gary reached over and placed a comforting hand on his wife's arm. The gesture made me smile. Greg would have done the same thing to me.

Gary glanced around. "Your husband home? I'd like to meet him."

"He's off playing basketball. He plays twice a month in a wheel-chair league." For some reason I couldn't explain, I tacked on, "We're not much on going to church."

The pastor laughed. "Not to worry, Odelia. We're not here to proselytize, just to see how you and Lily are holding up."

"Lily's not here either."

Alyce looked alarmed. "The county didn't take her into protective custody, did they?"

"Yes and no," I answered truthfully. "Lily is now under the authority of the county but is still with my friends. They know some of the higher-ups and were granted permission to keep her at their home until her family could be located."

"That's wonderful," said Gary with obvious relief. "A much better solution to an overcrowded children's home."

"Yes, my husband and I are going over there later for dinner and to visit with Lily."

Alyce looked about ready to cry. "It must have been just awful finding Connie like that."

"The police told you I found her?"

She nodded, her eyes cast down. "I'm glad it wasn't me who found her. Sometimes Erica had me drop things off at her house." Alyce visibly shivered.

"Did they say anything about Hank Holt?" I asked, wondering if the police had disclosed that bit of information during their questioning.

"Only if I had ever met him," Alyce answered, "which I hadn't." Her brows knitted with concern. "You don't think he killed his wife, do you?"

"Let's pray that's not the case," added Gary with deep concern. "The child has enough to deal with in losing her mother without her father being a murderer."

While the Allens contemplated their prayers for Lily, I kept my mouth shut. If the police were choosing to keep Hank's murder on the QT, I wasn't going to trample on their investigation. My plan was to stay off their radar as much as possible.

"Odelia," Gary said, swallowing hard, "could I trouble you for that drink you offered? I guess I'm a bit dry after my sermon this morning. Water would be just fine."

"You sure? I have some freshly made iced tea." I got to my feet.

"No, the water would be great. Thank you."

I looked at Alyce. "How about you, Alyce? Can I get you something?"

"No, but I would like to use your bathroom, if I may."

"Sure, I'll show you where it is."

I directed Alyce down the hallway that led to the guest room, our home office, and the guest bath. "It's the first door on the left." As she toddled off, I went into the kitchen to get Gary his drink. I'd just filled a glass with cold water from the jug we kept in the fridge when I felt something close by, like a ghost leftover from Halloween. I turned around, coming face to face with Gary Allen. Startled, I sloshed the water but managed to hang onto the glass.

"I'm so sorry, Odelia," Gary said, grabbing my arms to steady me. "I didn't mean to startle you. These darn shoes don't make a bit of noise. I should have at least cleared my throat."

"It's okay. Really." Grabbing a dish towel, I wiped the glass and handed it to him, making it necessary for him to unhand me. Then I dried my hands and dropped the towel to the floor to sop up the spill. "It's just water." I gave off a nervous laugh. "Now if our dog was here, he'd have that lapped up in a heartbeat."

Gary chuckled along with me but didn't move out of my personal space, nor did he take a drink of the water. His behavior almost made me wish Wainwright was home for other reasons. Just then the doorbell rang. I scooted past Gary to answer it. At the door was Dev Frye and Beverly, the woman he'd been seeing for quite a while.

"Hey, Odelia," Dev said. "Bev and I were on our way home from brunch and thought we'd stop by to see how you were, considering yesterday."

"Seems to be my day for company," I announced, trying to shake off the creepy feeling I'd gotten from Gary. "Gary and Alyce Allen are here. Alyce is Erica Mayfield's secretary." Just as I said her name, Alyce emerged from the hallway. She looked surprised.

"We've already met Detective Frye," Gary told me. He turned to Dev. "Nice to see you again, Detective. You here to question Odelia again?"

Beverly flashed a smile at all of us. I liked her. She was tall and slender and about my age. She'd been teaching high school for years and had a sharp wit that kept Dev on his toes. "We're here in an unofficial capacity," she said, nudging Dev lightly in his side. "Isn't that right, Dev?"

"Yeah, I guess," Dev confirmed with a shrug. "But you can't turn off being a cop like you can a spigot."

"The Allens dropped by to make sure Lily and I were okay," I informed Dev.

"We can see Odelia is in good hands," Gary announced, taking his wife's arm. "We should go, dear, and get back to the children."

As the Allens started to take their leave, I remembered something. "By the way, Alyce, I won't be in the office for a few days."

She looked at me through her oversized glasses like a spooked owl but said nothing.

"I've decided to take some time off. I've already left Tina a voice mail. If anyone needs me, have them e-mail me. I'll be checking it often."

"A few days off sounds like a great idea," Dev said as he helped Bev out of her coat.

"I agree with Detective Frye," Gary said to me. "Taking time off sounds sensible after everything you've been through. But if you need anything, anything at all, please call me or Alyce."

After the Allens left, I had a short but lovely visit with Dev and Beverly. With Bev's help, Dev managed to steer clear of talk of the investigation, at least until they were leaving.

"Mrs. Allen seemed somewhat squirrelly. Any idea why?" Dev asked, one foot out the door and the other still in my house.

I shrugged. "She's always a bit of a nervous Nelly, but I'm sure all this stuff with Erica Mayfield and her sister is making it a lot worse."

Dev and Beverly weren't gone but fifteen minutes when my cell phone rang. The display was Mark Baker's office number.

What in the hell did he want?

In the months since he'd come to Woobie, Mark had only called me on my cell once, and that was on a weekend to ask about a client file he couldn't find—a client I had always handled until Erica reassigned the matter to Mark.

I answered with a snarl, which was fast becoming my signature response to the phone. "What?"

"Charming way to answer the phone."

"I'm busy, Mark."

"Okay, I'll make it quick. A firm-wide e-mail just went out from Tina saying you won't be in for a few days. Any particular reason?"

"Since when are you the boss of me?"

"Just want to make sure you're okay. I saw Erica's house on the news. You didn't happen to be there when that went down, were you? After all, you do have some anger issues and a résumé for finding bodies."

I'm sure steam started coming out of my ears about then. Instead, I decided to be a smarty pants and answer his question with one of my own. "Been to Erica's house much, have you?"

"A few times to drop stuff off or to give her a ride when her car was in the shop." Mark paused. "You saying you've never been to Mike Steele's place in all the time you worked for him?"

He had me there.

"Why would you think I'd know anything about what happened at Erica's? It's not like we're BFFs like you two. All I know is what I saw on the news." I wasn't about to tell him anything, and it sounded like the police hadn't reached Mark yet to question him.

"Although expect the police to be grilling you about her. They've already talked to Alyce and me." Neither was I going to admit I was the one to find the body.

"I wasn't around much this weekend until just now," Mark told me. "The police will probably catch me tomorrow at the office."

I'd love to be a fly on the wall when the police questioned Mark, especially when Detective Fehring went after him. "Speaking of Erica, have you heard from her?"

"Not a word."

"Would you tell me if you had?"

"No, Odelia, I wouldn't. Not unless she wanted me to tell you." Another pause. A long one. "Listen," Mark finally said, "the real reason I called is I wanted to know some of the background on the Shane acquisition that went down last year. Erica wanted me to handle some cleanup on it. I'm in the office going over it this afternoon."

Kiss-ass. I didn't have any work, but he had enough to pull overtime. And on a matter I had handled with Mike Steele. I wanted to crawl through the phone and choke Mark on principle alone. I'll show him anger issues.

"I was going to ask you about it tomorrow," he continued when I remained silent. "But since you won't be in and it doesn't say when you'll be returning, I thought I'd give you a quick call now."

"And it didn't occur to you that I might be busy or have people over? It is the weekend. Some of us have lives outside the office." I looked down at the dirty towels clutched in my left hand. They were going into the washing machine with a bunch of their friends when the current load was done. Mark Baker was getting overtime on my client, and I was separating whites from coloreds. I wanted to scream. Greg and Steele were right—I needed to leave my job.

"Forget it," he snapped. "I'll figure it out on my own." It sounded like he was going to hang up without saying goodbye, which was fine by me, but instead he tacked on, "Hey, with Erica MIA, you still stuck with that kid?"

"Sorry, Mark. I've got people to see and things to do." *Click.*

"CHEESEHEAD SQUIRREL!" LILY SCREECHED as she launched herself into my arms. I clung to the little orphan like an octopus until she wiggled to be put down so she could make a flying leap at Greg. He picked her up and plunked her down on his lap and did a quick wheelie. She giggled with delight. We weren't the first greetings she gave. Those went to Wainwright.

In my hand was a small bag with the extra clothes I'd picked up at the Holt house and the tacky doll I'd gotten from Erica's. I pulled out the doll and showed it to Lily. She immediately snatched it from my hands and clutched it to her chest in delight. "Mummy."

"That's Mummy?" I asked her.

Lily wiggled back and forth with joy. "Mummy." Then she ran off into the den with Wainwright on her heels.

"I'm glad you brought that, Odelia," Zee said as we hung our jackets up by the back door.

We'd just moved all Lily's baggage from the van into the house, including the car seat. We'd only sent her to the Washingtons' with a change of clothes, thinking she was coming right back to our place. If there's one thing I've learned in all this, it's that kids seldom travel light.

"She had a nightmare last night," Zee continued, "just as you described—was crying 'Mummy' over and over."

"Who knew," added Greg, "that Mummy was a doll. And not a very cute one, at that. We thought she meant her mother."

"So did we," replied Seth. "Her scream in the middle of the night about set my blood to curdle. I'd forgotten about those kinds of nights. Our own had a few from time to time."

I stuck my nose in the air and sniffed. "Oh, Zee, you doll. You made my favorite, chicken and dumplings."

"It's perfect for a damp day, and I figured Lily would eat it. She likes chicken real well."

"What can I do to help?"

"Not a thing," Zee said. "The dining table is set, the salad's made, and we're just waiting for the food to be done." She turned to Seth. "Can you see Lily from where you are?"

He glanced into the den and nodded. "She's on the floor, playing with the dog."

Satisfied, Zee turned to me and Greg. "I almost had to call and cancel this visit," she told us, her voice low.

"What?" we exclaimed in unison. I followed up with, "Is Lily okay?"

"She's fine—in fact, her cold is almost gone—but we had a surprise visit from the county this morning," Zee explained. "Lily can stay with us, but they didn't want her upset by a visit with you and Greg. Seth had to do some fast talking to get them to change their minds."

"I don't understand." I grasped to make sense of it. "We're not planning on upsetting the child, and I'm not a suspect in her parents' murders."

"Keep your voice down, Odelia," Zee warned. "Little pitchers have big ears."

"It's not that," Seth said, returning to the topic. "They felt it would upset her to see you and not be able to go with you. And on that, they're right. She keeps asking about Cheesehead Squirrel. She told them about Cheesehead Squirrel and the doggie and kitties."

We stayed in the kitchen, where we could talk softly and still keep an eye on Lily in the den. I took a seat at the table. In my head all the players and information twirled until I was dizzy.

"As soon as they find Lily's family," Zee said, picking up the explanation where her husband left off, "she's going to be handed off to them, and they didn't want her traumatized any more than necessary. Seth finally convinced them that a visit from you would be healthy for her since she's bonded to you so well."

I gave Seth a small smile of gratitude.

"They're trying to locate her grandparents now," he told us.

"What about her father's family?" asked Greg.

"The only lead they have are her maternal grandparents in the Caribbean. They still haven't located her aunt. And they have no information at all yet about her father's family."

Zee poured us all some iced tea. Taking my glass, I told them, "Alyce, Erica's secretary, and her husband came to visit me today to see how I was doing. Erica hasn't contacted her yet either."

"If they know, then the police are wasting no time question-ing folks," Seth said. "Makes you wonder what the police found out from that Baker guy, if anything."

"Speaking of which, Mark Baker called me today," I told them. "About some client file he was working on. It didn't sound as if the police had contacted him yet."

My dark thoughts spilled onto the table. "I can't help but wonder if Erica's dead, too." I looked at my husband and friends. "Doesn't it seem odd with the murder on the news that she hasn't popped up?"

"Unless she did the killing," Seth suggested.

"Odelia doesn't think that," Greg told him.

I took a drink of tea. "At least I'm trying not to think that way. I just can't see a motive for Erica killing her sister. She might not have liked the idea of the Holts adopting Lily, but that wasn't recent and shouldn't be a reason to kill." I shook my head. "No, if Erica's still alive, I think there's a good chance she's running from whoever killed the Holts."

Seth moved his head in agreement. "I think you might be on to something there, Odelia. She disappeared about the same time her sister did and her brother-in-law was killed."

I crossed my arms in front of my chest. "I'd love to get that weasel Mark Baker alone and make him talk."

"Down, girl," said my lawyer. "We don't need you going all gangsta on us."

Seth was right. Besides, I wouldn't have a clue how to torture someone. Maybe I could talk them to death. "You think Dev might tell us anything?"

"Doubt it," Seth answered. "He's too close to you and has to appear objective. If you become a suspect, he might not be able to work the case at all."

TWENTY

As expected, at the end of our visit, Lily did want to come home with us, but we managed, with just a few shed tears on her side and me managing to dam up my own, to convince her to stay with Zee and Seth. We promised we'd come and visit again very soon. We told Seth and Zee about my plans to stay out of the office for a few days. Seth thought it sounded like a good plan, and Zee told me to stop by one day to have lunch with her and Lily.

"Honey," I said to Greg as we were driving home, "I have an idea I want to run by you."

"About the murder?"

"No."

"About your job?"

"If you'd stop playing twenty questions, I'll tell you."

Greg shot a sexy grin my way, signaling I could talk without further interruption.

"What do you think about us adopting Lily?"

For a split second the van swerved, making me glad it wasn't raining and the road slick.

"Where in the hell did that come from?" Greg glanced over at me, but he didn't seem angry, just confused.

I shrugged. "I know we shelved the idea of adopting, but now I'm wondering if maybe we should step up and give Lily a home."

"Lily has a family, Odelia. You just can't snatch her from them."

"Erica won't want her," I argued. "She was against the Holts adopting Lily in the first place. And who knows about the grandparents. If they're retired and living in some tropical paradise, they might not want a little kid mucking up their lifestyle. If they're anything like Erica, they'll be happy to cut Lily loose, especially since she isn't their blood."

"True, but we don't know about Hank's family. They might be entirely different—very loving and happy to take Lily."

"I'm just saying, if Lily does become a free agent, I think we should consider it." I took a deep breath. "Unless you don't want to. This has to be a one hundred percent mutual decision."

"Agreed."

We rode the rest of the way home in silence. I took the time to calculate what it would mean to take on parenthood at this time in our lives. I don't know what was going on in Greg's mind, but I was equally thrilled and terrified.

We were just coming into the house when my cell phone rang. I checked the display, half expecting to see Carl Yates's name.

"That Carl?" asked Greg.

I shook my head. "It's Clark. He probably got my package and has questions."

After dropping my purse onto the kitchen counter, I answered the call. "Hi, Clark," I said to my brother as soon as I answered. "Did you get my package?"

"It's not Clark," the familiar voice said, "although he is standing right here."

"Willie!" As soon as I said the name, Greg perked up. "What a nice surprise. Greg's here and says hello."

"It certainly is a surprise, though I hardly think it's nice."

"What do you mean?" I had a sinking suspicion I knew what he meant. Willie Proctor had the uncanny ability to know everything about my life. He was like an eye in the sky or Big Brother watching over me.

I moved to a chair in the living room. Greg moved his wheel-chair next to me. "He knows about the body, doesn't he?" he asked.

Because I'm never quite sure where the mouthpiece is on my smartphone, I held my hand over the entire phone while I whispered to Greg. "He hasn't said yet."

When I put the phone back to my ear, Willie was saying something.

"I'm sorry, Willie, but I missed part of that. I was talking to Greg."

"Put it on speaker, then," Willie requested. As soon as I did, we heard a deep sigh. "Do I need to send Clark out there to keep an eye on you?"

"Absolutely not!" I protested. "I'm not a child. Besides, Greg's here."

"Okay, then, to keep an eye on the *two* of you?"

"And hey," I said with sharp indignation, "since when does my brother need your permission to visit me?"

"He doesn't. But maybe he needs to be there not as your family but in an official capacity as my head of security?"

"Are you mad because I asked for some fingerprints to be run?"

"Nice deflection attempt, little mama, but no."

"Then I have no idea what you're talking about."

"Oh, then my source was wrong? You weren't hauled in by the police for questioning in a murder?"

I hemmed and hawed. Next to me, Greg fidgeted. Not bothering to cover the phone, I leaned closer to my husband and said, "My phone's becoming Grand Central. Next time it rings, I'm not answering. And tomorrow I'm changing the number."

"We heard that," yelled a voice from the phone.

Cupping my hand, Greg pulled the phone closer to him. "Hey, Willie, it's Greg. About that police thing, we've got that under control. As usual, Odelia found the body but is not a suspect."

While he talked, I picked at a loose thread on the arm of the chair, then discovered another. One of the cats must have been using it as a scratching post. My money was on Muffin. Seamus was getting too old to be that ambitious.

"She won't be needing those fingerprints after all," Greg continued saying into the phone. "One way or another, Odelia's going to leave her job, so it doesn't matter if that Mark guy is sleeping with her boss or not."

"The hell it doesn't!" I stopped fussing with the loose threads and snatched the phone closer to me, falling headlong into the stampede of words flooding my mouth. "Willie, I still need those prints run. They could lead to the real killer. We don't know if the killer went after Erica, who's my boss and missing, and got her sister, Connie, by mistake, or even if Erica is still alive herself. But I'm pretty sure Connie and her husband were into some deep, dark stuff of their own."

"What do you care?" Willie asked in a voice as mellow as warm tea.

His question stopped me in my tracks. "Huh?"

"I said, what do you care, little momma? If you're leaving your job, this Erica will not be your boss any longer. And if you're not a suspect, then you have nothing to prove. You and Greg sit back and let the police do their job. That's what they're there for."

"But," I began.

"No buts about it, Odelia," Clark added, cutting me off. "Willie's right. Without a tie to that law firm, you don't have a dog in this hunt. There is absolutely no reason for you to put your life on the line for these people, so don't. They wouldn't do it for you. So stay out of this!" Clark's voice escalated until it pushed me back in my chair. Greg took the phone from me.

"Calm down, Clark," Greg said firmly. "No need to go all Nazi on Odelia. She's been through a lot these past few days."

Clark lowered his voice, but he wasn't through. "Asking me to run prints was one thing. I was happy to do it to help you keep your job. But now there's a murder, and that murder involves people at that firm. The sooner you get out of that damn place, the better."

"Yeah, I feel the same way," Greg said. "Mike Steele's an angel compared to these guys."

I jumped to Woobie's defense. "But we don't know the murder was connected to the firm. To someone *in* the firm, yes, but not the firm itself."

There was silence on both sides until Clark broke it. "Look, sis, I'm sorry I yelled at you, but I worry about you and Greg. You tend to rush headlong into trouble without thinking."

I leaned towards the phone. "I understand and appreciate your concern, Clark, but we're not rushing into anything. I just need those fingerprints run. If they confirm anything, I'll turn the information over to Dev Frye and step away. I promise."

"Just so you know." Willie's voice came through the line. "I've set the prints and DNA samples in motion. And I'm going to hold you to that promise of stepping away. In the meantime, just keep your head down. Both of you."

"They're right, you know," Greg said after the call was over. "We need to keep a low profile on this. Especially if we want a chance at getting Lily."

I did a double take. "You mean you want her, too?"

"Yes. I think it's a great idea."

Throwing myself into my husband's arms, I squeezed him tight. After a few seconds he pushed me back a bit and looked into my eyes. "But *only* if she is without a home. I will not condone taking her from her family or even trying to convince them to give her up. Understand?"

I nodded as I fought back tears.

"And you know," Greg continued, "we'll be put under a lot of scrutiny by the state and county officials and may not get her in the end. You ready for that roller coaster?"

Again I nodded. "Maybe they'll let us be her foster parents and see how it works out."

"You never know." Greg gave me a look that melted my heart. "You ready to be a full-time mom?"

"I don't know," I answered truthfully, "but if it's meant to be, I'll rise to the occasion."

Greg took me back into his arms and planted a kiss on my forehead. "I know you will, sweetheart."

TWENTY-ONE

It FELT ODD TO get up on Monday morning and not have to get ready for the office. Greg rolled over and told me to stay in bed. He wrapped an arm around me and nuzzled my neck. Normally that would be enough for me to toss any and all exercise plans aside, but this morning I was antsy and not inclined towards romance. After heartfelt apologies and a promise of a rain check to Greg, I got up, put on my sneakers, and left on my usual walk with Wainwright.

By the time we'd gone the few blocks to the beach, I began to regret my decision to leave my warm bed and hot hubby. It wasn't raining, but it was damp and chilly. I contemplated turning around but instead zipped my windbreaker high up under my chin and kept moving, glad that under it I'd layered an old sweater over my usual tee shirt. I hadn't slept well, even after a glass or two of wine with dinner. My brain was a kaleidoscope of people, events, and possibilities. Who killed Connie and Hank? Where was Erica? What was going to happen to Lily? These questions and others twisted and turned in dizzying patterns of bright colors and shapes, mingling with secondary shades representing my job situation and the relationship between Mark and Erica. I was hoping the brisk morning walk would clear my head and calm me down.

Wainwright didn't seem to mind the chill. He trotted ahead of me, his tail high, his step perky, setting our pace until we reached the beach. Once there, we traveled up and down the water's edge, getting our exercise, until I was tuckered out. We trudged back up to the sidewalk and plunked down on a bench facing the ocean. I wanted to sort a few things out before going home. Wainwright stretched out on the concrete next to the bench and kept a sharp eye on the gulls.

We hadn't been settled long when my cell phone rang. By the ring tone, I knew it wasn't Greg. He insisted I take my phone with me on my morning walks in case of emergencies, but so far, the only emergencies seemed to be him calling me to pick up a few pastries from the bakery on my way back.

I dug my phone out of the pocket of my windbreaker and looked at it. The display said the number was blocked, meaning the caller didn't want to be identified. Usually I don't answer those calls. The numbers of my friends, family, and coworkers were always displayed. A new caller with an unblocked number would at least show the number, but this number was specifically blocked. I was about to decline the call when I realized it might be Willie calling. We didn't have a direct number for Willie. He was still a fugitive from the law. But we did have a number to call if we needed him. Neither Greg nor I knew who or what the number reached, only that it had a Wyoming prefix and a mechanical voice telling us to leave a message. Although these days, should we need to reach Willie, we'd probably just call Clark. Considering Willie was running those samples for me, I moved my finger to the answer button.

It was not Willie.

"Odelia?" Although a question, the woman's voice was not hesitant. Nor was it a young-sounding voice.

I pressed the phone closer to my ear to hear better and asked, "Who is this?"

"A ghost from your past."

Humph. The last time someone said that to me, it had been Clarice Hollowell and had spelled trouble. But this wasn't Clarice. I knew her voice and, besides, she was currently a long-term guest of the California Department of Corrections.

"I'm not into playing games," I said, keeping my own tone firm. "Tell me or I hang up."

"It's Mother."

I doubted my mother, Grace Littlejohn, would ever call herself Mother. She was *Mom*. But even if she did, would she call herself a ghost from my past, no matter how appropriate? Then again, Mom was an eccentric and cranky old broad who lived in a time zone three hours ahead of mine. And if Clark was unreachable, she might call me to amuse herself. She'd done it before. But the voice didn't sound like hers either.

I ventured another comment. "Not my mother, you're not."

"It's *Mother*, Odelia," the woman stressed. "My, how quickly you've forgotten. I'm truly disappointed. I thought I was more memorable than that."

When I didn't answer, she added, "Need your house cleaned?"

When my brain clicked, matching the name with the reference, I almost threw the phone into the sea and ran all the way home. Let Mother Do It was a house-cleaning business that moonlighted as contract killers. I'd encountered them while on the trail of a missing Mike Steele. Mother, an older woman, was the leader of the organization.

"No." I moved the phone to my other ear and stared at the waves lapping the sand below me. "My house is just fine, thank you." I fought to keep my voice even.

"Are you sure?" she taunted.

I started to ask Mother how she got my cell phone number but stopped. If there was one thing I'd learned, both in my years working in the legal field and especially during my stint as a corpse magnet, it was how easy it was to find people and their contact information. All you needed was a shred of starter information and knowing where to look.

"I see you're married now."

Again, it was almost the same words used by Clarice when she'd shown up on my doorstep unannounced. It made me wonder if there was a script undesirables could buy and memorize when reconnecting to people in their past.

"My life is of no concern to you," I answered with my chin aloft in defiance, as if she could see it.

"But Odelia, you're wrong about that. Very wrong."

My chin dropped, and I swallowed hard. "Is this about settling old scores? About what happened back in that house?"

"Partially, but not in the way you might imagine. I need you to meet me today."

I snorted. "And what—walk into a trap?"

"*Tch, tch, tch.* If I had my cap set on killing you, do you really think you would still be alive? My crew and I are very good at what we do." Her voice vibrated with amusement. "If you want to live, you need to meet with me. Today. It's that simple. And you will not be ambushed. At least not by me and my people." Her voice had slipped from mirth into dead serious in the blink of an eye. "And you cannot tell anyone where you're going or bring anyone, not even that cutie husband of yours, or the deal about your safety is off."

I steeled my shoulders as I readied to ask the next question. "When and where?"

I HATED DRIVING INTO Los Angeles, especially during the week. I'd made good time on the 405 Freeway, but once I merged onto the 110 heading north, things bogged down. My portable GPS said I would arrive a few minutes after ten. I hoped it was right, because ten thirty was the time I'd set with Mother, and I didn't want to be late. I would have left earlier, but I had to get Greg out the door first and with as few questions as possible.

"What are you going to do today, sweetheart?" he'd asked over coffee and the cinnamon rolls I'd picked up from the bakery on my way home.

I'd picked up an entire box of rolls, muffins, and donuts, thinking I might be able to get Greg out the door faster if he was taking breakfast goodies to his staff. No such luck. Instead, he plucked out a fat bun for himself and settled at the table with his coffee as if he had no place to go and no special time to be there. I wanted to scream but knew if I behaved squirrelly, he wouldn't let up until he'd picked my brain for the reason.

"I was thinking of having a spa day. Might be nice after everything." I sipped my own coffee and tried to still the nervous tapping of my foot under the table.

"That's an outstanding idea," announced my hubs. He took a big bite of his cinnamon roll and beamed at me. "Why don't you see if Zee wants to go with you? I'm sure you can find a sitter for Lily for just a couple of hours."

"I thought about that," I lied. "But I think I'd rather go alone and just detox in silence."

With a full mouth, he nodded in agreement. He swallowed and washed it down with coffee. "After what you've been through these past few days, I understand. And you deserve it."

I hadn't actually lied to Greg—I *was* going to a spa. That's where Mother had said to meet her. She'd given me the name and address. Curious, I'd looked the place up. According to its website, the Olympic Spa was in the Korean section of Los Angeles, not far from downtown. Although I'd heard about them, I'd never been to a Korean-style spa before. The services looked inviting, but I doubted I would be partaking of any. Mother probably planned on having a small, intimate meeting with me in a van in the parking lot.

I must be out of my freaking mind. All the way there, that phrase played over and over in my head like an annoying ditty from a sitcom.

As directed, I pulled into the parking lot behind the spa. An attendant took my keys. The lot was nearly empty, and there was no sign of Mother anywhere. The area around the spa was seedy, and so was the outside of the building, which was covered in graffiti. It was a far cry from the frou-frou spas Zee and I frequented in Orange County. But all that changed once I entered the building.

After walking down a narrow and nicely decorated corridor with bamboo wall coverings and Asian pottery and prints, I came to a reception counter. Behind it were two cute Korean girls in their late teens or early twenties. Both wore black leggings and black tee shirts with SPA DIVA spelled out across their chests in rhinestones.

"Are you Miss Odelia?" one asked in heavily accented English with a lyrical undertone.

"Yes."

She flashed me a 100-watt smile. "Your friend is inside waiting. Have you been here before?"

"No, I'm afraid not."

"First, no cell phones, please."

I pulled mine out and turned it off.

She showed me through double doors to a small area of stacked cubes with doors. "Your shoes, please." She pointed at my flats. I kicked them off, and she stashed them in one of the cubbies, shut the little door, turned a key, and pulled it out. "You are locker fifty-two." She handed me a hot-pink, curly plastic key ring with two oddly shaped keys—one that went to the shoe cubby and another. She pointed down the hallway towards two closed doors. "The one on the left is the restroom."

Finished with that chore, she showed me into a large room. In the middle were two sofas and some chairs in a grouping. Two middle-aged Asian ladies clad in thin cotton robes the color of wet sand were sitting on one of the sofas. They chatted quietly while sipping from paper cups. On the left-hand wall were several vanity areas with hair dryers, tissues, and lotions. To the right was a slightly raised stage with green tiles. My guide pointed to it. "That is our jade floor," she explained. "The floor is heated. After treatments ladies like to nap on it."

I nodded, wondering how in the world people could nap out in the open like that, warm tiles or not.

Next she pointed to the left, to a steamy glass door that divided the vanity area. "That is bathing area. You must take shower before using pools. Understand?"

Again, I nodded. Showering before using pools was spa etiquette no matter where you were.

"Some lockers are behind there." She pointed to an area partially hidden by a wall behind the sofas. "Yours is over here." With a sweep of her arm, she pointed to an area in an alcove to the right of the jade floor. "If you have any questions, please ask."

"Do I need to pay you?" Most spas allowed people to use their facilities without booking massages and other services, but there was always a small fee involved.

"Your friend pay for you. If you want to book something else, please see me at front desk." She gave me a slight bow and left.

I stood there in my stockinged feet, my tote bag in one hand, the jellied squiggly key ring in the other, and wondered what I was supposed to do next. The door to the bathing section opened, and two women walked out into the lounge area—one Asian, the other Caucasian. Both were naked as jaybirds, although the Caucasian woman was half wearing a thin cotton robe like the ladies on the sofa. The other had only a towel thrown casually over her shoulder. She strode over to the vanity, totally unfazed by being naked in front of strangers, before finally wrapping the towel around her body.

"Odelia, over here."

The voice came from the locker area. I took a few steps in that direction and peeked. Seated on a bench was a pudgy woman wearing one of the cotton robes. She was in her late sixties, possibly even seventy, with short hair the color of a dead field mouse. She smiled at me, showing small, stained teeth. It was Mother.

She looked the same as when I'd last seen her, except then her hair had been permed into tight, tiny curls and was gray. I didn't know how much money she made being a contract killer, but she really needed to spend some of her dough on a better dye job and a dentist. Then again, I probably needed to spend my money on some brains.

She waved me forward and pointed to one of the tall, narrow wooden lockers. "Your locker is right here."

When I hesitated, she added with a soft giggle, "Don't worry, I'm not gonna bite." She leaned towards me. "This is an informational meeting, Odelia, and you're going to thank me for it in the end."

Mother stood up. "Now get out of those clothes." She opened the locker with number 52 on the front and pulled out a cotton robe. "And put this on." She shoved the robe at me, hitting me in the chest. "There are towels in here, too. Bring those and the locker key, that's it."

I clutched the robe in front of me as if I were already naked. "Do I have to get undressed? Can't we just go somewhere for a nice cup of coffee?"

She laughed softly. "Not only will the hot tubs do you a lot of good, Odelia, but if you're naked, I'll know you're not wearing a wire. And in a place like this, I'll be able to spot anyone who might be coming along for the ride."

"I didn't tell anyone I was coming here," I assured her. "Not even Greg, my husband."

"Maybe not, but you never know who might be following you. You have quite a bevy of men protecting you, and this is a women-only spa. It's dead here on Monday mornings, so our conversation will be private enough." She started past me. "Now hurry up," she snapped. "I don't have all day."

I FOUND MOTHER WAITING for me in the lounge area. She was seated on a wicker chair, sipping something from a Styrofoam cup. The ladies seated there earlier were gone.

"They have this wonderful earthy tea here." She gestured with the cup towards a small kitchenette I hadn't noticed before. "It's right over there. Make sure you grab a cup before you leave. It's very cleansing." Next to her were two bottles of water. "Here," she said, handing me one. "They only have a drinking fountain for water, so I always bring my own. The place isn't fancy-ass like other spas, but I guarantee you'll be a new woman when you leave."

The robe barely covered my bulk. With one hand, I held the front together. With the other, I took the water. "Just so I leave alive."

Mother fixed me with steely eyes. "If you die here, it won't be by my hand."

She led me through the steamy glass door. Once on the other side, I felt as if I'd entered a different world—someplace foreign and primal. The bowels of the spa weren't large or fancy, but the beige wall tiles and floor radiated cleanliness. There were very few people.

To my left, two hot tubs were sunk into the granite floor. The whirlpool jets made them look like soup cauldrons bubbling over a medium flame. Open showers, divided only by small partitions with no doors, were in an alcove just behind the tubs. To my immediate left and to my right were chest-high walls. Behind them were massage tables. On one table, a naked African-American woman was lying facedown while her body was scrubbed hard by a Korean woman wearing nothing but a black bra and black boy-cut panties.

On another, a bulky blond was on her back, receiving the same treatment from a different attendant. Nearby, other attendants, dressed the same, stood ready.

Mother nudged me and indicated the scrubbing process. "You should try that sometime. It can hurt like hell if you're not used to it, but when they're done, your skin feels like a newborn's ass."

Up ahead and to the far right was another pool, but no steam came from this one. Straight ahead were two rooms with glass doors and windows, which I took to be steam rooms or saunas. Running down the middle of the entire area was a low granite trough with faucets at the end. Next to one, a small, naked, elderly Asian woman sat on a low plastic stool and scrubbed herself. While I gawked, she put down the scrubber and picked up a plastic bowl. Filling the bowl with water from the trough, she splashed it over her body. The water ran off her onto the floor, where it disappeared into one of the many floor drains. The place was heavy with humidity and a natural earthy odor.

"Shut your mouth, Odelia, or you'll catch flies."

The words startled me. For a moment I'd forgotten I was with Mother. I snapped my gaping mouth shut with an audible thud.

"Put your robe and water here," she directed, pointing to a set of cubes, each with numbers corresponding to our keys. "But take your large towel so you'll have something to sit on in the steam room. And you might want the smaller towel for wiping your face. The key ring goes on your wrist or ankle."

Without hesitation, Mother stripped off her robe. She wasn't as large as I was, but her torso was plump and without much definition, like a fire plug of soft cream. She walked away from me and headed for the showers without so much as a pretend blush, but not before I noticed a long, jagged scar running along her right side from her breast to the back of her waist.

Everyone was naked, except for the attendants ... and me. I'd never been naked in a public place before. It even took me a while to get used to being naked under a sheet while getting a massage. Then again, the robe I was wearing wasn't exactly meeting in the front, so it's not like I wasn't already offering up a peep show. After slipping the key ring around my wrist and clipping my hair up, I yanked off the robe, stashed it in the cubby marked with a 52, and followed Mother before I could change my mind. She said she had things to tell me—life and death things. *My* life and death things. Now was not the time to succumb to body issues and modesty.

After we showered, Mother stepped into one of the hot tubs. Holding the railing, I stuck a toe in. It was super hot and smelled funny—not bad but organic, like rotted leaves in the woods. I wrinkled my nose.

"It's a special tub," Mother told me. "The water is infused with mugwort tea. It's very cleansing and good for all kinds of things. The other is a mineral hot tub."

I glanced over at the other tub. Sitting in it were the two women who'd been in the lounge area upon my arrival. I took a few more steps down into the bubbling hot water, followed by a quick plunge, realizing the sooner I was under water, the less public my body was.

"Okay," I said once I was seated on a submerged ledge next to my friendly neighborhood contract killer, "what's this cloak-and-dagger stuff about?"

Mother glanced around to make sure no one was within earshot. "A new assignment hit my desk yesterday," she told me. "One I think you should know about."

In spite of sitting in a boiling pot of tea, a chill ran down my spine. "Someone after Steele again?"

"No, not him."

"Dev Frye, the Newport cop?"

She shook her head.

I racked my brain. "It's not William Proctor you're after?"

Again with the slow back and forth of her head. "Think closer to home."

I squeezed my brain together to get some juice out of it. Then panic struck. "Please say it's not my husband."

Mother slapped the water with the palm of her hand. "For God's sake, Odelia, I thought you were smarter than this, much smarter. But you're either dumb as a post or living in denial. It's *you*, you little ninny," Mother hissed above the sound of the bubbling water. "Someone hired me to kill *you*."

TWENTY-TWO

My natural instincts were confused. They didn't know whether to choose fight or flight. Instead, I simply slid under the hot water, hoping it was all a bad dream. When my need for oxygen outweighed my need to forget, I emerged, sputtering and gasping for breath. Mother was still beside me. She rolled her eyes as I wiped the water from my face with a hand.

"I thought you said you weren't going to harm me!" I finally squeaked out.

I edged away from her, wondering how fast I could haul my big ol' behind out of the deep hot tub. Suddenly, being nude didn't bother me. To save my skin, I'd be willing to run bare-ass naked down Olympic Boulevard all the way to downtown LA. Then again, being naked was as helpful to me as it was to her. There was no place Mother could hide a weapon that wouldn't be inconvenient or painful. She could try to drown me, but there were people just a few feet away.

"If I were doing my job, you'd be dead already."

She moved towards me. I flinched.

"Relax," Mother said, moving past me in the tub. "Let's cool off and hit the steam." She caught my eye. "Unless you prefer the dry sauna."

I had trouble finding my voice but finally managed to push out an answer. "No, I prefer steam."

"Good, me too." As she got out of the tub, Mother pointed to the tub on the far side, the one not steaming. "The tub over there is a cold water plunge," she explained. "But I prefer to cool off under a shower. That one is difficult to get in and out of with aging knees."

I nodded in understanding. My knees weren't bad, but they were not as sturdy as they used to be. Together we returned to the showers, this time taking cooler ones. After, I grabbed my towel and trailed after Mother as she led the way into the steam room.

I love steam rooms. I could have really gotten into this place had it not been for the worry of death hanging over me like an anvil suspended with thinning rope.

The steam room was empty. We put our towels down on the tile bench directly across from the door and put our butts on them. I noticed Mother never took her eyes off the door. It reminded me of Willie. Like Mother, he was always aware of his surroundings. I guess being a criminal will do that to you.

Mother got the ball rolling. "Seems, Odelia, you've stuck your nose into something you shouldn't have. But that's the norm for you, isn't it?"

I shot her a worried look.

"Don't be so surprised," she said. "After what happened the last time we met, I've kept a casual eye on you and your shenanigans. I didn't want you messing up my business again." She chuckled. It was deep and came from a dark place. "Frankly, I'm surprised no one has put a hit out on you before. Must be common knowledge that Proctor watches over you."

Her terrifying words were warring with the relaxing nature of the herbal steam. My body didn't know whether to slum into a tranquil stupor or break out in hives. I mopped the sweat from my face with the small towel. "Who wants me dead?"

"I can't tell you that, but I will tell you that I've decided not to take the job."

"Because of Willie?"

"For starters. I have no desire to tangle with him. He said he'd hunt me down if any harm came to you the first time we met. I'm playing it safe and assuming that threat is nonperishable. Besides, I like you, and I try only to take jobs that make the world a better place. Can't see where that applies to you and your nosiness."

"Why are you telling me this if you've decided against the … um … assignment?"

"Because I wanted to warn you."

"Then tell me who wants me dead." My voice started to climb like a child reciting scales.

Mother turned her eyes from the door and fixed them on me. "If it got out that I told you the name of my client, how long do you think I'd stay in business? Confidentiality and trust are major parts of my reputation."

She leaned close to me. Our bare, wet shoulders touched. "But that doesn't mean I can't point you in the right direction and let your busybody nature take its course. It's someone mixed up in this mess you're in right now, not someone from the past."

I took several deep breaths of the hot, muggy air, hoping it would clear my head as well as my sinuses. Next to me, Mother remained quiet. My life had been in danger before, but if someone was willing to hire Mother and her band of henchmen, what would stop them from finding another hit man to finish the job? Mother's warning wasn't stopping anything, just postponing it. And if they had killed the Holts, why were they outsourcing my death? Were they too close to me? Too easily suspected? Or…?

Without turning to Mother, I asked, "Did you kill Connie and Hank Holt?"

"I had a job to do."

My rising hackles overpowered my personal fear. I looked Mother straight in the eye and nearly spit on her. "Turning a small child into an orphan is not a job."

"There were two parts to the job I turned down." Mother didn't seem at all put out by my indignation. "I was to kill you *and* the child."

My heart almost stopped. I placed a hand over my chest and took several deep breaths. The thick air wouldn't go down. I needed to get somewhere cooler. I stumbled out of the steam room into the hot tub room, but it still felt claustrophobic. I felt someone take my arm and guide me towards the showers. It was Mother.

There were a couple more women taking baths than when we had gone into the steam room. They looked at me with curiosity but kept to themselves.

Mother stuck me under a shower nozzle at the far end of the shower area and turned on the water. It was ice cold against my hot skin. I jumped out of the way of the spray, but she pushed me back in and adjusted the water so it was cool but not cold. One of the attendants in a black bra and panties approached us.

"The lady, she okay?" she asked.

"She's fine," Mother assured her. "I think it was a bit hot for her in the steam room." After receiving a small smile and nod from me, the woman bowed and left us.

"Listen to me, Odelia," Mother whispered with urgency. "Listen to me if you want to live and save the child."

When she saw I was listening, she shut off the water. "Here's your towel. Dry off. I've got more to say."

Following orders, I dried off, grabbed my robe and water, and followed Mother back out to the lounge area. She directed me into a corner of the stage area with the jade floor. I slid down the wall to the floor, which was warm and toasty but not hot, and drank down half the bottle of water in one go. Mother left and returned with two cups of the tea. We were the only ones around.

"Here," she said, handing me one of the cups. "This will help."

With shaking hands, I raised it to my mouth. It was hot and tasted like it had been steeped with potting soil, but I took several sips, one after the other. There were a bunch of blankets and small square pillows stacked against a nearby wall. Mother grabbed one of the blankets and placed it over me.

"It will be too hot," I protested.

"Trust me, you'll love it. It's like returning to the womb."

Obviously she'd never met my mother.

Once I was covered, Mother slid down to the floor, her back to the wall, next to me. There was something unsettling about being taken care of by a killer, but I didn't raise a fuss. She had more to tell me, and my panic over her news had settled enough to understand that the better I listened, the more likely Lily Holt would live. I undid my hair clip and combed through my wet hair with my fingers, waiting for more information.

Mother sipped her tea before starting. "The Holts are not who you think they are. They're definitely not that girl's parents."

"I know that. Lily was adopted."

"I'm not so sure about that either."

The tea in my cup sloshed. "What are you saying? That Lily was kidnapped by the Holts?"

"Not by them specifically, but she's the key to something sinister. Why else would someone want a three-year-old dead?" Mother looked into my eyes. "I don't kill kids, Odelia. I got an order to take the Holts out. After doing some due diligence on them, my crew did just that."

"Did you also ransack their house?"

Mother looked surprised. "The Holt house? No. Might have been the people who hired us."

"What about Erica Mayfield?" I took more tea. Mother was right—it was soothing, and my body was as relaxed as a noodle, even if my brain was buzzing like a downed power line. "Were you supposed to kill her, too?"

"Yes, but she disappeared. We were watching the Mayfield house in case one or both showed up there. The Holt woman finally did on Friday night. She let herself into the house, and that's when we got her. The sister, or anyone else, was nowhere in sight. We did the job and left. Then Saturday evening I got a call to take you and the kid out—two job orders that didn't set well with me."

"I'm the one who found Connie's body."

216

She studied my face. Her own remained impassive. "Must be why they want you out of the way. They're probably afraid you know something."

"All I know is Connie dumped Lily on Erica and took off. Then Erica dumped the kid on *me* and took off. No one told me why or for how long."

Mother indicated my cup, which was now empty. "Want a refill?" I held it out to her. With a labored grunt, she got to her feet and went to the kitchenette. While she was gone I tried to piece things together, but I couldn't. It was just too bizarre.

"But here's the really odd thing," Mother said, holding out my refill to me. "I was about to turn the job down when another order came in on Sunday afternoon. This was just for you. They said to forget about the kid. They'd take care of her."

I threw off the blanket and struggled to get to my feet. It's not that I was drugged or anything, but I'm not very agile. Once on the ground, it took an effort to right myself. Think big turtle on its back, with four limbs flailing about. Finally I was on my feet and hurrying for the lockers, not caring that my hair was wet or that my robe was flapping open.

It took me several frustrating tries to get the key into the lock on my locker. I finally managed by holding the hand with the key steady with my other hand. I stripped off the robe and dressed as fast as I could. Mother opened a locker a few doors down and did the same.

"You have to tell me who hired you," I said to Mother as I struggled into my clothes. "I don't give a damn about your reputation." My voice was rising again. Mother flapped a hand in my direction, indicating for me to tone it down.

I looked around inside the small locker. "Where in the hell are my shoes?"

"In another locker," Mother reminded me. "You can't wear them in this part of the spa."

I shot her a dirty look before I started to root around in my bag for my cell phone. I had to call Zee. "Are you going to tell me the name of your client or not? Lives are at stake here."

"I've done my good deed for the day." She started to leave.

Crazed with urgency, I pulled a sharp nail file from my bag. Grabbing Mother by the arm, I slammed her against a locker and held the sharp point to the hollow in her throat. "Tell me who hired you."

She looked into my eyes and presented a slow smile of nasty teeth. Then it disappeared and I found myself on my knees, holding my throbbing wrist. The nail file was now in Mother's hands. I never saw it happen.

"You see this?" she said to me, her voice low and dripping with venom. She lifted her sweater and indicated the large scar I'd noticed earlier. "Fourteen years ago, my husband gave me this with a hacksaw. A year later, he was dead, and my career as a cleaning lady began." She threw the nail file to the floor. "I gave you a second chance at life, Odelia. I am giving you a chance to save that child. Don't bite the hand of the killer who set you free."

I pulled myself to my feet and shook out my wrist. It was bruised but not broken or sprained. "Lily's with a friend of mine. If they go after Lily, they might harm them both." I choked down bile. "They might kill them both."

"Then do something about it."

218

TWENTY-THREE

It seemed to take me forever to get out of the spa. I wanted to follow Mother but decided it was more important to call Zee. I turned
on my cell phone and tried not to dance with impatience while it
fired up. I punched the speed dial for her house, but the call went to
voice mail. I tried her cell and got the same. I grabbed my bag and
flew out the door, but was stopped by one of the two women at the
front desk. She pointed down. I didn't have my shoes.

I went back to the clothes locker where I'd left the key, then
found my shoe locker. I slipped into my shoes, happy I'd chosen
slip-ons instead of tennies. Again, when I tried to leave the spa, I
was stopped. Seems I was supposed to return the keys to the front
desk on leaving. I yanked open the door to the locker area, snatched
the key ring and keys from the shoe locker, and all but threw them
at the women on my way out.

Running up the long corridor to the parking area, I tried Zee
again and again got voice mail. When the attendant asked for my
parking ticket, I had to dig around for it. I could see my car just a

few yards away but knew they'd never let me have it without a claim ticket. More delays. I finally located it and handed it to the valet. When he retrieved my keys from a locked box, I snatched them out of his hands, threw several dollar bills at him, and ran for my car.

It was going to take at least an hour to get back to Orange County, possibly much more, depending on traffic. When I stopped for a red light, I hooked up my cell phone's earpiece. The last thing I needed was to be stopped by LAPD for talking on my cell. In spite of the law, people did it all the time, but it would be my luck to be pulled over and ticketed for it. The first call I made was to Seth's cell phone. When he answered, I let out a big sigh of relief.

"Seth, do you know where Zee and Lily are? I tried the house and her cell." I tried to keep my voice calm to not alarm Seth right off the bat. That would come soon enough.

"I think Zee was going to take Lily shopping today. She also said something about a carousel, so maybe they're going someplace else after."

The old carousel at the Newport Beach Fun Zone was gone, but there was a place where you could both shop and ride a carousel, and that was South Coast Plaza, one of the largest malls in the US. It was across the street from my office. I ground my teeth, thinking that if I'd been at work today, I'd have been closer and better able to help. Then again, if I'd gone to work, I would never have met Mother and found out Lily was a target.

"There are two carousels at South Coast Plaza, a large one and a small one," I told Seth. "You need to find Zee and Lily and get them somewhere safe. Try the large one first—Zee loves it."

"What's going on, Odelia?" The rising panic in Seth's voice was unmistakable, so I gave him the unvarnished truth.

"The people who killed the Holts are after Lily. I don't exactly know why, just that they are, and they won't think twice about hurting Zee in the process."

"Where are you?"

"I'm driving back from LA. I found out about this just now."

"I'm heading to the mall this instant."

"The big carousel is in the main part of the mall," I explained. "Go in the entrance by Z'Tejas and you'll be right on top of it. You know where that is?"

"Yes."

"I'm going to call Dev and Detective Fehring," I told him. "They can get some people looking for them, too." Seth's office was near Fashion Island—another mall. Unfortunately, it didn't have a carousel.

I called Dev Frye but only reached his voice mail. I needed to call Fehring but didn't have her number or the number to the Newport Beach Police Department handy, so I called Greg.

"Honey," I said, knowing sooner or later I would have to face the music and tell him about meeting Mother. Greg was going to go ballistic when he found out, but for now I needed his help. "Did you by any chance get a number for Detective Fehring the other day? You know, like a business card or something?"

"Actually, I did. Just in case. Why?"

"I'm in the car right now, but I need to speak with her. Can you call her and ask her to call me? I tried calling Dev but there was no answer."

"What's up, sweetheart? Did you just remember something important?"

"More like I just learned something important."

The other end of the call went silent, telling me my smart hubby was putting two and two together.

"I thought you were going to a spa, Odelia."

"I did go to a spa—sat in the hot tub, steam room, all the normal stuff." I felt awful fudging the truth, but I didn't want to get into an argument just now, not with Zee and Lily's lives on the line. There would be plenty of time for that later.

"Then did Clark call you with some news on those prints?"

"Um, not yet."

"Dammit, Odelia." Greg's voice swelled with irritation. "What's going on?"

"Greg, I just found out Lily's life is in danger, and maybe Zee's since she's with her. I'll explain the rest later, but I really need you to call either Fehring or Dev and have them call me so I can tell them what's going on."

Greg didn't push for an answer. He'd been mixed up enough in my exploits to understand as well as I did how important time could be in these situations. "Fine, but where are you now, and where are you heading?"

"I'm on the 5 heading to South Coast Plaza. After talking with Seth, I think that's where Zee took Lily. Hopefully no one followed them there. Seth is heading there now."

"And hopefully the crowds at the mall will provide some protection if they were followed. I'll tell Fehring to send someone over there right away." Right before Greg disconnected, he said, "I have no idea what you're doing on the 5, but for now, be safe."

I was losing it as I fought the traffic south to Orange County. It would move in fits and starts. We'd travel along at forty to forty-five miles per hour, then slow to fifteen or twenty. We never even got near the posted speed limit. Occasionally the cars and trucks around me would come to a stop altogether. On a good day, I hated traffic like this. Today it was unbearable.

As the minutes ticked by and my cell phone remained silent, I worried that maybe I wasn't getting any reception. Now was not the time for a no-bars situation. With my right hand, I picked up the phone. It was working fine, and all bars were evident. I put the phone back down on the passenger's seat and shifted in my own. Stuck on the freeway, I had to trust Greg to reach Dev or Fehring. And I knew if he couldn't reach them, he'd call the police station to make sure someone was heading for the mall. Then I remembered that the mall wasn't in Newport Beach but Costa Mesa. Someone would have to call the Costa Mesa police for help.

Relax, Odelia, before you have an accident.

When the phone did ring, I nearly wet myself. Touching my earpiece, I answered, hoping to hear Dev's voice. Instead it was Andrea Fehring. I hoped she could put aside her snotty attitude towards me long enough to listen and help.

"What's this all about, Ms. Grey?"

"Didn't my husband tell you? Lily is in grave danger."

"He told me, and we've called the Costa Mesa police to check out the mall. I'm heading there myself. But I can't help Lily and your friend without knowing what's going on."

I swallowed hard, knowing answering was going to open a can of worms. "There was a hit put out on Lily. I just found out this morning."

"And who told you that?"

I hesitated. Why couldn't Fehring just go to the damn mall and take care of Lily? "I'll tell you later—after Lily and Zee are safe."

"Tell me now, Odelia, or I'll call it all off, and your friend and the kid will be on their own."

"You wouldn't do that." I braked and stared at the bumper of the SUV in front of me. Plastered to it was a proclamation that the owner's child was student of the month at some Christian school. "Would you?"

"Try me. How do I know this isn't just some hoax imagined by an addled woman with too much time on her hands?" Her disdain for me was palpable—a hand reaching through the phone line to shake a finger at me.

"There have been two dead bodies so far," I said into my mouthpiece. "How many more do you need before you believe me?"

"What do you know, Odelia?"

"Where's Dev? Let me talk to him."

"You can't talk to him. He's in the hospital."

I stopped breathing. When my lungs went back to work a second later, I asked, "You mean Dev's *at* the hospital, right? Not *in* the hospital?"

"Wrong. Detective Frye is in the hospital. He's at Hoag right this minute. He was found unconscious in his home this morning. I was at the hospital when your husband reached me."

"What happened? Is Dev going to be okay?" I was taking deep breaths to keep from panicking.

"We don't know yet. So if you're pulling me away from my partner for a wild goose chase, I will personally make your life miserable in ways you can't imagine."

I knew she meant it. At this moment I wasn't sure who I feared more, Fehring or Mother. But I needed Detective Fehring's help right now, so she won.

"I know because the contract killer told me."

"The killer told you. You expect me to believe that?"

"Connie and her husband were both professional hits," I explained, trying to push aside my worry about Dev for the moment. "A hit was also put out on me and Lily."

"So why aren't you dead?"

"Let's just say the killer and I have a history." I took another deep breath and edged into the lane on my left, which seemed to be moving a smidgen faster. "Can't we talk about this later?"

There was a long silence on Fehring's end, but from the traffic noise in the background, I knew she hadn't disconnected. "Are you in contact with Elaine Powers?"

"Who's Elaine Powers?"

"I know your background, Odelia, so don't try to play me."

I protested, "I'm not playing you now or anytime, Detective Fehring. I have no idea who Elaine Powers is. Really."

"How about *Mother*?" Fehring pressed. "That name ring a bell? And I don't mean your own mother. I'm talking about the head of a notorious assassination crew. I believe you two crossed paths a few years back."

"Yes," I admitted. "Mother contacted me, but I've never known her real name. In addition to being hired to take out the Holts, someone hired her to kill me and Lily. She was also contracted to kill Erica Mayfield." I gave Fehring a summary of my meeting with Mother while I continued my hurry-up-and-wait travel down the freeway.

"Powers is lethal. Hard to believe you're still alive, no matter how warm and fuzzy your reunion." Fehring's tone wore a sneer like a raincoat. "Unless you had something to do with all this to begin with."

I smacked my steering wheel with the palm of my hand, triggering a loud, short blast of my horn. "I have nothing to do with the Holts or with Mother," I yelled. "Nothing. Nothing. Nothing." I smacked my horn with each word, not caring if the people around me thought I was in the throes of road rage. I was enraged, but at Fehring.

"Mother told me she doesn't kill kids. She also seems to have a soft spot for me. You know, like Dev Frye." I didn't know if throwing Detective Fehring's earlier words back at her made any impact on her thick skull, but I didn't care. "So she turned down the rest of the job." I took another deep breath and wished I was back in the hot tub. "I don't think Mother has found Erica yet."

After a pregnant pause, Fehring said, "We found out Mayfield left the country sometime Thursday night."

"Where did she go? To the Caribbean, where her parents live?"

"You don't need to know that."

I curled my lip at the phone.

"Where is Mother now?" the detective asked.

"I don't know. She disappeared like smoke as soon as she warned me. Now can we get back to saving the lives of Lily and Zee?"

"Where are *you* now?"

"Stuck on the 5, coming in from Los Angeles. I'm heading for South Coast Plaza."

"No," Fehring snapped. "Don't go there. The police will take care of Lily and your friend. If the killers are there and see you, it might complicate things."

"But—"

"No buts about it, Odelia. I forbid you to go to the mall."

"Forbid me? *You* forbid me?" I stomped my foot on the floor of my car, thankful I'd had the presence of mind to use my left foot and not my right, which was alternating between the gas and brake pedals, with an emphasis on brakes.

"You show up at the mall, Ms. Grey, and I will arrest you for obstructing justice. You got that?"

I didn't know if Fehring could do that or not, but I didn't want to test her on it. She already didn't like me and seemed like the type to hold a grudge. "Okay. I won't go to the mall. But I want to know the minute they're okay."

My phone gave off a tone that told me I had another call coming in. It was Greg.

"My husband's on the other line," I told Fehring.

"Fine. Just remember what I said about you going anywhere near that mall. For once I'm thankful for Southern California traffic. When you do get to OC, come straight to the police station. I have questions for you—lots of questions."

Yeah. Yeah. Yeah.

TWENTY-FOUR

"Honey," I said as soon as Greg was on the line. "Detective Fehring just told me Dev is in the hospital."

"Yeah, she told me the same thing. I'm trying to find out what's going on, but no one will tell me anything. Don't know if it's because he was attacked or if he's ill. I even tried calling Beverly but just got voice mail. Are you still on your way to South Coast?"

"Fehring forbade me to go to the mall. She wants me to come to the station for questioning."

I could have sworn my husband was stifling a small laugh. "Are you going to listen to her or be pig-headed and go to the mall anyway?"

"I'm not sure. She really chafes my hide."

"I know. She's all sharp edges. But I want you to listen to her."

"But it's Zee, and she's in danger because of me."

"No, she's not, Odelia. Because of you, she'll be safe. No one knew Lily would be in danger when the Washingtons agreed to take care of her."

"Well, seems you'll both get your way. Traffic on the 5 is moving so slow, the mall will be decorated for Christmas by the time I get there."

My phone was at about 50 percent power, so as soon as I finished talking with Greg, I dug into my glove compartment and found my cell phone charger for the car. It was easy to set up, considering traffic was hardly moving. The last thing I wanted was another dead phone incident, especially now.

The rest of the way to Orange County the phone was silent, but that gave me time to try to work through what was going on. The Holts were into something bad—so bad it got them killed and their house tossed. And whatever it was, Erica probably knew about it, and that's why she fled. I even sort of understood why they wanted to get rid of me. If they knew I had been inside the Holt house and had found Connie's body in Erica's house, they might think I know more than I really do and/or had found something incriminating. And what about poor Dev? Was he also a victim of Mother's team, or was his being found unconscious just a coincidence?

I was worried about Dev. In the years I've known him, he's always been strong as a bull. The idea of him lying in the hospital made me sick to my stomach, but I pushed it aside to think about Lily. I couldn't help Dev, but I might be able to figure out why Lily was such a threat. The child couldn't blow her own nose or eat with her mouth closed. She could barely speak to be understood. Had she seen something she shouldn't have, and the bad guys were afraid her memory might be triggered at a later date?

And why had they suddenly pulled the contract for Lily's death off the table and said they would take care of it themselves? If they were watching carefully, they must have known she was with me.

So why tell Mother to kill me and not Lily? I was so lost in this dilemma, I almost didn't notice the car in front of me stop suddenly. Slamming on the brakes, my torso shot forward, only to be jerked back in place by my seat belt. The sharp jolt also loosened my brain. According to Mother, she had received a contract to take out both me and Lily. Then on Sunday afternoon it was revised to just me. In that short time period, what had happened to change their mind? The only thing I could think of was that Lily was no longer in my custody. She'd gone to stay with the Washingtons. Whoever was putting out the contracts must have known that.

As traffic started up again, I thought about who would have known Lily was with someone else. Mark Baker, for starters. Alyce and Gary. The cops. Racel knew Lily was elsewhere on Friday during the day. Even Carl and Steele knew that I'd handed her over to Zee. I couldn't imagine any of these people having motives against a three-year-old.

When I was almost to the mall, I pulled over to the curb and parked. No Parking signs were posted all along the street, but I didn't care. From where I was, I could see the sprawling complex with its acres of parking and stores and restaurants paying homage to conspicuous consumption. Somewhere within the walls of that retail city, my best friend and a helpless little girl could be riding painted wooden horses and not realize their lives were in danger. Or they could have been found and spirited away by now.

My desires were answered when my cell phone rang. The display said it was Seth. I didn't bother saying hello. "Are they okay?"

"Yes, Odelia, they're fine. The police contacted mall security, who found them riding the carousel, just as you suspected. They were escorted to the mall office until the police could get there and take custody of them. I got there just after they were taken to the office."

"And now?"

"We just arrived at the Newport Beach Police Station. They're trying to figure out what to do with them to keep them safe until this all blows over."

I started weeping with relief.

"Thank you, Odelia," Seth continued. "Your fast thinking might have saved their lives."

"Don't thank me, thank Elaine Powers."

"Who is this Elaine Powers? The police asked us if we knew her."

"You don't. And, trust me, you don't want to know her."

As soon as I hung up from Seth, I called Greg. It went straight to voice mail, telling me he was on the phone. He was probably trying to find out more about Dev. I left him a voice mail, letting him know Zee and Lily were safe and that I was heading to the police station to see them and to answer more questions. I told him not to worry, that I'd call later.

I couldn't wait to throw my arms around both Zee and Lily, and hopefully find out what I could about Dev. I had just turned the key in the car's ignition when my cell phone sounded another familiar tone. It was Clark.

"Hey, bro." With Lily and Zee safe, my voice had definitely turned a bit more upbeat.

Clark's tone didn't match mine. "We got the prints back." His voice was gruff and short.

"And?"

"You sitting down?"

"Yeah, I'm in the car."

"Pull over and park."

I was getting worried by the direction of the conversation. "I'm already parked." I turned off the engine.

"We picked up prints from the deodorant. They belong to Carl Yates."

"That's impossible! What would his prints be doing on toiletries at Erica's house?" Clark waited in silence while the answer sunk into my skull on its own.

"No. No. No. It can't be," I insisted. The idea that Carl was cheating on his lovely wife with bitchy Erica made me want to gouge my eyes out—or Carl's.

"But," I said into the phone as I tried to make sense of the information, "if he were sleeping with Erica, why would he have me looking into a possible affair with Mark Baker?"

"Jealousy, sis. Maybe he suspected something. Just because Carl was having a fling with her doesn't mean she wasn't also doing her paralegal."

Oh, gawd! Now I wanted to gouge my brain out along with my eyes.

"I was used." Anger bubbled up like oil heating in a skillet. Any moment smoke would come out of my ears.

"Probably. But there's more."

"Don't tell me you found Steele's prints, too. I couldn't take that."

"Nope, but we did find something interesting when we ran the prints on that coffee mug from Baker."

He paused like an awards presenter building anticipation before revealing the winner. I hate that on the Oscars and the Emmys and didn't appreciate it now. I growled into the phone.

"Keep your blouse on," Clark said. "This is serious stuff." He paused again, and I about lost my mind.

"The prints don't belong to any Mark Baker."

I dropped my annoyance like a hot potato and paid closer attention. "Who do they belong to, then?"

"We don't know."

"But I saw him use that mug myself. Could it be he got this far in his life without being printed?"

"Whoever he is, he's been printed. But his name isn't Mark Baker. Our print guy says the prints are in the system, but the identity is classified."

What? My mind imploded with the unexpected information. "Since when does a paralegal need a false identity?"

"Odelia," Clark began, speaking in a measured voice, "whoever this guy is, I'll bet he doesn't have a long background in your line of work. He could be a former government employee who needed a new identity for security reasons. Or he could be in witness protection. He might even be undercover—deep undercover."

"Undercover? At Woobie?" I shoved my surprise aside to think. "I do know that he wasn't with Hamlin-Hawke long before the merger. Maybe a year or so at the most."

"Maybe he was undercover at Hamlin-Hawke and got caught up in the merger before his assignment was complete."

"But an undercover like this wouldn't be local, would it? It would have to be federal."

My brother went silent. He was either digging through his considerable past experience as a cop or had some info he wasn't sure he wanted to share.

"Odelia, whatever this is, I'm pretty sure it's federal. I'm guessing he's either undercover for some federal agency, probably the FBI, or he's in witness protection. Either way, this situation could put him in danger if he's discovered."

"But if he's an undercover fed, why was he so nasty to me? He wanted me to lose my job!"

"I have no idea, unless it was to keep his cover intact. If he's in WITSEC, it could be he's just an offensive guy." He went silent for a moment. "And here's something else to keep in mind, sis. There are basically two kinds of WITSEC witnesses—regular folks who were unfortunate enough to see something they shouldn't have and criminals who turned snitch on bigger criminals. If this guy is under federal protection, let's hope he's the former and not the latter."

"Geez, Louise!" I ran a hand through my hair, which had dried on its own into a flat, stringy mess.

"I'm coming out there."

"No, Clark, I'm fine," I assured him. "The police are on this. They have Lily in custody for her protection, and I'm on my way to the police station right now."

"Why would she need protection? I thought Zee had her."

Oh, crap. Clark didn't know about the contracts put out on me and Lily, and I didn't want him to know. If he did, he'd fly here from Arizona sporting a big red cape, with Boy Wonder Willie by his side. Or maybe it would be the other way around.

"Oh, by the way," I said, trying to break Clark's focus, "Dev is in the hospital. We don't know why, just that he was found unconscious at his house."

"I'm very sorry to hear that. He's a good man. Was it job related or illness?"

"Don't know yet. Greg's trying to find out. I'm hoping I can learn something more from his partner."

"Now, getting back to the question you don't want to answer: what's up with Lily and police protection?"

I tapped my foot, wondering how much I could say without saying too much. Clark was far from a dummy and, like most career cops, could read between the lines as if it were in a large font. "We have reason to believe she's in danger, so the police took her into custody for the time being. Zee's with her, and I'm heading there now."

"Danger from the creeps who killed her parents?"

"Yes."

"Do they know yet who killed her folks?"

"Not exactly."

"Meaning?"

"I gotta run, Clark. Wouldn't want a ticket for talking on the cell while driving."

"You told me you were parked." Thick pause. "Dammit, Odelia, what are you not telling me? Or do I have to call Greg to find out?"

"Greg doesn't know!"

Oh, gawd. In the heat of the moment I had slipped, giving Clark more to chew on. Why couldn't my brother be a pharmacist?

"Know what? And don't you dare hang up on me, Odelia, because I'll think the worst."

"It couldn't be much worse, Clark." I hung my head, accepting defeat. "The Holts were killed by a contract killer, and there was a contract also put out on Lily."

"What?" he yelled. "A hit put out on a three-year-old? That's despicable, even for a professional assassin."

"The contract killer turned down the job on Lily." As soon as the words were out of my mouth, I regretted them.

"And how do you know that?"

"She told me." I said the words and ended the call. Let him chew on that for a while. I was tired of being grilled, although I worried he would immediately call Greg. I wanted to tell my husband myself after everything had calmed down. And no doubt Clark would discuss it with Willie, and Willie would figure out it was Mother who'd received the job order. I was only glad I had stopped talking before I mentioned the hit put out on me.

TWENTY-FIVE

"I THOUGHT YOU WERE out today?" Joyce asked as she scanned my stringy hair and casual attire.

"I am, but I forgot something." I stopped in front of Woobie's reception desk and lowered my voice. "Don't tell anyone I'm here. I just want to get in and out."

She nodded her understanding as she answered a call.

It was just after one thirty. In most law firms, staff and attorneys take lunch anytime between noon and two o'clock. Attorney, department, and committee meetings are often held during the lunch hour, and staff members stagger their lunch times depending on workload and daily demands. By two the place would be back in full swing. Unless he was tied up in a lunch meeting, Carl Yates preferred to take his lunch around twelve thirty, and he usually went out to a nearby restaurant. I knew today was not one of his usual department lunches. If Carl was running true to form, he'd just be getting back from lunch or would be shortly.

After what Clark had told me over the phone, there was no way I was not going to have a heart-to-heart chat with Carl Yates as soon as possible. From my illegal parking spot by the mall, I could see our office building. I didn't think twice. I turned the car key and headed to the familiar parking structure on autopilot.

I went down the hall towards my office but had no intention of making that my destination. I didn't want Alyce to see me. She usually took earlier lunches and would be back at her desk by now. Instead, I cut through the file room. It was the heart of the office, along with the copy center, and a natural shortcut to the other side of the office suite. I slipped in one door and out another at the far end and found myself just steps from Carl's office. Peeking around a file cabinet, I saw that Ani, Carl's secretary, was not at her desk. I looked in the other direction and saw no one in the hallway. With a few strides, I was in Carl's office. It was empty. I partially closed the door and took a seat across from his desk. Carl would be inside before he spotted me.

I didn't have to wait long. I heard footsteps just outside the office, then the door opened wide. Carl came in, his head down, his attention glued to the document in his hand.

"Shut the door, Carl."

His head shot up at the sound of my voice, and he stood rooted to the ground like a deer caught in headlights on a dark country road. His shock only lasted a second, but it was gratifying. I had trusted this man for years, and in the end he'd played me for his own purposes. The gloves were off. Knowing I'd already planned to leave Woobie was going to make this a lot easier.

"Come in, and please shut the door," I repeated. "I have information for your ears only."

Carl shut the door and took his seat behind the desk. "I'm surprised to see you today, Odelia. I'd heard you were going to be out for a few days."

"Yes, that was my intention, but I forgot something on Friday, so I needed to swing by." Without hesitation, I went straight into the topic on my mind and hopefully his. "I'm sure the police have already questioned you about what happened at Erica's house."

He nodded, but his eyes studied me, reading me and my body language like he would a hostile witness on the stand. "Yes, how tragic about her sister. Of course, I told them there's no way you would have done such a heinous thing."

"That's true, and I didn't. But did you also tell them I was snooping around with your blessing and encouragement?"

"Seems the police already knew that, so you must have been the one to tell them." He paused. "I wish you hadn't. It puts me in a very precarious situation here at the firm." He picked up a pen and made a pretense of jotting down a note.

"Funny thing about that," I said, making myself comfortable.

Carl was trying to maintain his position of authority over me, but it wasn't working. He was no longer my boss, even if he didn't know it yet. Nor was I about to grovel in the hopes of obtaining good references. We were on equal footing, and it was liberating.

"Did you explain, like I did," I continued, "that you were only concerned with helping me keep my job?"

"Of course I did, Odelia." He leaned back in his expensive ergonomic chair with the ease of a man used to calling the shots. "I told the police and the other partners how Erica saddled you with her niece and threatened your job." His lips parted with a paternal smile. "And I told them how you ... I mean we ... wondered if there was some inappropriate monkey business going on."

"And what about Mark Baker? Do you know if the police and the other partners questioned him about it yet?"

Carl shook his head. "I have no idea. I know the police want to question Mark, but they can't seem to locate him. He didn't call in sick this morning but was simply a no-show." He shrugged. "I hate to say this, but maybe he had a hand in killing Erica's sister. Maybe he and Erica's fling went sour, and Connie got in the way."

Mark had called me Sunday from the office, then today, the day the police want to talk to him, he goes missing. Something told me we might never see him again. My money was riding on him being in witness protection, and hopefully the common citizen type.

Carl tapped the pen on the arm of his chair. I remained still in mine, even though I wanted to leap across the desk at the man who had once attended my wedding.

"I think it's a good idea that you're taking a few days off, Odelia. Let this blow over. I'll talk to the partners. They'll see that you always were the best choice for the corporate paralegal job."

"And what about you and Erica?"

The pen stopped tap-tap-tapping. "Excuse me?"

"When the police questioned you, did you tell them that saving my job was just a cover for you using me to find out if Erica was double-timing you with Mark?"

"That's preposterous."

"Really? Then how did your fingerprints get on intimate items in her home?" I wanted him to think his prints were found in several places.

Carl leaned forward. "Are you threatening me with bullshit, Odelia, after all the years we've worked together?"

"It's not bullshit. There were prints, and they were identified. Once the police get them, it's just a matter of time before your name hits the suspects list."

"I did not kill Connie Holt. I've never even met her."

"What about Erica? Don't you think she'll talk as soon as they start to question her about your relationship? They've located her, you know. She was running for her life."

Carl blanched. "Certainly you don't think Erica was afraid of me?"

"No, I don't, Carl. She was running because of something her sister was involved with and she probably knew about."

"Odelia, please. This will destroy my marriage."

His comment made me want to barf. Why is it cheating spouses never think about the destruction of their marriage *before* they get between the sheets with someone else? It only seems to occur to them when they're caught, and then it's someone else's fault when they end up in divorce.

"You should have thought about that before you boinked Erica, not now."

Carl hit a button on his phone. Through the speaker I could hear Ani, now back at her desk, answer. "Ani," Carl said into the phone, "please hold all my calls. I'm in a meeting and not to be disturbed for any reason."

At that moment my brain cracked open and light flooded through its crevices, bringing partial illumination, like a shade half raised. "If you and Erica were involved, then she was trying to convince you to vote in favor of keeping Mark over me. It never even occurred to you that she might be sleeping with Mark until I suggested it, did it? That's why you changed course and sent me out to dig up whatever dirt I could about them. This was never about saving my job but about satisfying your own sick curiosity."

"That's not true, Odelia. Erica never turned me against you, even though she tried. In spite of our personal relationship, we never agreed on the paralegal situation." He ran the hand without the pen over his chin, squeezing his lips forward between his fingers. "But, yes, I saw an opportunity to look into your suspicions."

I leaned forward, my chest almost on his desk. "You mean to have me look into them without you getting your hands dirty. If I got caught, you could just pass it off as me being my usual snooping self to save my job. The partners would buy that in a New York minute, no matter what I said to the contrary. Attorneys always stick together when it's between one of their own and staff."

"Odelia, I'm sorry." Carl dropped the pen on the desk. "I'll fix this, I promise, but we have to come up with a story about those prints."

"What's this *we* business?"

I really didn't think Carl had anything to do with Connie's death or with the contracts to kill, but if he and Erica were involved intimately, there might have been some useful pillow talk.

"Someone's trying to kill me, Carl. I think that takes precedence over your infidelity. You know anything about that?"

His eyes widened. He took off his reading glasses and stared at me even harder than before. "What?"

"Someone put out a contract to kill both me and Lily Holt. And there's a hit out on Erica right now, too, probably by the same people who paid to have Connie and her husband whacked. What do you know about that?"

He waved his hands over the desk as if calling a base runner safe. "Absolutely nothing! I can assure you."

"What do you know about Lily Holt, besides her being Erica's niece?"

He gave my question serious thought before answering. "I know the child's adopted."

"I heard Erica wasn't too keen about the adoption. Why was that?"

"Erica mentioned it a few times, usually after we'd had a few drinks. She often said the adoption was going to bite her sister in the ass one day."

"That's an odd thing to say, don't you think?"

"Very odd. I always thought it was because Erica didn't like kids in general or Lily specifically. She was like that, you know. Once she got it in her head she liked or didn't like someone, she wouldn't change her mind. That's what I think happened between you two. For some reason you rubbed her the wrong way, and she wanted you gone. And she usually got what she wanted."

"Like you?"

His head drooped. "I'm not proud of this, Odelia."

"Carl, my life's been threatened. The life of a small child has been threatened. Two people are dead. If you expect me to give you pat-pat-there-there sympathy, you're seriously mistaken. What else can you remember?"

"Fair enough." He closed his eyes tight. When he opened them, he said, "To be honest, I always thought from the way Erica talked about it that the adoption was illegal."

Mother had hinted at something like that, making me wonder exactly who was Lily Holt, and why was she important enough to kill over? And how did the Holts get her in the first place?

TWENTY-SIX

AFTER TELLING CARL NOT to talk to anyone about what we had discussed, I started down the hallway towards the front entrance at a speed-walking pace. As I moved, I dug around in my purse for my cell phone. About the time I reached the elevators, I realized I'd forgotten it in the car.

I needed to call Fehring as soon as possible, so I scooted back through the reception area and this time really did head for my office. Alyce was surprised to see me.

"I forgot something on Friday," I said before she could ask the obvious.

Once in my office, I closed the door and picked up the phone. Damn! Without my cell phone's contact list and list of recent calls, I was at a loss for numbers. So I called Zee's cell, one of the few numbers I had memorized, and hoped she would answer. She did.

"Zee, where are you?"

"We're still at the police station, bored out of our minds, but at least we're safe. They might let us go home soon, but not without police protection. Would you believe the mall cops dragged me and Lily off the carousel in the middle of a ride?"

"Zee, listen to me. Is Detective Fehring around?"

"Yes, she was just here a minute ago, checking on us."

"Get her on the phone right now. It's important. I'll hold."

I aged five years waiting for Fehring.

"Odelia," came the snide voice through Zee's phone. "You're supposed to be here at the station. Do you need a police escort to remind you?"

"Listen, Detective Fehring, I think I just found out something important about Lily."

"I'm all ears."

I could tell by her tone that her attitude was at war with her listening skills, but I pushed it aside for Lily's sake.

"I think Lily was adopted illegally. Maybe that's why people are after her."

"How do you know this?" The snotty tone was replaced by all business.

"Mother—I mean Elaine Powers—said something about it to me earlier today, and just now Carl Yates told me he thought the same, based on things Erica Mayfield said to him. And, by the way, Carl Yates was having an affair with Erica Mayfield."

"And just how do you know that?" She was listening, but I could tell her patience was strained.

"He confessed it to me. I'm at my law firm right now."

"Very interesting. Mr. Yates left out that tidbit when we spoke to him."

"Can you find out about Lily's background through fingerprints and stuff like that?"

"We'll certainly try. Any idea how long the Holts had her?"

I racked my brain until the Quinn sisters came to mind. "Yes, friends of Connie's told me Lily was adopted about a year or so ago. Does that help?"

"It's a good start. We'll search missing kids reports filed during that time period. Good work, Odelia."

I wondered if I should say anything to Fehring about Mark Baker. I was tempted to let sleeping dogs lie, considering what Clark had discovered, but I knew Fehring would have my hide if she found out I was withholding information. Besides, I had promised Willie and Clark I would go straight to the police if any information cropped up from those prints.

"There's one more thing," I told Fehring. "It's about Mark Baker. Have you talked to him yet?"

"No, we haven't been able to reach him. Is he at the office with you now?"

"No. He didn't show up to work today, and I think I know why. I have reason to believe he's either an undercover fed or maybe in witness protection. Either way, he's not who he claims to be."

"And how do you know that?" I was sure she was as tired of asking that question as I was of hearing it.

"I can't tell you this minute."

There was a long, deep gust of angry air on the other end of the phone.

"Look," I said, hoping to calm Fehring down, "I promise I will tell you everything once I get to the station." When she didn't answer, I added, "I'll bet when you went to Mark's home address, you found a mailbox place, didn't you?"

"All I can say, Ms. Grey, is that we have a lot of work to do, and you have a lot of explaining to do. A hell of a lot."

"How's Dev?" I wanted to know his condition, but I was also eager to get myself out of Fehring's crosshairs.

"He had a heart attack. Now, get into the station—and that's an order."

I tried to get more info on Dev, but Fehring hung up.

Just as I was about to leave my office, my eye caught on Lily's drawing pinned to my bulletin board. It seemed like years since I'd hung it there, not just a few days. Drama enough to last a lifetime had occurred since. At that time I was only concerned with wiping Lily's nose, calling Erica on her crap, and saving my job. Now I was worried about saving Lily's life and my own. But today my eyes were catching something more than the loss of a more innocent time. The picture was taken out of a coloring book. It was a large outline of a playful kitten and a ball of yarn. Lily had colored the animal, both inside and outside the lines, with various colors not usually found in fur, and she had given it a crude hat. I went back around the desk and leaned towards the picture to get a closer look. The cat was definitely wearing headgear—an uneven blob with points. It had been colored yellow and pink, but mostly yellow.

I picked up the phone again and dialed Zee. "Hey, Zee, is Detective Fehring still nearby?" A second later, Fehring was back on the line.

"You'd better not be calling to tell me you've been sidetracked on your way to the station, because I swear I'll send a cruiser to pick you up, handcuffs and all."

"No, I'm on my way," I assured her. "But I think I have a lead on where to start with Lily. When you're looking through missing kids reports, start with Wisconsin."

"Wisconsin?"

"Yes." I studied the drawing again. "It's just a hunch, but if it pays off, it could save you a lot of time."

"Sure, why not? Wisconsin it is."

As I made my way out of my office, I gave the drawing one last look. Cheesehead Squirrel thanked Cheesehead Kitty.

TWENTY-SEVEN

My stomach was growling, reminding me I hadn't eaten anything since that cinnamon roll and coffee with Greg this morning. Opening a lower desk drawer, I pulled out a box of Thin Mints, newly purchased just a few weeks before from a Girl Scout troop stationed in front of the grocery store. I opened the carton and tore into one of the double packs. I polished off a handful of cookies, nearly swallowing them whole, and washed it all down with water from a bottle on my desk. Next to my computer monitor was an apple. It wasn't a cheeseburger, but it was shiny and inviting just the same. After returning the cookies to the drawer, I picked up the apple and got ready to hit the road to the Newport Beach police station.

I was going to ask Alyce if she'd seen or heard from Mark Baker, but she wasn't at her desk when I came out of my office. I jotted a few words on a neon lime sticky note saying I'd let her know when I would return to the office and stuck the note in the middle of her monitor to make sure she saw it.

After a quick stop by reception to let Joyce know I was heading out, I stepped into the foyer to wait for the elevator. Once in the elevator, I took a bite out of the apple. It tasted so fresh, especially after the cookies, I nearly swooned. By the time I reached my car on the fifth level of the parking structure, I was nearly done. After taking one last bite of the apple, I walked over to a trash container and deposited the core. It was one of those heavy concrete and gravel boxes that held a metal liner. My car was parked halfway down the end lane, with many empty stalls between me and it.

Each floor of our parking garage is level and flat, with several long, wide aisles. Parking stalls line both sides of the aisles and the outer edge. The up and down ramps were at the far end, the two enclosed stairwells kitty-corner to each other. Two elevators were located midway on each floor. I liked parking on the fifth level. I usually parked on the outside end facing the next office building. Since most of the cars on this level were bunched near the elevators, and it wasn't as crowded as the lower levels, there was less chance of my car being dinged or wedged in by other people's bad parking. Usually my car was by itself, like today.

As I started for my car, I aimed my key fob at the vehicle to unlock it, but the lights didn't flash, nor was there the familiar click of the door being unlocked. I stopped in my tracks, wondering if I had locked it when I'd arrived. I had been in such a rush to get into the office, I could have forgotten. Or maybe the battery in my key fob was weak, and I needed to get closer for it to work. Another more sinister idea was starting to seep into my thoughts just as I heard someone call my name with urgency.

"Odelia!"

I jumped and spun around to see Carl Yates trotting towards me from the elevator. His shirt sleeves were rolled up, and his tie was askew.

"Did you remember something else?" I asked him as I dug around in my bag looking for something with which to wipe my hands. In surrender, I used the legs of my jeans.

Without warning, Carl grabbed me by my shoulders and shook me, not hard but enough to gently rattle my teeth. "Odelia, in my office you said something about the police—that once they had my prints I'd make the suspects list. Does that mean the police don't have my prints yet?"

Leave it to a master litigator to catch all the nuances in a conversation. Had Carl not been so distraught, he would have picked up on that on the spot, not twenty minutes later. The question was, should I tell him the truth? No, they didn't have the prints, but they do know about the affair. Instead, I played possum and said nothing. Carl's tall. I'm not. I tipped my head back and latched my eyes onto his. They were wild and desperate and not at all the eyes of the confident man I'd known for so many years. I became alarmed.

He shook me again, this time with more vigor. "Tell me, damn you!"

In all the years I've known and worked with Carl Yates, he's put an arm around me with affection. He's kissed my cheek at holidays and at my wedding. He's patted me on the shoulder for a job well done and shaken my hand in congratulations. But never has he touched me or spoken to me with violent intent. I struggled out of his grasp.

"Carl, you're losing your mind."

"I have to know if the police know yet about the affair."

Holding my tote bag in front of me like a shield, I backed up in the direction of my car, taking it slow, as if backing up from a rabid dog. The stairwell was much closer, but Carl could easily jump me as I tried to go down the flights of stairs. "Are you involved in this mess in other ways, too?" I asked him.

"Odelia, I can do things for you if you cooperate. I can save your job. Pay you cash. Anything to keep this under wraps and away from my wife."

His wife, Louise, was a nice woman and not someone I wanted to hurt, but it was too late, and keeping her in the dark was not in my job description. Neither was taking bribes to cover an infidelity. It quickly occurred to me that Carl seemed only concerned with his wife finding out about him and Erica. It indicated to me that he didn't have anything to do with the murders or whatever Erica and her sister were involved with, only indiscretion. Of course, I could be wrong, especially considering I was more intent at the moment in saving my hide.

"You don't understand, Odelia." He took a step towards me. I took another two steps back. As I hugged my big bag closer, my fingers felt something familiar through the leather of the side pocket.

"Louise and I are going through a bad patch. It happens. It's going to happen to you and Greg one day, trust me. We've even talked divorce. But if we divorce under these circumstances, she could ruin me and my relationship with my children, and you know how important my children are to me. Keep me out of this, and I'll make it worth your while."

Keeping my eyes on Carl, I slipped my fingers in the side pocket of my tote bag and eased out the pepper spray. He was so hell-bent on his mission, he didn't seem to notice. When I took another step back, I glanced over my shoulder to make sure I was still on track to reach my car, wishing that today I had parked closer to the other vehicles. In that split second, Carl stepped close enough for me to smell his lunch—something spicy.

"Stay back, Carl," I warned. "You're scaring me."

"Odelia, I'm desperate. Please tell me where I stand in this mess."

He lunged to grab my shoulders again, but this time he wasn't successful. Just as one of his large hands touched my shoulder, I pulled out the pepper spray, leaned back, and hit the plunger. The stream hit him on his nose, but enough of the mist shot upward into his eyes to be effective. Carl howled and grabbed his face.

I took the opportunity to make for my car, but I didn't get far. Carl, in his rage and frantic struggle to see, had reached out with one hand and grabbed my sweater. I twisted and turned to free myself, but he had a good grip and was reeling me in like a tuna. Changing my course, I turned to face him again, the pepper spray ready to go, when he went limp in my arms and slid to the ground.

I stared down at my fallen boss as a red stain grew across the white, crisp back of his expensive shirt. I heard a scream, but it took a few seconds before I realized the cry had come from my mouth. I started to scream again, but the sound was cut short as a bullet struck the concrete wall to my left, sending tiny shards into the air. Both times I never heard the shots and couldn't tell where they were coming from.

I didn't want to leave Carl. I didn't even know if he was alive or dead, but I couldn't help him if I was also down. Staying low, I dashed for the garbage can and hunkered down behind it just as another shot exploded into the wall again. I was torn: should I make a run for the stairwell or my car? The stairwell was closer, but my phone was in my car. I also didn't know from which direction the shots were coming. And if the shooter chased me into the stairwell, it would be like shooting fish in a barrel.

Peeking out from behind the can, I tried to scan the parking garage, but all I saw were vehicles parked for the day while their owners toiled inside the connected high-rise office building. Visitors never parked on the higher levels. Considering it was just mid-afternoon, it might be a while before anyone came to retrieve their ride. That was both good and bad news. The last thing I wanted was unsuspecting office workers walking into a sniper situation, but it also meant no help was on the way. And if I didn't hear the shots, neither did parking security. For the time being, I was on my own with nowhere to go. The shooter was probably using some sort of silencer, which made me think contract killer. Mother may have turned down the job, but it was just a matter of time before another hired gun would take the opportunity to make a buck. The only good thing was that Lily was safe.

A moan invaded my thoughts. It came from Carl. He was still alive, but there was no way I could drag him to the safety of either the stairwell or the car. I hoped he wouldn't move too much and cause the shooter to aim better next time. Fish in a barrel be damned, I had to try the stairwell. The car was simply too far away. Leaving my bag behind the trash can, I dashed to the stairwell and grabbed the door handle. It twisted and turned in my hand, but the door was jammed. As a shot hit the wall next to me, I dove back to the precarious safety of the garbage can.

I had to head for the car and the phone. It was my only option. If I was lucky enough to reach it, maybe I could start up the car and use it to give cover to Carl before the killer moved in to finish us off.

Taking several deep breaths that I realized might be my last, I made ready to dash to my car. I knew I was a big target, but I had to try. Doing nothing meant certain death. I had taken only a few steps, bracing myself against a bullet I was sure would find its mark, when the back door of my car flew open and a man shot out of it at the speed of a human bullet train. It was Mark Baker. In his hand was a gun, and he was headed straight for me.

I staggered backward until I fell next to Carl. I froze where I was, waiting for the inevitable, for Mark to gun me down—paralegal to paralegal. Either he was involved in the same mess as the Holts or he *really* wanted to keep his job. As I scooted back on my butt, my leg hit something. It was the pepper spray canister I'd dropped when Carl slumped into my arms. I grabbed for it, clutching it like life itself, and aimed it at Mark. He saw it and turned his head, raising an arm against the burning spray just before tackling me and sending me flat on my back on the greasy concrete floor. At the same time, a couple of bullets flew over our heads. Once again I didn't hear the shots, just a high-pitched whizz followed by the sharp sounds of concrete being struck.

I struggled to push Mark off of me.

He held me down. "I'm not the one shooting at you, you fool." He got off of me. "Come on," he ordered.

Before I was even halfway to my feet, Mark was pushing me back towards the garbage can while he shot his gun towards an unseen target. One of his bullets struck the back window of a parked car, the sound of shattering glass singing backup to the blast.

"Wait here," he barked. "Help's on the way."

"But Carl." I started to go back to the fallen attorney, but Mark stopped me with a hard jerk to my arm.

"Keep directly behind this can and give thanks that whoever that is can't shoot worth a damn."

Following his order, I hugged the garbage can to me like a long-lost love. Mark covered me from behind, his chest pressed hard against my back. I could feel his head bobbing side to side, his gun at the ready, as he kept watch of both vulnerable sides.

What paralegal certification program did he learn this from?

I heard sirens—not close but closing in—and hoped they were heading this way and would arrive in time to save us. A few more bullets whizzed by, one hitting the garbage can close to my hand. I yanked it back, my heart in my throat. The shots were followed by the sound of footsteps hitting the pavement at a fast clip, then the roar of an engine. A white van pulled nosefirst out of a parking slot at the far end of the parking structure close to the exit ramp. Instead of leaving, it headed our way.

Mark ran forward to meet it. After taking cover behind a parked car, he took shots at the windshield. It exploded. The van swerved and clipped the back ends of a couple cars to its left. The air filled with the sound of gun blasts, breaking glass, and mangled metal. I slapped my hands over my ears. The van slowed down but kept coming. From the passenger's side, a man took aim at Mark. As the van got closer, I recognized Gary Allen. Driving the van was Alyce.

Mark held his gun steady with both hands and shot at the tires, hitting one. Alyce fought to keep control of the van as it neared us, but the van tipped and swayed like a drunk. I could hear Gary yelling to her. Through the broken windshield I saw him grab for the steering wheel.

As the van passed Mark, it lunged far to its right. Both Gary and Alyce were trying to wrangle the heavy vehicle around the end of the aisle and keep it upright. Thankfully, it was now heading away from us. Just as the van cleared the end of the aisle, it tipped onto its right side and slid across the concrete until it smashed into the only parked car in the area—my car.

When the scraping of heavy metal on concrete stopped, it became eerily quiet, followed a few seconds later by the gut-wrenching screams of a woman from inside the van. Mark approached the van, keeping his gun steady on the vehicle.

I went to Carl just as I heard something crash against the door to the stairwell. The door caved, and officers dressed in flak gear burst through it, guns drawn. Some rushed past me towards the van. Two covered me.

Several police vehicles entered the parking level and raced towards us, sirens blaring. They came to a stop, blocking aisles and surrounding the fallen van. A plain sedan and two paramedic units followed. Fehring jumped out of the unmarked car. Mark no longer had his gun on the van but held it loosely aloft, both of his hands in the air, until he was unarmed by one of the cops.

Carl was still breathing, but barely. I held his hand, ignoring Fehring, until the paramedics took over. Once assured Carl Yates was in good hands, I went back to the garbage can, leaned over it, and threw up.

TWENTY-EIGHT

THE JOINT. THE SLAMMER. The clink.

I'd been down this road before, and it wasn't any easier the second time around.

"You okay, Odelia?"

I looked up with surprise at Fehring. "You just called me Odelia, not Ms. Grey."

Fehring offered a half smile of truce as she handed me a soda. She handed the one in her other hand to Seth, who once again was acting as my counsel. Greg was waiting outside the interrogation room, pacing in his wheelchair. The police had allowed Zee and Lily to go home with police protection.

This time I wasn't being questioned about a dead body and my connection to it, but I had spent the past few hours being debriefed, sharing everything I had learned and knew with the police. In return, Fehring was bringing me up to speed, though I'm sure she wasn't disclosing everything. But to be fair, neither was I. I had only said that my half brother, a former cop who now worked high-level security for the private sector, had run the prints. I left William Proctor out of everything.

I popped the top off the soda. It was my third, and I was feeling the buzz of the caffeine and the rush of the sugar. Fehring had brought me a sandwich earlier, but I was only able to nibble at it. Although I'd hardly eaten all day, I wasn't hungry, just happy to be alive.

"I still can't believe Alyce and Gary Allen are kidnappers." After taking a drink, I looked up at Fehring with alarm. "Their own kids—what about them? Are they theirs or…" I let my words trail off.

"We're looking into that," Fehring told us. "The Allen woman claims they are hers by birth, but we're not exactly taking her word for it without proof." Fehring took a seat. "That's why they tossed the Holt house. In addition to trying to find Connie Holt, they were looking for Lily's adoption papers and birth certificate, knowing close scrutiny would show them to be fake."

"Have you located them?"

"Not yet, but we're hoping Erica Mayfield can help with that. According to Alyce, Erica knew Lily's adoption was illegal, though she didn't know or want to know where the child came from. She said Mayfield even went over the paperwork for her sister. My guess is it's in a safe-deposit box somewhere."

"If Erica knew about the illegal adoption," Seth added, "she's going to lose her law license, especially considering the child was kidnapped."

I nodded in agreement. The California bar was going to have a field day with this. "Where's Erica now?"

"Still out of the country. We're trying to get her back here before she slips through our fingers and disappears."

Fehring stretched. It was early evening, and like us, she'd been going over the mess for hours. "Seems the Allens ran a small but very lucrative black-market baby ring. Desperate but well-heeled couples would find their way to them through discreet referrals and put in an order for the type of child they wanted—things like eye and hair color, gender, even age up to a certain point. The Allens would look for a child that matched the description, generally somewhere far away from where the adoptive parents lived, and would snatch the candidate."

I shuddered, and not for the first time in the past few hours. "Basically, the Allens were operating a child chop shop, like organized car thieves."

"Basically," Fehring agreed. "According to Alyce, they've been doing it for years and saw it as God's work. They would remove a child from a poor or bad environment and relocate them to a well-to-do family where they would have the best education and opportunities."

"You mean sell the child, don't you?" My words were laced with disgust.

"Yes," Fehring said, "they would sell the children. Alyce is still in shock, but we've been getting pieces of information out of her all afternoon. Seems they've had several aliases and have moved around—no telling what we're going to find once we start really digging. We're working on her now about any records they might have kept on other children. We're also going through their home with a fine-tooth comb."

Alyce had been driving the van while Gary did the shooting. What the police had gleaned so far was that as soon as she saw me back in the office, Alyce had called Gary and alerted him to my whereabouts, then joined him to lie in wait for me in the garage. They had used Mother's services to get rid of the Holts, but when she refused the job to finish me off, they decided to become do-it-yourselfers. It was as yet undetermined what they had planned for Lily. When the van tipped and crashed into my car, Gary had been crushed to death, leaving a shell-shocked Alyce to spill the story.

Seth shook his head, still as stunned as I was over everything. "How did the Allens get hooked up with the Holts, and why did it turn bad?"

"Apparently," Fehring explained, "the Holts had been trying to adopt but were unsuccessful, something Alyce learned after coming to work for Erica. She and Gary approached them, and the Holts grabbed at the chance to become parents. According to Alyce, Hank Holt came to Gary several months ago with an idea to expand the operation. He wanted in as a partner, but Gary balked at the idea, believing he was doing the Lord's work and not in the business of selling people for profit."

"Talk about denial." Seth took a deep breath of disbelief.

"Exactly," said Fehring. "When Gary refused to let Hank in, Hank threatened to expose the operation. Gary Allen reciprocated by threatening the entire family, Lily included. Learning that, Connie Holt panicked."

I ran the information around in my head. "So she left her daughter in Erica's care and disappeared, hoping the Allens wouldn't dare touch Lily if she were in the care of someone else."

Fehring nodded. "That's what we think, but can't be sure. Although I doubt Connie expected Erica to bring Lily into the office, where Alyce had access to her."

I ran a finger down the side of the cool soda can. "And since Erica knew the adoption was bogus, she worried about her own skin, dumped the kid on me, and took off. She never wanted any part of Lily. Maybe she hoped the Allens would take her and bump me off in the process—a twofer."

"Could be," Fehring agreed with a nod of her head. "We also think Connie got hit when she came out of hiding to check on Lily."

The three of us sat in silence a moment. Even seasoned Fehring seemed lost in the bizarre facts of the case.

"Your hunch was right, you know." I looked across the table at Fehring when she spoke to me. "Lily was from Wisconsin. How'd you know?"

I felt my lips part in a small smile, even though I wasn't feeling cheerful. "Cheesehead," I explained. "Lily used the term *cheesehead*. At first I thought it was just a little kid's imagination, then I realized she had to have learned it somewhere. It wasn't a foolproof lead— she could have heard it on TV—but it gave you someplace to start."

"We've contacted her parents. They're on their way here now."

Seth blew out some air, thinking, I'm sure, about his own kids. "They must be shell-shocked. I know I would be."

Detective Fehring leaned forward. "Lily's real name is Aurora, Aurora Sanger. Her parents are Pat and Kate Sanger. She also has two older brothers. At the time she was taken, her father's business had gone under, and the family had lost their home. They were bunking with relatives, trying to rebuild their lives. It was exactly the type of situation the Allens looked for when shopping for kids. I'm happy to say the Sangers are back on their feet now."

"I can't imagine the pain the Sangers went through." I took a drink of soda. "Do you have children, Detective Fehring?"

She hesitated, weighing how much of her personal life, if any, to share. She didn't strike me as the chatty coffee-klatch type. "Yes. I have a daughter, Chelsea. She's thirteen going on thirty-five. Some days I want to ship her off to Borneo, then something like this happens and I want to put her under lock and key to keep her safe."

"I hear ya," responded Seth. "Felt that way about my own."

"And what about Mark Baker?" I asked.

After the shooting, Mark had been spirited away in a patrol car, as I had. I caught a glimpse of him at the station hours ago but had not seen nor heard anything about him since. All I knew was that while he was hiding in my car, he'd used my recharging cell phone to call the police when he saw I was in danger.

"He's being processed," is all Detective Fehring surrendered.

"But who is he? The way he handled that gun and the situation, he had to be professionally trained by someone. And what was he doing in my car in the first place?"

Andrea Fehring might have told me about her daughter, but I could tell from the set of her jaw she was giving up squat about Mark Baker, although it was confirmed he was not having an affair with Erica. Nor was he having an affair with Racel. I had brought up that I thought someone was hiding in Erica's bedroom when I was there with Racel and that maybe it had been Mark. After questioning, Racel admitted that it was her boyfriend from school and that Erica had threatened to fire her if she had him over, so he hid when I arrived.

Next to me, Seth cleared his throat. "Considering how this Baker character was after Odelia's job, then was found hiding in her car with a gun, I think we deserve an explanation, even if he did save her life."

"I agree." The comment did not come from Fehring, but from someone opening the door. It was Mark Baker. He slipped inside and stood next to the table. "You do deserve answers, Odelia."

Mark was still dressed in the same shirt and slacks he'd been wearing during the shootout, but now a badge of some kind was fastened to his belt.

"You're a cop?" I asked, my question a mixture of wonder and wariness.

"Special agent," he corrected. "My agency had suspicions about the Allens but no proof. We picked up their trail in another state and followed them here. I went undercover at Hamlin-Hawke to get close to Alyce, who seemed to be the weak link of the operation."

"So you knew Lily was a black-market adoption?"

He moved his head back and forth with two short jerks. "No, not until now. When I saw how detached Erica was towards her niece, especially after her sister disappeared, and how interested the Allens seemed to be in the child, I was worried they were going to kidnap her and sell her off."

Seth leaned forward. "So you thought she might end up a new product for their service?"

"Yes," answered Mark.

I pointed a finger at Mark. "That's why you kept asking me where she was?"

"Yes. I was relieved when you got her out of the office."

"That still doesn't explain why you were in my car, ready to ambush me."

Mark casually put one foot up on an empty chair like he owned the place. "After Erica's sister was murdered, I knew things were coming to a head and you might be in danger. After I saw you drive into the parking garage when you weren't even supposed to be at the office, I decided to intervene and get you out of the way myself."

"You were going to kill me?" My voice climbed the ladder to hysteria.

"No, not at all," Mark assured me. "My plan was to get you somewhere safe, either willingly or by force."

"But—" I started, but Mark cut me off.

"And that's all I can tell you."

A silence settled over the room. Seth and I exchanged looks before Seth turned to Mark. "Thank you. My client and I are satisfied."

Mark put his foot back down to the floor and started for the door.

"Not so fast," I said just as he put a hand on the doorknob. I got to my feet. I had hoped to jump up with showy indignation, but the bumps and bruises from being thrown to the ground had rendered me slightly decrepit. "If you were undercover and obviously not a career paralegal, why were you so gung-ho to take over my job and my office? Were you even qualified to be there?"

Mark first looked at Fehring, then at Seth, who said, "I think that's a fair question." Fehring seemed to agree.

Mark gave me a tight-lipped smile. "First of all, I do have a paralegal certificate. I was a paralegal for the agency before I got into field work. That's one of the reasons they chose me for this assignment." He left the door and moved closer to me. "After the merger, we did background checks on all Woobie employees. We were worried your habit of playing amateur sleuth would get in the way of our investigation. Since Erica wanted you gone, it was easy to play along with her and get you out of the way before you got in ours. It wasn't personal, I assure you."

"Yeah, yeah, you said that before, but being thrown under a bus is very personal to the person wearing the tire tracks."

"I'm very sorry, Odelia." Mark's face softened. "For what it's worth, it was a shitty thing to do, and you are definitely the better paralegal." He leaned forward and whispered, "You're not a bad investigator, either. But you didn't hear me say that."

CARL YATES WENT STRAIGHT from the parking garage into surgery. Last we heard, he was going to be okay, but it would be quite a while before he was well enough to go back to work. He didn't seem to have anything to do with the Allens' baby-buying scheme, only bad judgment when it came to his pecker.

Dev would be out of commission for a while, too. He'd gotten up Monday morning as usual but felt horribly ill and had shortness of breath. He called 911 but blacked out just before they arrived. That afternoon, about the time I was being gunned down, he underwent bypass surgery.

TWENTY-NINE

"Sweetheart, you okay?"

I didn't respond to Greg but remained still. I was in the guest bedroom, lying on top of the bed—Lily's bed—with the drapes closed. I was moping in the dark, wondering about what might have been had Lily not had a family who loved and wanted her. Not that I wasn't truly thrilled that the Sangers got her back. We'd met them briefly a few days after they'd arrived in California to retrieve the daughter they'd thought was lost forever.

Detective Fehring had asked us to come down to the station, saying there was some final paperwork to go over. I called Seth to see if I should have him by my side, and he said he and Zee had also been called in. When we arrived, Fehring escorted the four of us into a small room and introduced us to the Sangers, a quiet, bookish couple in their thirties. With them were their two sons.

"Cheesehead Squirrel!" Lily broke away from her parents and latched herself onto my thick leg. I squatted down and gave her a long, firm hug. When I stood up, Kate Sanger threw herself into my arms, sobbing words of gratitude. With tears running down his face, her husband pumped all of our hands with vigor.

"The Sangers wanted to thank you," Fehring explained, "for helping get Aurora back safe and sound."

I wondered if the police had told the Sangers there had been a hit put out on their three-year-old, or if they had let that tidbit of information slide for now. They couldn't keep it a secret, not if Alyce Allen went to trial, but now might not be the best time to disclose everything. Either way, I certainly wasn't bringing it up.

We had a short but lovely visit. Just before we parted, Lily handed me the sad little bear in the torn tutu—the one she'd called Mummy.

"I bought Mamie for Aurora just before she disappeared," Kate Sanger explained, stroking her daughter's head. "It was her second birthday, and it was all we could afford. I think she wants you to have it."

I clutched the bear named Mamie, not Mummy, as I wallowed in the bed Lily had once slept in and thought about the little girl who had started out being an annoyance with a head cold and become a piece of my heart.

Greg wheeled closer to the bed. "You know, sweetheart, we could still adopt."

I shook my head slowly side to side. "I'll be okay, Greg. Really, I will."

My husband reached out and fingered my hair, running his palm down to cup my cheek. He understood all too well.

"I think you and I are fine just the way we are. Don't you?"

Greg nodded and smiled. "Yes, I do." He leaned forward and kissed me on the lips.

"Who was at the door?" I asked. I had heard the doorbell, followed by Wainwright's usual barking, just minutes earlier.

"Steele's here. He's concerned about you. You feel like seeing him? If not, I'll send him on his way."

I took a deep breath. "No, I'll see him. Why don't you hand him a beer and give me a minute to freshen up."

Greg kissed me again and left the room.

GREG AND STEELE WERE in the kitchen, both with bottles of beer in their hands. It was Friday night. Greg hadn't been home from work long, and Steele looked like he'd just come from the office. I hadn't returned to work yet, and when I did, I was going to give notice. There was no way now I would ever go back to Woobie. There were just too many recent bad memories. I wanted to remember Woobie as it had been before the merger.

Steele raised his bottle in my direction. "TGIF, Grey. It's been a very long week, hasn't it?"

Greg handed me a beer, and I took a seat next to Steele. I clinked my bottle against his. "Felt more like ten years instead of a week." I took a long drink.

On the table in front of Steele was a ten-by-fourteen-inch white envelope. On the address label was the Hamlin, Hawke, Boer, and Yates logo with my address.

"What's that?" I asked.

"Your layoff package." Steele pushed the envelope towards me. "And it's quite generous."

"They laid me off?" I couldn't believe it. Indignation raised its ugly head. "How dare they!"

Greg put a hand on my arm. "But you said you weren't going back. This is a good thing, sweetheart. You said so yourself a few days ago that the ideal thing would be for them to lay you off so you could collect the money."

"I know it doesn't make sense." I took another swig of beer. "I don't want to return, but I also don't want them to cast me aside like I'm excess baggage. Besides, with Mark gone, they now need a corporate paralegal."

"Exactly," stressed Steele. "After all the hullaballoo with Carl and the shooting, I called a few of the old Woobie partners I knew would be straight with me. Seems the partnership had decided in favor of keeping Mark over you after all, but now that he's disappeared, that decision is moot."

I tapped the envelope. "But this is a layoff package."

"Yes, it is." Steele assured me. "And it's dated last Friday. Carl was supposed to lay you off with everyone else but held off, partially because he was determined to change the decision and keep you on for his own purposes."

Steele paused to let the information sink into my thick skull. "So the ball's in your court, Grey. You can go back to that hellhole or you can take the money, have a nice summer, and come work for me in the fall." Steele sounded confident about the last part.

"But with Mark Baker gone, there's no longer a duplication of positions. Why would they give me that choice? Why wouldn't they just wait for me to quit, which any fool would know I would do under the circumstances? Then it would cost them nothing."

"I'm guessing," said Greg, giving Steele a sly look, "that someone pressured them into keeping the layoff in play."

I looked at Greg, feeling the confusion take form on my face. When I swung my eyes back to Steele, it all fell into place. "You bullied them into giving me the severance money?"

"*Bullied* is an ugly word, don't you think?" Steele took another swig from his bottle. "I just reminded them about everything that happened to you, and all at the hands of one partner or another."

"So you threatened to sue them on my behalf?" I couldn't believe my ears.

"*Threatened* is another ugly word, Grey. And, besides, I wasn't authorized to negotiate a lawsuit or anything on your behalf. All I did was make a few calls to people I knew and had worked with for many years and casually remind them of everything you've done for the firm and everything the firm had *recently* done to you."

I leaned back in my chair, not sure what to think. "Unbelievable."

Steele gave me a shit-eating grin. "This morning Boer called and set up a meeting to hand me this personally."

"Boer," said Greg, "always struck me as a good guy."

"He is," Steele assured him. "He's a decent guy and a sharp attorney. He's appalled by this whole mess."

Steele turned to me. "Boer said to tell you he's deeply sorry and would love to continue working with you, and I know he meant it. He assured me your layoff was by no means unanimous among the partners. But he'd also understand if you don't feel the same way about coming back."

I picked up the envelope and opened it. Inside was a multi-page letter explaining the terms of the layoff, insurance issues, vacation time accrued, and other bookkeeping matters of separation. It was dated last Friday. With it was a large check in the amount I'd expected based on what Kelsey had told me. There was also another check, dated today. My eyes popped like two balloons when I saw the amount. With it wasn't a letter but a release and confidentiality agreement.

"What's this for?" I waved the second check at Steele.

"It's your bonus for a job well done."

"Woobie doesn't give staff bonuses in March or in this amount, and since when do bonuses come with confidentiality agreements?"

Steele smiled like he'd just checkmated someone. "I convinced them to pay it earlier, considering."

I handed the second check and agreement to Greg. "This is a payoff," he announced after looking it over, "plain and simple. They're afraid she'll sue and know she has good cause."

"That firm," Steele explained to us, tapping an index finger on the table to emphasize his point, "is facing serious issues right now, starting with a federal investigation into whether or not Erica Mayfield, an equity partner, knew about and participated in a black-market baby ring operated by another employee. Carl Yates is probably going to get dragged into it as well, considering his relationship with her. Along with the feds, there will be a state investigation and one by the California Bar. A lawsuit by Odelia is small potatoes compared to all that." He leaned back in his chair. "They want this problem to go away so they can focus on the other stuff."

I ran a hand over my weary face, then took the check back from Greg. I studied it with mixed emotions. Woobie had been my family for decades. I felt relieved to have an out but heartsick by the turn of events. "This will bring Woobie to its knees."

"Most likely," Steele confirmed. "This layoff package and bonus are predicated on you accepting the layoff. If you turn it down and return to work on Monday, it all goes away, and you'll have to take your chances with the survival of the firm."

Even though I knew what I had to do, I turned to Greg for support. "What do you think I should do, honey?"

Greg flashed me his killer smile. "Take the money and run, sweetheart—all the way to the bank."

THE END

www.MidnightInkBooks.com

From the gritty streets of New York City to sacred tombs in the Middle East, it's always midnight somewhere. Join us online at any hour for fresh new voices in mystery fiction.

At midnightinkbooks.com you'll also find our author blog, new and upcoming books, events, book club questions, excerpts, mystery resources, and more.

Midnight Ink Ordering Information

 Order Online:
- Visit our website, www.midnightinkbooks.com, select your books, and order them on our secure server.

 Order by Phone:
- Call toll-free within the U.S. and Canada at
  1-888-NITE-INK (1-888-648-3465)
- We accept VISA, MasterCard, and American Express

 Order by Mail:
Send the full price of your order (MN residents add 6.875% sales tax) in U.S. funds, plus postage & handling to:

Midnight Ink
2143 Wooddale Drive
Woodbury, MN 55125-2989

Postage & Handling:

Standard (U.S., Mexico & Canada). If your order is:
$24.99 and under, add $4.00
$25.00 and over, FREE STANDARD SHIPPING

AK, HI, PR: $16.00 for one book plus $2.00 for each additional book.

International Orders (airmail only):
$16.00 for one book plus $3.00 for each additional book.

Orders are processed within 2 business days.
Please allow for normal shipping time.
Postage and handling rates subject to change.

Too Big to Miss

BOOK ONE

Too big to miss—that's Odelia Grey. A never-married, middle-aged, plus-sized woman who makes no excuses for her weight, she's not Superwoman—she's just a mere mortal standing on the precipice of menopause, trying to cruise in an ill-fitting bra. She struggles with her relationships, her crazy family, and her crazier boss. And then there's her knack for being in close proximity to dead people…

When her close friend Sophie London commits suicide in front of an online web-cam by putting a gun in her mouth and pulling the trigger, Odelia's life is changed forever. Sophie, a plus-sized activist and inspiration to imperfect women, is the last person anyone would ever have expected to end her own life. Suspecting foul play, Odelia is determined to get to the bottom of her friend's death. Odelia's search for the truth takes her from Southern California strip malls to the world of live web-cam porn to the ritzy enclave of Corona del Mar.

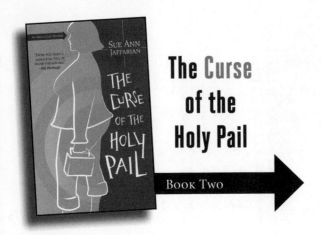

The Curse
of the
Holy Pail

Book Two

I s the "Holy Pail" cursed? Every owner of the vintage Chappy Wheeler lunchbox—a prototype based on a 1940s TV Western—has died. And now Sterling Price, a business tycoon and client of Odelia Grey's law firm, has been fatally poisoned. Is it a coincidence that Price's one-of-a-kind lunch pail—worth over thirty grand—has disappeared at the same time?

Treading cautiously since her recent run-in with a bullet, Odelia takes small bites of this juicy, calorie-free mystery—and is soon ravenous for more! Her research reveals a sixty-year-old unsolved murder and Price's gold-digging ex-fiancée with two married men wrapped around her breasts—uh, finger. Mix in a surprise marriage proposal that sends an uncertain Odelia into chocolate sedation and you've got an unruly recipe for delicious disaster.

Thugs and Kisses

BOOK THREE

With the class bully murdered at her thirtieth high-school reunion and her boss, the annoying Michael Steele, missing, Odelia doesn't know which hole to poke her big nose into first. This decision is made for her as she's again swept into the action involving contract killers, tangled relationships, and fatal buyer's remorse. Throughout this adventure, Odelia deals with her on-again, off-again relationship with Greg and her attraction to detective Devin Frye.

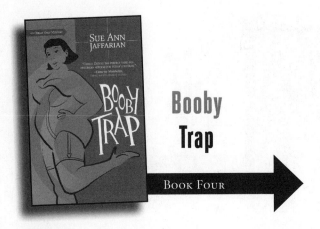

SUE ANN JAFFARIAN

"Odelia Grey is the perfect tart and underdog—superglue for today's woman."
—Annette Mahon, Sews to Die Series author

Booby Trap

BOOK FOUR ➤

Could the Blond Bomber serial killer possibly be Dr. Brian Eddy, plastic surgeon to the rich and famous? Odelia never would have suspected the prominent doctor of killing the bevy of buxom blonds if she hadn't heard it directly from her friend Lillian—Dr. Eddy's own mother!—over lunch one day. This mystery gets even messier than Odelia's chicken parmigiana sandwich as Odelia discovers just how difficult—and dangerous—it will be to bust this killer.

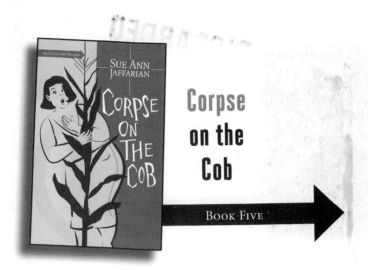

Corpse on the Cob

BOOK FIVE

What do you have to lose when you go searching for the mother who walked out of your life thirty-four years ago—besides your pride, your nerves, and your sanity?

Odelia finds herself up to her ears in trouble when she reunites with her mom in a corn maze at the Autumn Fair in Holmsbury, Massachusetts. For starters, there's finding the dead body in the cornfield—and seeing her long-lost mom crouched beside the corpse, with blood on her hands...

C

ing
frie
Cla
my
tha